Holiday Brides

JEWEL AMETHYST
FARRAH ROCHON
STEFANIE WORTH

LEISURE BOOKS NEW YORK CITY

A LEISURE BOOK®

October 2009

Published by

Dorchester Publishing Co., Inc.
200 Madison Avenue
New York, NY 10016

ISBN 10: 0-8439-6319-0
ISBN 13: 978-0-8439-6319-9
E-ISBN: 978-1-4285-0757-9

Printed in the United States of America.

10 9 8 7 6 5 4 3 2 1

Visit us online at www.dorchesterpub.com.

Holiday Brides

CONTENTS

From SKB with Love

Jewel Amethyst

This story is dedicated to my Kittitian friends and family both at home and abroad who have touched my life in a special way. May God bless you all.

Chapter One

Venetta David sat in the darkened living room, an untouched glass of Johnny Walker Blue label in her hands. Tears rolled from the sides of her brown almond-shaped eyes, matting her long lashes together, and streamed down her milk chocolate cheeks. She gazed at the bottle sitting in the ice bucket. She and her husband had received the bottle as a wedding gift ten years ago and took a shot of it each year on their anniversary. Tonight was their anniversary—and the anniversary of his death.

She held the photo of her late husband and sobbed aloud. She could still see his face, pale and twisted from painful chemotherapy, smell the antiseptic, and hear the beeping of the monitors in his hospital room.

MJ reached up and touched her face lovingly. "You will be all right," he whispered hoarsely. "I want you to go on when I'm gone. Remarry and have kids." He smiled weakly.

"You are not going to die," Venetta assured him, kissing his palm. "We will find you a match and you'll get that bone marrow transplant. We are going to grow old together."

MJ smiled and took her hand in his. "I love you, V." He closed his eyes as he mustered the strength to ask for water.

It had taken Venetta less than a minute to fetch the water, but when she returned to the room, he was lifeless, the cardiac monitor had flat-lined. MJ was gone, but for the first time in months there was a peaceful pain-free expression on his face. Her soul mate had gone to heaven.

Venetta got up from the couch, placing the glass of liquor on the side table. Venetta had known Michael David Jr., since prekindergarten. She told her mother, "MJ and I are going to get married when we're twenty and have lots of kids."

A year later MJ and his family moved away. They needed to be near a good affordable children's hospital for treatment. He had leukemia. They returned to Baltimore when he was in ninth grade; his leukemia had been in remission for several years. That was when Venetta and MJ started dating.

When MJ was eighteen, his leukemia returned. That same year they married, knowing that Venetta could be widowed shortly. It was a wonderful five-year marriage.

Christmas was always special. As long as strength permitted, MJ would cut a beautiful pine that they decorated together. Every year he hung a sprig of mistletoe on the ceiling and kissed her every time she walked under it. He invited friends and relatives over for Christmas parties. He'd died on their fifth anniversary, less than a week before Christmas. Since then Venetta never celebrated the holiday.

The sound of the doorbell ringing interrupted Venetta's sad reverie. She dried her tears and straightened up herself before answering the door.

"What are you doing here?" Venetta exclaimed, surprised to see her longtime friend and coworker Kerina standing outside her door.

"Interrupting your annual pity party," Kerina responded exuberantly, stepping into the dimly lit room. She flipped the light switch, immediately flooding the room with bright overhead flights. "We are going to celebrate Christmas."

"You know I don't do Christmas," she said curtly.

"That's why we'll celebrate it in a warm place," Kerina said, stretching her long jean-clad legs out on the couch.

Venetta joined her, straddling the arms of the couch. At five feet six inches, Venetta was two inches shorter and a few shades darker than her biracial friend. Whereas Kerina was slight, Venetta was a curvy size 8, with a well-rounded derriere, emphasized by the lowrider black jeans she wore. Her oversized sweater that once belonged to her husband concealed full breasts.

"You finally won the lotto?" she asked, turning to face Kerina, her shoulder-length relaxed hair falling carelessly over her oval face.

"That would have been even better, but no. I just won an all-expense-paid vacation for four to the Caribbean" she shouted excitedly, holding up the tickets and flyer in her hands. Kerina had a penchant for entering contests. She played the lotto religiously, called in to radio stations for giveaways, and even auditioned for *American Idol* knowing full well that she sounded like a strangled cat when she sang. "And *you* are coming with me."

"Don't you have a husband and two adorable kids to take?"

The twenty-eight-year-old mother of two shook her head. "Mark is committed to spending Christmas at his mother's house again this year. She still refers to me as 'that woman,' calls my children little bundles of germs, and Mark is too much of a wuss to stand up to her."

"So who else is going?" Venetta questioned, feeling excitement creep in.

"Sheridia and Janelle. It'll be a girls' week out."

"Kerina, you know how I spend Christmas . . ."

Kerina gasped in exasperation. "It's been five years. Do you think MJ really wants you to spend Christmas crying at his grave? You are getting on that plane with Sheridia, Janelle, and me and we are going to have a sunny Christmas in . . ." She turned the flyer around and read aloud. "SKB . . . St. Kitts."

Chapter Two

"This is paradise!" Janelle exclaimed, inhaling the jasmine-scented air as the four friends stepped onto the Robert Bradshaw International Airport in St. Kitts.

The tiny airport sat on a small hill and offered panoramic views of the city of Basseterre and its surroundings. Lush green fields of sugarcane swayed in the warm gentle breeze. In the near distance the waters of the Caribbean Sea beckoned, sparkling like myriads of tiny diamonds in the warm sunshine. Gentle rolling hills kissed by the sea and vibrant grassy plains all lay spread out like a banquet table, giving a feeling of peace and tranquility. The air was clean and perfumed. The sky, a pure cloudless blue, seemed close enough to touch.

"Wow," Venetta exclaimed, taking a last look at the panorama before entering the white minivan that served as a taxicab.

They drove along a narrow two-lane road on the way to the hotel. As they approached a roundabout with a statue of Queen Victoria, the taxi stopped. A crowd surrounded the vehicle. A brass band mounted on a truck pulled by an agricultural tractor approached playing frenzied soca music while the throng of people jumped and danced in the street.

"What's happening?" Venetta asked the cabdriver.

"It's a precarnival jam," the cabbie responded calmly. "We'll have to take a back road."

"Wait," Sheridia called. "Can we come out? I want to see this."

"Sure," the cabbie responded, pulling onto the side of the road. "Just be careful. It's easy to get swept up with the crowd. I'll wait here."

The girls exited the vehicle and watched amused as locals danced, gyrating their hips as if they were boneless, and jumped waving rags in the air.

"That's called wukking-up," the cabbie explained, noting Sheridia's interest.

"Wow! I want to do that," Sheridia shouted.

The cabbie shouted in reply, "If this is your thing, you've come at right time. From Christmas Eve until January second is our carnival season. You will be seeing lots of street jamming, partying, parades, and shows."

"Do you have a schedule?" Janelle, the organizer, asked.

The cabbie fished a glossy flyer from his glove compartment and handed it to Janelle. "If you want year-round action, you can go to the Strip. It's close to your hotel. There are lots of bars and clubs with live music and DJs. You can get anything you want there."

After a few minutes enjoying the crowd Venetta sighed, "Guys, this is interesting, but it's been a long day. We should go to the hotel and rest—or at least check in."

"I totally agree," Kerina concurred.

"Party poopers," Janelle and Sheridia, Venetta's co-workers and friends, grumbled as they piled into the minivan and drove to the hotel.

The hotel was located on the beach at the entrance of the narrow Southeast Peninsula. The girls checked into their two-bedroom suite with a view of the Atlantic Ocean. On the other side of the peninsula was the Caribbean Sea. As the girls unpacked, Kerina pulled out her cell phone and began dialing.

"I'm calling Deborah Demming. She was my roommate in college who just happens to be a local."

"Think she'll know the hot party spots?" Sheridia asked excitedly. Sheridia was the accomplished party girl, spending most of her weekends going from one club to another.

"I don't know. She *was* quite a party animal in college, but she's married now with a family."

"I didn't know you had an island roommate," Venetta said. She and Kerina had been friends since college. Unlike Kerina, who led the typical college life living in dorms and off-campus apartments with multiple roommates, Venetta had been married and living with her husband, first with his parents and later in their own town house.

"You met her before. Slim girl with a tiny waist and big backside always wearing short, loud clothes."

"Oh, Debbie Bryan. I thought she was from Jamaica."

"Don't let her hear you. She's very touchy about that."

After a short conversation on the phone Kerina announced, "Debbie is meeting us at the Strip tonight and taking us on an island tour tomorrow."

The others gave an excited whoop, while Venetta said quietly, "Count me out. I'm taking an early night."

Chapter Three

Venetta strolled barefooted along the darkened water's edge. The sand beneath her feet was warm and compact as the water lapped around her ankles. The half-moon reflected on the water surface like myriad tiny mirrors, adding to the tranquility of the deserted beach. The only sounds she could hear were the waves rolling gently at her feet and the occasional chirp of night creatures.

"Sharks come ashore to spawn at night." A soft deep voice with a rhythmic Kittitian accent broke the peace. "They can nibble at your feet."

Venetta looked toward the sound of the voice, startled. There, sitting on an overturned sailboat, was a brown-skinned man in his late twenties. He had some of the nicest dreadlocks she had ever seen.

The man left his perch and strolled over to Venetta. He was about five eleven and athletically built. He wore white slacks and his colorful batik shirt was unbuttoned. Beneath it was a black T-shirt with the words *Kittitian Pride* inscribed over the outline of a steel pan. As he came closer she could see his angular face was devoid of facial hair.

"Is that really true?" she asked the stranger uncertainly.

"That's what my mother told me when I was little," the man responded, falling into step with Venetta. "Of course now that I'm grown I believe it was just a tale devised to keep me from the beach at night."

Venetta chuckled and glanced up at the handsome stranger. He had a slightly flared nose and full lips. She could see his eyes were the highlight of his face. They were large and dark brown, crowned by long curled lashes. In his eyes was a twinge of sadness that made him look vulnerable.

"So, what's a beautiful lady like you doing all alone on the beach at this time of night?" he asked in his soft, deep, accented voice.

"I can ask you the same question."

He chuckled. "Fair enough. I come here to unwind and meditate."

"Same here."

He walked along beside her, hands in his pockets, his unbuttoned shirt fluttering carelessly in the breeze. "It's not a good idea to be alone on a deserted beach at night."

The thought had occurred to her as well. "I know. I'm heading back to the hotel now."

"I'll walk you back," he volunteered. "So what brings you to St. Kitts at this time of year?"

"Christmas break," Venetta answered without hesitation.

"Let me guess, you're a teacher."

Venetta stopped and smiled. "Yes. Is it that obvious?"

He nodded. "Your use of the term 'Christmas break' was a dead giveaway. We teachers think in terms of breaks."

Venetta gathered that he was also a teacher. "What level?" she asked.

"High school chemistry and physics. You?"

"Languages. Middle school French and Spanish."

"So, where are you from?" the man asked, as the lights of the hotel got closer and brighter.

"Baltimore, Maryland."

"I used to live in Maryland, College Park area. I went to UMD. Graduated seven years ago."

Venetta was surprised again. "It's a small world. I graduated six years ago. Were you in the teacher education program?"

"Nah," he laughed lighty. "Engineering. I did a bachelor's in chemical engineering, but when I returned to SKB, I couldn't find anything in my field, so I became a teacher."

They reached the entrance of the hotel and stepped into the dimly lit lobby. The attractive young man turned to Venetta and asked, "Can I buy you a drink?"

Venetta was hesitant. Standing and talking to him was comfortable and she was enjoying herself, but having drinks was like a date. She thought of MJ and experienced a twinge of guilt. "I'm afraid I'll have to pass," she said politely.

Venetta was pleased he amicably accepted her rejection. They remained standing in the lobby, sharing stories of teaching adventures and nightmares. Half an hour later he said, "We could have been finished with our drinks by now."

Venetta looked at the time on her watch: 10:35. "One drink," she said, and walked with him to the bar.

He ordered a Carib beer while she ordered a virgin piña colada. There was no way Venetta was consuming alcohol with a man she just met in a foreign country. She'd heard too many stories.

As they sipped drinks and casually chatted, a calypso medley of Christmas carols began to play.

As if reading her mind, her new friend asked, "So, how do you celebrate Christmas when you are not gallivanting around the globe?"

She thought for a moment of her depressing Christmas ritual. "I don't," she answered.

"Religious reasons?" he questioned.

"No. I just no longer find joy in it," Venetta said, then quickly changed the topic. "How do *you* celebrate Christmas?"

"For Kittitians, Christmas and carnival are deeply entwined with lots of dancing and drinking and parades. But Christmas Day is a quiet religious experience with most people going to worship and then dinner. For me it's all about the food."

"Really? Tell me," Venetta urged.

"There are some foods and drinks you enjoy only at Christmas. And it's not uncommon for people to drop in unannounced for their 'Christmas,' which just means cake and sorrel."

"Sorrel?"

"It's a drink made from a flower that only blooms around December. You've got to try it." He indicated to the bartender to serve Venetta the drink.

The bartender poured the bloodred drink and placed it in front of Venetta. "It's not alcoholic, is it?"

He shook his head.

Venetta drank the tangy drink. It was deliciously refreshing. They talked and laughed for a long time, and for the first time in years, Venetta was enjoying the company of an intelligent and funny man. Finally Venetta looked at her watch. It was past midnight. "I guess I have to call it a night," she said to the young man apologetically. "Thanks for the drinks. It was very nice meeting you."

His eyes followed her as she glided gracefully toward the lobby. It had been a long time since he enjoyed the company of a woman like that. She was intelligent, interesting, and certainly easy on the eyes. He'd seen many people traverse deserted beaches alone and had never had the urge to approach any one of them. He had no idea why he'd had the desire or even the courage to approach this stranger tonight, much less invite her for drinks. Maybe it was because she looked so much like the way he felt.

"I see you sweating de touris'," his friend Darren teased, approaching. "What's her name?"

"Didn't ask," he responded with a shrug.

"Another half-assed attempt at moving on. At this rate, you may as well join the seminary," Darren said, shaking his head.

He laughed without mirth and swirled his beer. "There'll never be another Sharon."

Darren looked at him long and hard. "You're right. Sharon was unique. So quit looking for her and find yourself another woman. I saw how you looked at that lady. You got a thing for her."

"What's the point? She'll be gone in a week."

"Then have some fun making hay while the sun shines," he said, slapping him on the back.

Chapter Four

"Don't tell me you spent all evening at the hotel bored and alone," Deborah asked Venetta the next day as they strolled through Independence Square. They were going on an island tour and their second stop after leaving the hotel was downtown Basseterre. Their first was at Deborah's house not too far from the hotel. Venetta felt as if she was transported to the nineteenth century. The two-story town houses all had stone bottom and wooden upper floors with intricately trellised balconies.

The girls sauntered around Independence Square with its shady tropical trees and radial walkways leading to a fountain in the center. On the east side of the square rose the twin spires of the Cathedral of the Immaculate Conception and the Courthouse, while the west side boasted the National Bank and several businesses. Art galleries, restaurants, and cute little stores occupied the north and south sides of the square.

"When you all left, I took a walk on the beach. I met a cute local guy and we went back to the hotel for drinks."

Kerina, Sheridia, and Janelle burst out laughing simultaneously. "Yeah, right!" Kerina added.

"What's so unthinkable about her having drinks?" Deborah asked incredulously. "She's widowed, not dead."

"That's because you don't know Venetta," Kerina quipped as they approached the Circus. The Berkeley monument with its large clocks and drinking fountains loomed ahead in the center of the roundabout. It was the widest street Venetta had seen on this island thus far. People moved around doing their Christmas shopping at a rather leisurely pace. Others stood in the middle of the street interrupting the flow of traffic to hold loud conversations.

"So what's his name?" Deborah pressed.

Venetta hesitated. It was only then she realized they had never exchanged names. "I don't know."

"See, it's all in her imagination," Kerina said.

Sheridia laughed. "I guess you met the phantom of the beach."

"Whatever," Venetta muttered as the girls headed toward Port Zante with its cruise ship berth and many souvenir shops and restaurants on the waterfront.

The waterfront was packed with people. Vendors sold fresh produce from the backs of pickup trucks, trays, and crocus bags lying on the ground. Men with carts sold snow cones. Fishermen, with boats no bigger than canoes, sold tropical fish from the seawall to loud patrons. A ferry horn sounded as it unloaded throngs of people coming from the neighboring island of Nevis. Buses, not much larger than minivans tooted musical horns as they departed from the bus terminal. Despite the chaos, the people moved around unhurriedly as if time did not exist.

The girls stopped for a drink of coconut water served by a chiseled shirtless young man just outside the market. After they drank the refreshing water, the man chopped the coconut in half with a machete and they scraped the meat.

On the way back to Deborah's Nissan Xtrail, they ran into two shirtless men in cutoff pants pulling a cart, blowing a conch shell, and shouting at the top of their lungs, "Getcha ballahoo, getcha conches!"

The five girls left Basseterre on the narrow main road, driving past fields of sugarcane waving in the breeze. Lush green cloud-capped mountains stood on one side, while the sea lay on the other. As they drove past Bloody Point, Deborah told them the story of the planned uprising by the indigenous Caribs against the British settlers and their betrayal by a young woman in love with one of the British leaders. "They massacred the entire Carib population," she said. "The blood of the Caribs ran down this river for days. That's why it's called Bloody Point."

The girls visited the Carib petroglyphs, the only remaining evidence of the existence of the indigenous people on the island, and drove up to the entrance of the rain forest to Romney Manor, the home of Caribelle Batik. There they saw Sea Island cotton transformed into beautiful waxed and tie-die designs. Kerina went crazy purchasing outrageously expensive batik wear for her husband and kids.

On the way down, they met a prepubescent kid riding a donkey.

"Can I get a ride?" Janelle asked the little boy. A few minutes later the American girls were all taking turns riding the donkey and laughing. It was an exhilarating experience.

"What are you guys doing tonight?" Deborah asked on the way up the steep winding road to Brimstone Hill Fortress. It was a majestic fort built on a hill that stuck out from the central mountain range. The stone beauty took a hundred years to build on the backs of African slaves, and was the center of many wars fought between the British and the French, who shared the island. Just before the entrance they saw green vervet monkeys swinging from branch to branch in the canopy of trees.

"Nothing yet," Janelle replied.

"Good. Christmas Eve is at my mother's place."

Venetta sat on a large cannon, the wind blowing in her hair, drinking in the panoramic view of Sandy Point and the surrounding areas, while Janelle took endless photos. She could see as far as the islands of St. Eustatius and Saba. She loved the quiet tranquility and the sounds of the birds chirping in the distance. Her mind wandered to the attractive stranger she'd met the night before and she wondered who he was. Deep down, she wished she could see him again.

"Come on, let's go," Deborah urged, heading to the parked SUV.

Even with stops at various tourist attractions, elegantly preserved plantation houses, abandoned wind-powered sugar mills, and Deborah's grandmother-in-law's tiny wooden shack where they ate cassava bread, the tour around the island took less than three hours. When they returned to the hotel, they all hit the beach, sampling the crystal-clear waters of the Caribbean Sea. As Venetta looked at the tiny fish visible in the clear green waters, she again thought about the stranger whose mother had given him the tale of sharks biting his feet at night and smiled. She wished she had gotten his name.

Chapter Five

The Christmas Eve party at Deborah's mother's house was not what Venetta had expected. The louvered windows were unadorned, and Mrs. Bryan was still baking cake and brewing sorrel while her husband did last-minute repairs in the backyard. The atmosphere was jovial as people laughed and chatted, greeting one another, merrily wishing compliments of the season. However, instead of people staying, folks came, and ate quickly, before heading downtown to the opening of carnival.

Mrs. Bryan greeted the women. "Don't be strangers," she said to them. "The food is on the table and in the kitchen. Drinks are in the fridge, enjoy yourselves."

Venetta looked at the different large silver pots with goat stew, goat water, black pudding, souse, and conch stew and remembered her "phantom's" words, *It's all about the food.*

She feasted on peppery soused pigs' feet and goat water, a boiled goat head. Sheridia, afraid to try anything with goat, ate the conch stew only. Janelle and Kerina sampled a bit of everything.

As Venetta sat on the railing of the veranda eating her goat water, she heard a soft, deeply accented voice behind her. She turned around, expecting to see the man she'd met on the beach last night. Instead she found herself face-to-face with a young clean-cut man in his late teens.

Deborah brought the man toward Venetta. "This is Dexter, the youngest of my five brothers."

Though disappointed, Venetta greeted him brightly.

As they said their good-byes to head downtown, Mrs. Bryan said to them. "You have to come by for Christmas dinner tomorrow, and I am not accepting no for an answer."

"Of course we'll be here," Janelle answered for everyone. "Is there anything we should bring?"

"Yes," replied Mrs. Bryan. "Your bellies."

The women laughed and headed toward the shoreline where the opening ceremony of carnival was taking place. Wooden booths serving all manner of delicious-smelling food lined the waterfront, which earlier today had been filled with market vendors. A band played on the stage, while folks danced or wandered from vendor to vendor. On every corner, whole chicken legs smoked on barbecue grills made of oil drums, and folks walked around with Carib beers in their hands, drinking openly. It was a giant party, and certainly a very different way of spending Christmas Eve than Venetta had ever experienced.

Surprisingly, stores were still open, and locals were milling about doing their last-minute Christmas shopping. As Deborah led them back to Mrs. Bryan's house where her SUV was parked, they saw a group of old men with banjos on the front porch of a neighbor's house singing, "Good morning, good morning, this is Christmas morning." The group simultaneously looked at their watches and realized it was past midnight.

"Merry Christmas," they said to each other, exchanging hugs.

Later that night, as Venetta lay in her bed, she thought of Christmas and the pain that often accompanied it. However, with the party atmosphere, the casual happiness of the people, the entire island-Christmas feeling, she realized that she was looking forward to celebrating the holiday. And for the first time in years her mind was not on MJ, but on the "phantom" she had met at the beach.

Chapter Six

"Merry Christmas!" Mrs. Bryan greeted with warm hugs. Venetta was surprised by the change in the small bungalow. The windows were now adorned with red and cream satin and lace curtains, the doorways covered by drapes, and in the kitchen doorway hung a wooden beaded curtain. A fully decorated artificial Christmas tree, under which lay a porcelain nativity scene, stood near the front window overlooking the veranda. Even the sofas that were worn and threadbare last night were covered with new red velveteen slip covers and beautifully crocheted cream chair backs. A red damask tablecloth hid the scars on the large dining table that was elegantly set with cream and gold place mats, napkins, and delicate china. A banquet of delicious food graced the table: savory turkey, honey-glazed ham, stewed beef, curried mutton, rice with pigeon peas, yam pie, veggie casserole, green banana salad, breadfruit logs, fried plantains, salt-fish balls, and more. Venetta's mouth watered at the savory sights and delicious scents emanating from the table.

She had awoken this morning with the usual Christmas trepidation and had considered forgoing this dinner. She wanted to bury her head under the covers; that is, until she saw the bright sunlight streaming through the glass windows of the hotel room. Instead of succumbing to depression, she donned her bathing suit and jogged to the beach, where she let the waves and surf wash away her anxiety.

When she returned, her traveling companions were still asleep. Venetta then made a quick decision. She called a taxi and visited a local church for Christmas service. It was inspiring and for the first time in five years, Venetta was looking forward to Christmas dinner with excited anticipation.

One by one Mrs. Bryan introduced the girls to her husband, an ebullient man with a growing paunch. He invited them to sample hard liquor as he chatted and laughed nonstop in heavy dialect the Americans could barely comprehend. She next introduced them to four of her five sons and their families, who were in attendance. Her youngest daughter, Deborah's only sister, was at a university in England and did not make it home this year for Christmas.

"Where's Sean?" Mrs. Bryan asked Deborah.

"Late as usual," she commented, adding another dish to the already crowded table.

"This place is beautiful, Mrs. Bryan," Venetta complimented. "When did you do all this decorating?"

"Sometime between midnight and dawn," she responded before rushing off to attend to the buffet.

The friends joined the buffet, talking, laughing, and having a good time.

Venetta stood piling her plate with food when over the softly playing Christmas carols, she heard a soft, deep, familiar voice behind her. "I told you it was all about the food."

Her heart skipped a beat. Slowly, she turned. There he was, dreadlocks neatly held back in a rubber band, a wide smile on his face.

Before Venetta could respond, Deborah came over to

him and slapped him behind the head. "About time you showed up. Venetta, this is my brother, the perpetually late Sean Kevin Bryan." With that, Deborah flitted off.

"Finally a name to fit the face," Sean said to Venetta, extending his hand.

Her right hand occupied with the piled plate, Venetta extended her left. "Nice to meet you—again. You never told me your name."

"And you never told me you were married," he responded, observing the wedding band on her finger.

Venetta, suddenly self-conscious, felt her face flush. "I . . . I . . . that's because I'm not married, not anymore," she stuttered.

"Divorced?" Sean asked, filling his plate with food.

"Widowed."

After a beat, he apologized. "I'm really sorry to hear that. How long?"

"Five years." Venetta looked up at him, expecting him to say something about moving on. "I know it's a long time to still be wearing the ring, but . . ."

"No need to explain yourself, Venetta," he said kindly. "Only you know your pain and only you can tell when you're ready to move on."

Venetta searched his eyes. He was sincere. He understood. She breathed a sigh of relief.

As Venetta sat next to her friends, Janelle leaned over. "Who's that cute guy with the dreadlocks you were talking to?"

Venetta smiled. "That," she said, "is Sean Bryan, Debbie's brother. He's also the *phantom of the beach*."

When Venetta looked up, Sean was standing next to her.

"Phantom?" he questioned after she introduced him to her friends.

"Long story," Venetta answered with a blush. Sean encouraged the women to try some konky, a pudding made with grated sweet potato, coconut, and cornmeal wrapped in banana leaves and boiled.

After dinner, some of the men sat in the backyard under the shade of a guinep tree playing dominos. The kids opened presents and played with toys, the younger adults engaged in a boisterous game of Taboo, and Deborah challenged Kerina, Janelle, and Sheridia to a game of Monopoly. Venetta wandered into the backyard, observing the different fruit trees that occupied the area. Out of the corner of her eye, she saw Sean coming toward her, two dessert plates in his hands piled with goodies.

"I thought you'd want dessert," he said. "I don't know what you like, so I brought you a little of everything. There's potato pudding, bread pudding, pineapple upside-down cake, coconut tart, and that's black cake . . . not chocolate. I'd go easy on the black cake. Debbie made it and she's been known to put enough wine in it to drunken a man."

"Thanks." She smiled. "By the time you're finished with me I won't be able to fit into my jeans."

"That's okay. Kittitian men like a little flesh on the bones," he joked. Venetta laughed lightly.

Sean escorted her around the yard, pointing out the different fruit trees before settling on the veranda.

"So, why did you refer to me as the 'Phantom of the beach'?"

Venetta smiled. "When I told my friends that I met a nameless local on the beach, they dubbed you a phantom."

"I guess that makes me the Frigate Bay Jumbie."

Venetta laughed, having learned earlier from Mr. Bryan that jumbie was the Kittitian word for "ghost." They remained outside on the veranda, talking and laughing, until the sun descended behind the mountains and the silver half-moon took its place.

"So, this is the way Kittitians spend Christmas," Venetta observed. "I like it."

"This is just the beginning. At midnight there are usually parties that culminate in j'ouvert jamming."

"Sounds like fun."

Sean stole a quick peak at Venetta. She was indeed a very beautiful woman and he liked her. He quietly contemplated his friend's advice to make hay while the sun shone. This year, like every other, he got invitations to various Christmas parties, but it had been years since he'd attended one. He stole another glance at her, standing in the moonlight, her hair pulled back in a ponytail, high cheekbones giving her face a wide youthful appearance, and full lips. He looked at the way her red silk sheath dress hugged her curvaceous figure, ending just below the knees, revealing well-toned calves. Maybe . . .

"Would you like to go to a party later?" he asked quickly before he could chicken out. "It's walking distance from here."

Venetta swung her head around to face Sean. "I . . . I don't know . . . I . . ."

"It's okay," he reassured her. "You don't have to feel pressured or anything. I don't usually go to them. I just figured you might want to experience St. Kitts carnival from a local perspective."

Venetta brought her eyes up to meet his. Their eyes held, and Sean could see anxiety. He almost regretted asking her, causing her conflict.

"Yes," she responded quickly and decisively. "I'd be happy to go to the party with you."

Sean's face lit up in a bright smile. Just then Deborah came out onto the veranda, her husband, Leroy, and three-year-old son in tow.

"Sean, can you keep Xavier with you tonight? We want to take the girls to the National Bank party."

Sean looked at her apologetically. "Sorry, Debbie. Leave him here with Mother. I'm taking Venetta to that same party."

"What!" both Debbie and her husband exclaimed in surprise.

Debbie turned to Venetta and laughed. "I don't know what magic you've been working, but it's been years since we've been able to drag Sean to a party."

Chapter Seven

The party was held on the upper floor of the National Bank Building on Central Street, overlooking Independence Square. It was a fun party with great calypso and reggae music, tons of Carib beer, and the local rum, CSR. While Kerina, Sheridia, and Janelle immediately hit the dance floor, Venetta and Deborah stood with a group of girls discussing local politics. Apparently politics was a big emotional affair in this country, and Venetta watched in amusement as the mild discussion morphed into a heated debate.

Sean handed Venetta a malted beverage. "Wanna dance?" he invited, extracting Venetta from what was now a shouting match between some of the ladies. Leroy did likewise, taking Deborah to the dance floor.

Venetta was anxious. "I haven't danced in a while," she explained to Sean, "so forgive me if I crush your toes."

"I wouldn't worry about that if I were you. With calypso, anything goes."

Sean was a graceful dancer, which made Venetta a little self-conscious. As they danced, though, Venetta got caught up in the music and was soon matching his movement.

"Join the train," Sheridia shouted to Venetta as the partiers formed a train and danced around the room. Before Venetta knew it, she was in the train, her hands on Sheridia's shoulders, Sean's hands on her shoulders, and moving around the dimly lit room dancing to the latest Kittitian calypso tunes.

Hot and sweating, Venetta walked out onto the crowded balcony for fresh air. It was almost four in the morning. From afar she heard the music of a band on the street, signifying the beginning of j'ouvert. The balcony suddenly emptied out as folks left the party to join the bands. As the party wound down, the DJ played slower reggae and R & B.

Deborah joined Venetta on the balcony, a Rum and Coke in her hand. "So you're my new sister-in-law," she teased. "Good thing we already like you."

"Hold your horses. We had a few drinks, we attended a party . . . aren't you putting the cart a mile ahead of the horse?"

Deborah took a sip of her drink. "Sean doesn't have casual relationships."

"I just met him two nights ago."

Deborah smiled calmly. "I know my brother," she said, patting Venetta on the shoulder before exiting the balcony.

A few minutes later, Sean joined her on the balcony. The first rays of dawn streaked across the sky, and various tunes from multiple bands could be heard in the distance wafting on the wind. Inside, dance hall reggae was being played.

They remained alone on the balcony in companionable silence for a while. Venetta's mind raced. She found herself much more attracted to Sean than she'd anticipated, but to be called "sister-in-law" was a stretch. Plus he never even made a pass at her. For all she knew, he was probably just being a gracious host, nice to all foreigners. Face it, he treated her just as warmly as his parents and

most of the locals they'd met thus far. Deborah was probably reading way more into it than there was.

The reggae was replaced by lovers' rock and the song
"Tempted to Touch" belted out over the speakers. Without
asking, Sean took her hand in his, placing the other around
her shoulder, and they began to dance to the slow, smooth
rhythm. Venetta's heart thumped wildly against the walls
of her chest. It had been a long while since she'd been this
close to a man. She could smell his cologne through his
shirt. Venetta raised her eyes to his. Their eyes met and
held. On his lips was a soft calm smile and for the first time
since meeting him, Venetta saw no sadness in his eyes.

Sean drew her closer to him, his arms wrapping around
her in an embrace as their bodies melded together, moving to the slow rhythm. She rested her head on his shoulder, and closed her eyes, submitting to the flood of
complicated emotions that threatened to overwhelm her.
She could not decipher whether it was nostalgia from a
time past, the ambiance of the music and the beautiful
sunrise in the distance, or the attraction she felt for this
man she'd met less than two days ago. Suddenly she was
afraid . . . afraid of the emotions she was feeling, afraid of
the throbbing feeling growing in her body.

Venetta raised her head and gazed wide-eyed up at
Sean. His eyes were closed, a dreamy expression on his
face. Slowly he opened his eyes, staring deeply into Venetta's. He brought his face closer to hers, his eyes silently
asking permission to kiss her.

After a lifetime of cautious living, and years without
MJ Venetta for once wanted to throw caution to the wind
and just submit to the flood of desires lying just beneath
the surface. Her lips parted, slowly. Locked in each other's
embrace, in the soft light of the early dawn, swaying to
the music, hearts pounding in their ears, Sean and Ven-

etta were oblivious of the loud music of the band on the street down below them until the balcony was suddenly flooded with people. Self-consciously, they released each other without a kiss. And the strange thing for Venetta was, she really wanted to kiss him.

Chapter Eight

From the balcony, Sean and Venetta watched two bands, coming from opposite directions. The throngs of revelers dressed in simple colorful costumes, some with mud-painted bodies, blended together as the musicians played their sweetest music to entice the dancers. The lead singers of both bands took turns taunting each other using metaphors and hyperboles to describe the sweetness of their music, encouraging the revelers to choose the better band by showing their best "wuk-up." The dancers responded with frenzied dancing. On the balcony, folks were wild with excitement.

"It's a clash of rivaling bands," Sean explained. "Whoever leaves with the most people has bragging rights."

"Why are we still here?" Sheridia asked, leaning dangerously over the crowded balcony. "Let's join the jam."

Deborah looked at her as if she were crazy. "Not when there is a clash. I have no intention of being trampled."

Finally one band moved west on Central Street, taking most of the revelers with them. The other band moved in the opposite direction, promising to "whip them" on Last Lap, the last day of carnival festivities. As the music faded into the background and the crowds thinned out, Sean, Deborah, Leroy, and the three friends left the building and walked toward crowded Fort Street in the early morning light. The aroma of freshly baked bread filled the air.

The group stopped to get breakfast from a Rastafarian selling out of a van on the side of the road. They walked along the main road, sipping foam cups of steaming bush tea, an aromatic herbal blend of balsam, lemon grass, and sage, and munching on fresh bread with stewed salt fish. As they neared the stone walls of the historic Anglican church, a band approached surrounded by hundreds if not thousands of dancers. Soon the group found themselves being swept along with the crowd of sweat-drenched bodies.

Sean placed his hands protectively around Venetta's waist, ensuring that they remained together. Venetta looked around and realized she was separated from her friends. They followed the band being pushed, shoved, and pressed along. Before long, they found themselves jamming in the streets along with the crowd of revelers.

"This is fun!" Venetta shouted to Sean, grinning as they jammed along with the crowd. It was midday when Sean and Venetta finally left the band. Venetta was hot, sticky, and exhausted, but had never had more fun in her life.

"Let's go by Mother's to get my ride. I'll take you back to the hotel," Sean suggested, leading Venetta up a narrow crowded road.

A troupe of scantily clad men and women with painted bodies hung around sitting on the side of the road. In the middle of the road, a man dressed in a red bovine costume lay on the ground. Two kids in dog costumes pounced around excitedly as spectators formed a ring around the activity. An old bearded doctor, dressed in colonial garb with a crooked cane, limped toward the downed bull.

"Is he all right?" Venetta asked.

"It's just an act. Wait, you'll see what happens next."

The doctor poked the bull with a giant needle. The

bull wriggled on the ground, and then slowly stood up. Next he reared his head and dashed madly into the surrounding crowd, holding on to young girls and "wukking-up" on them. Venetta laughed loudly.

"That is the Bull," Sean explained, laughing. "It is a reenactment of a story that supposedly took place on a plantation sometime in the late nineteenth or early twentieth century. The doctor is Dr. Walk-an-Chook."

Venetta laughed as the bull and his crew dancing to the music of a string band ran off to another performance. They continued walking along the road, the midday sun becoming almost unbearable. Despite all the excitement, exhaustion was setting in. Venetta had been awake for more than twenty-four hours and she was hungry and tired. "I'm beat," she said. "Let's go."

Venetta and Sean heard an exciting roar go up from the painted troupe. They turned around just in time to be dowsed with water from a fire hose. Venetta screamed as the cold water drenched her from head to toe. The mud-painted troupe members were jumping and laughing in the water, the paint and mud being washed from their bodies and into the open drain.

Venetta looked at her dress already ruined from the jam. She was soaked to her skin. She looked at Sean with his black T-shirt clinging to his lean, well-developed chest. They burst out laughing.

"I'm sorry about your dress," Sean apologized between peals of laughter.

"It's okay," Venetta responded, still laughing. "This is the most fun I've had in a long time." She grabbed Sean's hand and half dragged him into the stream of water.

Sean looked at her and smiled, happy to see her having such immense enjoyment. She was like a child in her excitement, and it was infectious.

By the time they arrived at Mrs. Bryan's house, the intense sun had dried their clothes. Mrs. Bryan took one look at Venetta's ruined dress and raised her eyebrows at Sean inquisitively.

"We were jamming," he explained to his mother, knowing what she was thinking. "We got caught in the annual wash-down."

Mrs. Bryan offered them a meal of dumpling and stewed codfish, with mashed green bananas.

"This is delicious," Venetta complimented. "You have to give me the recipe. And the one for that black cake."

Mrs. Bryan said with a sly smile, "Sure. You'll have to learn to cook Kittitian food soon anyway. My son loves his oil-down salt fish."

"Mother!" Sean exclaimed.

It was almost one in the afternoon when the couple headed out, but they were waylaid by a troupe of masqueraders in multicolored costumes adorned with mirrors and wooden headdresses with peacock feathers performing outside the gate. After the performance, Mrs. Bryan invited the group onto the veranda, where she served cake and sorrel.

Venetta was surprised when Sean led her to a red Kawasaki Ninja. "This is my ride," he said, straddling the sleek motorcycle and revving the engine. "Hop on."

"I've never ridden on a motorcycle before."

"There's a first time for everything," he shouted over the noise of the revving bike. "My car broke down on Christmas Eve. With all the holidays, I don't think it'll be fixed before next year. But this is pretty safe and fun. You can use my helmet if it'll make you more comfortable, but there's no law here requiring it."

She smiled and hopped onto the motorcycle, declining the offer of a helmet. They rode on back roads through

rows of little bungalows and across fields of sugarcane
until they came to the hotel. With the wind in her hair
and her arms wrapped tightly around Sean, Venetta felt
liberated. It was a feeling of carefree exhilaration that
made her want to scream out loud. It was a feeling she
cherished long after he left and she drifted off to sleep
with a smile on her face. Indeed she was happy she'd accepted Kerina's trip to St. Kitts. She was even happier
that she had met Sean.

Chapter Nine

Venetta awoke to the sound of excited chatter and off-key singing. She opened her eyes to see Kerina on the phone singing a lullaby to her children, while Sheridia and Janelle prepared to attend a show.

"What time is it?" Venetta asked, stretching and clearing the cobwebs from her eyes. She had no idea what time her friends had returned to the hotel as she had been in a deep exhausted sleep.

"Almost eight, Sleeping Beauty," Sheridia replied, tossing a pillow at her. "We're going to the Talented Teen Pageant. Wanna come? Or do you have some secret rendezvous with your phantom?"

"I saw them all cozy on the balcony at the party," Janelle said, joining in the teasing.

"Oh, shut up." Venetta blushed and tossed the pillow at Janelle.

Kerina ended her phone call. "Count me out on tonight's activities. I'm going to grab a bite and hit the sack by ten."

"I'll join you," Venetta said.

Venetta and Kerina headed to the hotel dining room where they dined on a buffet of seafood and listened to a live steel orchestra.

"So, what time did you guys get back?" Venetta asked.

"Around three. Sheridia and I followed a band until it

packed up. Of course we got lost. Everyone we asked for directions kept telling us to go up the road, or across the road or by the some cock-and-hen tree. So we walked until we bumped into Mrs. Bryan's neighbor, who escorted us there."

"Where were Janelle and Debbie?"

"At Mrs. Bryan's house—worried. So, what did you and big brother *phantom* do? I want all the juicy details."

Venetta smiled as she reflected on her groundbreaking day. "We jammed until midday, saw a bull, masquerades, and got soaked in the annual wash-down. My dress was ruined, I rode on a motorcycle for the first time in my life . . . and I had the time of my life."

Kerina raised her glass. "Here's to St. Kitts and Venetta's liberation."

Before Venetta could respond, a waiter delivered a virgin piña colada. "Compliments of SKB," he said, placing the cherry-topped drink in front of Venetta and motioning toward the band.

"Compliments of St. Kitts?" Kerina asked, confused.

Venetta looked around, and there in the steel orchestra was Sean. He waved his drumsticks at her and smiled. Venetta returned his smile, her heart doing double flips, and turned to Kerina. "No. Compliments of Sean Kevin Bryan."

"Wow!" Kerina responded. "I think he really likes you. And he's cute, too."

"Can you keep a secret?" Venetta asked, and Kerina nodded. "We almost kissed today."

"Hey, maybe it's the beginning of something."

"Kerina, I'll be gone in a few days. I can't begin something," Venetta said with a sigh.

"Something begun here doesn't have to end here."

"I don't think long-distance relationships work."

The band had finished playing and the players were packing up. "Don't look now, Venetta, but your phantom's coming this way."

Sean approached the women with his friend Darren in tow. Both of them wore identical colorful batik shirts over the T-shirts marked *Kittitian Pride*, which Venetta now realized was the uniform of the steel orchestra. He greeted both and introduced Darren.

Darren shook Venetta's hand cordially, then slowly, seductively brought Kerina's hand to his lips. In his deepest, most seductive voice that could rival Barry White's, he crooned in a fake American accent, "I must have died and gone to heaven. Angel, where have you been all my life?"

Kerina smiled sweetly and answered just as seductively, "Living in Baltimore with my husband and two kids."

Both Venetta and Sean observed the exchange, trying not to laugh aloud.

Darren was not so easily dissuaded. "Your husband must be one lucky man. But he's there, and I'm here. What are you doing later?"

"Going back to my hotel room, slipping into something nice and sexy, calling my husband, and having some steamy P.S." With that, Kerina strutted out of the dining room, mouthing to Venetta, "Have fun."

Darren turned to Venetta and asked, reverting to his Kittitian accent, "What's P.S.?"

"Phone sex," she responded, laughing out loud. Sean couldn't contain his laughter any longer and doubled over in laughter.

Having decided to head to the bar for some drinks, Sean turned to Darren. "Care to join us?"

"Nah," Darren responded. "You two enjoy yourselves. I'll probably go check out the action at Shoreline." He then turned to Venetta before taking leave. "Sean is one of the good ones."

Sean smiled as he and Venetta took up perches on the bar stools. "Don't worry about Darren. He's a flirt who chases anything in a skirt. He'll get over it. What are you drinking?"

"I'll try something a little stronger tonight."

"I didn't realize you drank," Sean commented.

"I only drink when I'm with people I trust," she responded.

"I'm honored."

Sean ordered a martini while Venetta turned to the bartender and asked, "What do you recommend?"

"Sex on the Beach is always good," the bartended responded.

Venetta's face flushed.

"It's a drink," Sean whispered in her ear.

"Of course," she responded, slightly embarrassed at her overreaction.

As they sipped their drinks leisurely, Venetta asked Sean, "How long have you been playing the steel pan?"

"I started in junior high. Never realized how much I enjoyed it until I went to college. So when I came back, a few friends and I got together, raised some funds, and *Kittitian Pride* was born."

"Where do you find time?"

"That's the advantage of teaching. Between the short days and the holidays, you do have time for hobbies," he responded, finishing his drink. "Let's get some fresh air."

This time Venetta did not hesitate as he led her to the darkened quiet beach. She had no idea what to expect, but she was looking forward to being with him.

Chapter Ten

Sean and Venetta strolled along the starlit beach, hand in hand, Venetta's long blue cotton skirt swirling around her calves. They observed a lone boat on the water, hearing distant music sailing on the wind.

"I had a really wonderful time today," Venetta said.

"Me, too. It's been a while since I participated in j'ouvert."

"Why?"

"It's a long story. I'm also pretty busy with the band this time of year."

"Do you play for the street parades, too?"

"Occasionally, like this year, we'll play for the parade of troupes and Last Lap, but most of our engagements are at hotels, tourist ships, or on the Strip. We even play at beach weddings."

"Beach weddings," Venetta mused dreamily. "As a teenager I dreamed of marrying on a beach. I would wear a long flowing off-the-shoulders cotton dress, and flip-flops. My bridegroom would dress like a pirate in black pantaloons and a white bell-sleeved shirt, and my bridesmaids would have coconut shell bras like *The Little Mermaid*, and Hawaiian sarongs with orchids in their hair."

"So did you?"

Venetta shook her head no. "We were completely traditional—white satin gown, MJ dressed in tuxedo, and bridesmaids in impractical pink satin dresses. It was in a church."

"What was MJ like?"

Venetta looked up at him questioningly. Most of her friends discouraged her from constantly talking about MJ. "Why?"

"Because I want to get to know you and he was an important part of your life."

Venetta smiled, a warm feeling enveloping her. "He was a wonderful person. Warm, generous, adventurous. Can you believe we met in preK? I think I was in love with him even then, but we didn't start dating until high school. He liked traveling, but mostly to cold places. He liked snow and winter sports. And he loved Christmas. Every year he would . . ." Venetta looked up at Sean. He was watching her intently, apparently hanging on to every word. "Am I talking too much?"

Sean shook his head. "How did he die?"

"Leukemia." Venetta walked toward the water, her eyes glistening with unshed tears. She removed her shoes and dipped her toes into the warm ocean. "He had it as a child. It came back when he was eighteen. We were married just after. I guess I expected it, but it's still difficult."

"I know," Sean said, looking at her as if he felt her pain.

"What about you, have you ever been married?"

"No," he responded. "I came close, though."

They resumed walking along the darkened beach in companionable silence, listening to the waves roll at their feet. With each look, with each softly spoken word the attraction between them grew. He took her hand in his as they stopped under the shade of a coconut palm.

"Look at the horizon," Sean directed.

Venetta gazed across the waters as the moon, a great

orange semicircular block of cheese, rose where the sky met the sea. It was difficult to tell where the moon ended and its reflection on the water began.

"That is beautiful," she breathed, awed by the splendor of nature.

"You're beautiful," he whispered, turning her around to face him.

Sean gazed down at Venetta and tenderly moved a strand of hair from her face, tucking it safely behind her ears. He gazed into her wide eyes. Slowly he brought his face close to hers.

Venetta put her hands around Sean's neck, gazing into his large eyes. She saw in them everything she was feeling. She trembled slightly as his full lips came close to her own. She felt his wine-sweetened breath on her face, and closed her eyes. Their lips touched ever so gently. Sean caressed her lips with his own, sending shivers down her spine. Slowly he released her lips, searching her eyes. Venetta smiled. She'd never kissed anyone besides MJ. It was beautiful.

Instantly, Venetta reached up and kissed him again, her lips caressing his. Tenderly he parted her lips with his tongue, sweetly exploring her mouth. Venetta felt her body come alive, a feeling she hadn't experienced in years. She responded with fiery passion, raising her tongue to meet his, exploring the deep recesses of his mouth. A soft moan escaped her lips as her passions ignited and their kiss deepened. He pulled her into a tighter embrace, his chest against her soft breast, his hands running through her hair, a gasp escaping his throat.

He released her lips. They remained in a tight embrace under the half-moon that now bathed the beach in silver.

Venetta looked up at him. "You know I've never done that before."

"Done what?" he whispered hoarsely.

"Kiss a man I've known less than three days."

"Neither have I," he responded. "In fact, I've never kissed a man."

Venetta laughed and poked him in the ribs. He sucked in his stomach and grabbed both her fists in his hands, laughing lightly as he did. He pulled her toward him, placing her arms around his waist. "I feel like I've known you all my life," he whispered to her, nibbling lightly on her ears.

"Me, too," Venetta replied, glancing at her watch.

He noticed and paused his kisses. "Are you ready to go back to the hotel?"

Venetta was not ready for the night to end and shook her head no. "Where do you live?"

"Just up on that hill," he responded, using his head to motion the direction. "Walking distance from here."

"Let's go there," Venetta suggested boldly.

Sean ran his hands tenderly through Venetta's hair. "Are you sure?"

She nodded her head, a lump the size of a grapefruit in her throat as her heart threatened to break through the walls of her chest. "Yes."

Chapter Eleven

Venetta was surprised by the grandeur of the brightly painted multifamily home on the hill. They climbed a flight of stairs to a wraparound porch on the second floor that Sean occupied. From there they could see exotic views of Frigate Bay Beach, Bird Rock, and low-lying Basseterre. As they entered the house with its large picture windows, Venetta realized it was built so that every room on this floor was a room with a picturesque view.

The house was built with open, easy flowing space. The spacious living room with high ceilings and ceramic floors were separated from the dining room and eat-in kitchen by a wide archway. The dining room was separated from the kitchen only by a bar, giving the illusion of one large open room.

"May I look around?" Venetta asked, proceeding to explore the elegantly built house. Each room had an exit to the porch. Most of the intricately designed furniture and cabinetry was made of white pine and stained in a honey oak color.

Venetta wandered into the master bedroom, where a queen-sized wood framed bed lay unmade and covered with clothes. The matching dresser was cluttered with an assortment of colognes, envelopes, and receipts. Even the nightstand was cluttered with books and papers. Venetta looked at a clearly embarrassed Sean and raised her eyebrows inquisitively.

He shrugged sheepishly. "If I knew I was having visitors I would have tidied up."

She smiled as they walked back to the living room. "How can you afford this on a teacher's salary?"

Sean handed her a CD case. On it was a photo of himself minus the dreads beneath the title, *Notes from S.K.B.* He popped a CD into the stereo set. His deep voice, smooth and clear, crooned a blend of reggae, calypso, jazz, and soul that seemed to create a genre all its own. "And I rent out the two downstairs apartments to Ross University students."

"Wow, you are talented. Do you compose your own songs?"

"I compose, arrange, sing, make and market the CDs," he said proudly.

Venetta sinking into the comfortable leather couch turned the case over in her hands. It was dated three years back.

"Haven't composed anything new recently," he said sadly.

"Why?"

Sean did not respond. Instead, he led her by the hand across the neatly landscaped backyard to a small louvered workshed. In it was furniture in various stages of completion and scraps of wood. At one end of the shed were bits of craft made of wood with high-gloss latex finishes. Some contained postcards in the guitar-shaped outline of St. Kitts, others contained photos.

At the other corner of the room was a little alcove, with a bench and an easel. Cluttered on the bench were sketches of furniture pieces and cupboards. What attracted Venetta's attention most was the back wall of this alcove. Almost every square inch was filled with framed photos of a stunningly beautiful young lady.

Venetta felt a twinge of jealousy. "Who is she?" she asked him quietly, wondering if the kiss they had shared just minutes ago was a mistake.

"That's Sharon. She is . . . was my girlfriend." Sean looked at the photos fondly, much the same way as she'd idolized MJ's photos just a week ago.

She recognized the emotion. "What happened?"

His voice was barely a whisper as he spoke. "We met as teenagers. She was Darren's half sister by his father's side. The moment I saw her, I knew I was in love with her and did every idiotic thing I could to get her attention. She was warm, sensitive, creative, and funny. It took her a while to come around, but when she did it was magic." He smiled nostalgically. "She lived with her grandmother then, who didn't approve of her dating anyone. So she would pretend to go visit her father and Darren would sneak her out to see me. We saw each other secretly for a year. By the time we were at the local college, we were officially a couple—Sharon and Sean, Sean and Sharon. We did everything together. Then she went to college in Jamaica and I went to Maryland. Everyone said our relationship wouldn't survive the distance, but it did."

A sad wistful look replaced the dreamy expression as he continued. "We had big plans for our lives together. Marriage, kids, the works. Then one day, Sharon discovered a lump under her armpit. I encouraged her to see a doctor. After all, her mother had died of breast cancer. But Sharon hated doctors, and routinely did self breast examinations. She insisted the lump was an allergic reaction to a deodorant she used. Instead she tried all kinds of natural and herbal remedies to get rid of the lump. It took her a full year to finally visit a doctor."

Sean's voice faded to barely a whisper as he tried

desperately not to shed tears. "That's when we learned she had stage-four metastatic inflammatory breast cancer—the kind that couldn't be detected by breast examinations. The doctors gave her six months to live without treatment, a year and a half to two with aggressive chemotherapy. She opted to forgo any treatment. A year later, three years, four months, and three days ago, she died, and so did part of me."

Venetta felt tears sting her eyes. She felt his pain. Now she understood why he was able to understand her hurt at losing MJ. Now she understood why his eyes were sad, even soulful; why his folks thought he was reclusive. Venetta put her arms around Sean, embracing him. "I'm so sorry," she whispered.

They walked back to the house in silence and sat on the brown leather sofa. "I guess that's why you no longer write?" Venetta asked quietly.

Sean nodded. "Sharon was the inspiration for most of my songs. In the evenings, she would stand at her easel drafting her plans while I arranged the music and tested it out on the keyboard . . . she couldn't draw in quiet." He smiled reflectively. "She was such a great architect. She designed this house. It was supposed to be our dream home. My father and brothers built it and I did most of the joinery and woodwork in it. After her diagnosis, before the house was completed, I asked her to marry me. She said, 'What's the point? I'll be dead in a few months.' I guess she accepted it better than I did."

Venetta nodded. She could relate to that. "While I was running around trying to find a bone marrow match, MJ was making funeral arrangements for himself."

He ran his hands through his locks. "I guess few people understand what it's like, the pain, the anger, the helplessness. I remember being so mad at her for not fighting more, for refusing the chemotherapy. It's only now I finally understand her reasoning. She didn't want to spend her last days at some hospital in Trinidad, away from her friends and family just to extend her life a few months. Sometimes I wish I could turn back the hands of time and undo it all."

Venetta nodded in total understanding. "Most of my friends think I should just move on. It's not that easy. There's the part of your life that you know you'll never get back, and then there's the—"

"Guilt," he finished simultaneously with her.

"As if you betray their memory by thinking about another."

They looked at each other and smiled, both thinking the same thing. "Did you feel guilty when I kissed you tonight?" Sean asked.

Venetta shook her head and Sean let out the breath he was holding. "It was beautiful."

They sat in silence on the couch next to each other, the stereo playing softly in the background. They were kindred spirits having gone through familiar suffering and now understood each other. He took her hand in his, interlacing their fingers, and drew her close.

"You are very special," he whispered, touching his forehead to hers. "You're the first person I've gotten close to since Sharon."

Venetta closed her eyes, feeling the warmth of his breath on her face. He kissed her eyelids, her cheeks, and then possessed her lips. Slowly his tongue probed her mouth, sending Venetta's heart pounding wildly against her chest, making her weak in the knees. Venetta responded to his kiss passionately, sweetly exploring his mouth, her entire being alive. He pulled her closer, his kiss intensifying as he gently caressed her shoulders and the nape of her neck, sending shivers down her spine. Venetta caressed his shoulder and back, feeling the ripple of muscles beneath his shirt. He released her lips long enough to send a tiny trail of kisses down her neck and chest.

A moan escaped Venetta's lips as Sean tenderly caressed her breast through the thin fabric, making her wild with desire. She quickly removed his T-shirt, gasping at the lean cut of his chest muscles and his hard-packed abs. He possessed her lips again, his long fingers expertly unbuttoning the tiny buttons on her loose-fitting cotton blouse.

Sean looked at Venetta lying on the couch, her blouse opened, revealing full breasts barely covered by a black lacy bra. He stared at her intently. He sent tiny wet kisses up her flat, well-toned stomach while caressing her legs.

Venetta arched her body invitingly. She was burning with desire and wanted to be connected to Sean in every way possible. Her breathing labored, her body on fire, she moaned aloud.

Suddenly Sean stopped, shuddering.

"Don't stop," she pleaded passionately.

Ignoring her pleas, he slowly rebuttoned her blouse. His voice was hoarse when he spoke, "Let's go before we do something we're both unprepared for."

Venetta gazed into Sean's eyes and realized he was speaking of both emotional and physical preparedness: protection. It was something she had never taken into consideration with MJ. They had both been virgins when they married, and years of aggressive cancer treatment had left him infertile.

That was when the recognition of their actions hit her. She was about to make love to a man she'd met just three days ago.

* * *

They walked back to the hotel in silence. Venetta thought about the evening. Had anyone told her she would be in that compromising position with a virtual stranger, she would have told them to get their head examined.

"You okay?" he asked as he escorted her to her hotel room.

Venetta nodded.

"Venetta, you have no idea how hard it was for me to control myself tonight. I want to make love to you, but I don't want to hurt you."

Venetta nodded and smiled. "What we're doing is crazy. We just met and in a few days I'll be back in Baltimore. But, Sean, I feel closer to you than I've felt to anyone in years. It feels right and . . . What I'm trying to say is, maybe we should just enjoy each other's company, no strings attached, regardless of where our passions lead us."

Venetta turned to face Sean as they stood outside her hotel room. He stroked her face with his finger.

"You've seen the tourist's St. Kitts and you've seen Debbie's St. Kitts. Tomorrow I'd like to show you *my* St. Kitts. I'll take you to my favorite place."

Venetta nodded before he gave her a passionate kiss good night. "See you tomorrow," she whispered, her heart wanting to explode in her chest.

Venetta entered the door and leaned against it trying to make sense of all that had happened in these few days on the island and the passionate kisses she had shared with Sean tonight. *This is crazy*, she thought to herself, *but I think I'm falling in love with you.*

Chapter Twelve

With hair flying freely in the early morning wind, Venetta and Sean zipped uphill on his Ninja over rugged dirt paths between fields of sugarcane. They stopped in an estate yard next to a large concrete cistern that formerly supplied water to the old sugar estate. An oxidized copper basin and ruins of an old sugar mill stood adjacent to the cistern. Cattle, sheep, and goats dotted the hillside, grazing on the dew-kissed grass.

Sean parked his bike next to the cistern. A woman in tattered clothing with several bare-bottomed children filled buckets of water and carried them on their heads to the ramshackle village below. He removed a backpack from the storage compartment of the bike and slung it over his shoulders. "We'll continue on foot from here," he announced in his singsong Kittitian accent, walking a few feet into the cane fields. He returned a few seconds later with two sticks of sugarcane. "We'll need these."

They plodded through a narrow dirt track with rows of dasheen, yams, and sweet potatoes on one side, and shade trees bordered with the large-leafed elephant ears on the other. Intermittently they spotted a lone peasant farmer under the shade of a corrugated metal lean-to who would greet them with a hearty, "Morning, morning." They spotted a few folks on donkeys with hampers loaded with crocus bags of produce. From there they could hear bits of conversations floating on the wind from the tiny wooden shacks in the village below.

Soon the fields that Sean referred to as "grungs" gave way to rows of cacao and large fruit trees. He stopped to pick a yellow cacao and a ripe custard apple sitting on a low-lying branch. Twigs crackled under their feet as they walked along the gentle slopes.

The landscape transitioned from gently sloping drier dirt-packed paths lined by fruit trees to moist steeply inclined leave-strewn paths. The trees got taller and formed an interlocking canopy; ferns and ginger lilies made up the underbrush. The soil beneath their feet got softer and darker, and a damp musty smell of rotting leaves pervaded the air. They were now in the rain forest.

Venetta leaned heavily on the stick of sugarcane as she navigated the narrow muddy path. Vines hung from trees, and the mountain doves sang melodious tunes. There was little sunlight except for the occasional breaks in the forest canopy. Venetta could hear the trickle of mountain streams in the distance.

Sean helped her up a narrow stepped path between two tree-filled ravines. "Those are ghauts," Sean explained, "temporary rivers that flow only in times of heavy rains."

After a grueling uphill trudge, they finally began walking downhill, slipping and sliding on the muddy hillside. Abruptly they came to a stop in a valley. Venetta looked around and shivered, her light khaki shorts and aqua tank top no match for the cool, damp mountain air. Fog hung low over the mountainside, lowering visibility. "Is this it?" Venetta asked, disappointed. She had expected an exotic view.

"Just wait a minute," Sean replied patiently, placing his light fatigue jacket over her shoulders.

In the twinkling of an eye the mist, like a veil, lifted, revealing a sparkling crater lake of crystal-clear water. The sun reflecting off tiny ripples on the surface sparkled like diamonds in a tiara. Ferns of all shapes and colors, and tiny fragrant flowers, framed the edge of the lake. The sky, clear and blue, looked close enough to touch. A lone red bird swooped overhead, the flutter of its wings breaking the serenity of the day. From the tall trees on the mountainside a mountain dove cooed melodiously, its song echoing off the sides of the crater.

"This is beautiful," Venetta whispered reverently. "When I picture heaven with its Crystal Sea and streams of living waters, this is what I imagine."

Sean slipped his arm around her. "This is DuDon Pond, my favorite place in the world."

Venetta stooped down and dipped her hand in the water. It was ice cold. Sean filled an empty bottle from his backpack with water.

"This is a crater lake. If you dive in the middle you can go all the way down into the volcano," Sean said.

"Really?"

"I don't know," he chuckled, and Venetta pushed him playfully.

He caught her hands in his. "I can think of more exciting uses for those hands."

They both laughed and walked around exploring the edges of the wide lake. The long hike made Venetta hungry and her stomach growled loudly.

"What's that sound?" Sean asked.

Venetta laughed out loud. "Just my stomach rumbling."

Sean removed an old blanket from his backpack and spread it on a small grassy area beside the pond. He removed two paper plates and a plastic dish, filling the air with the scent of fried fish. He dished out some small fishes fried dry and little biscuitlike pastries.

"I'm not much of a cook, so I'm afraid we'll have to settle for fried ballahoo and johnnycake."

Venetta took a bite. "Peppery, but okay."

He poured her a drink. When Venetta tasted it, it burned her mouth, forcing her to down the water from the lake. "What's that?"

"Ginger beer."

Venetta had drunk it before at Mrs. Bryan's house, but it was definitely not as potent as this one. "Tastes nothing like your mother's own," she said, clearing her throat.

"I guess I should have made it a little milder," Sean laughed. "My culinary skills are extremely limited. Mother spoilt me. She lives close enough to the school so I can pop over for lunch and stop by for dinner."

"So you only know how to make breakfast," Venetta teased.

"Hey, I do make a mean soup."

Venetta finished eating and washed her hands in the cool lake. "Now I need something sweet to combat all that pepper."

"I'm sweet," Sean joked. "So is sugarcane." He used his knee to break the stick of sugarcane and peeled it with his teeth. Venetta looked at him incredulously. Sean smiled and handed a piece of peeled sugarcane to her. "This is the way Kittitians eat sugarcane."

Venetta chewed on the cane, enjoying the sweet juice. "So, what's in the soup?"

"Everything but the kitchen sink. I'll show you sometime before you leave."

The thought of leaving saddened Venetta. "I'm not

looking forward to the cold weather or the short dark days of winter that's still in Baltimore. I'm having so much fun here, I don't want to leave."

Sean opened the creamy custard apple and shared it with her. "Then stay."

"What would I do here?"

"Teach. We need language teachers."

Venetta sighed. "Sean, I have a life in the States. My job, my friends, my family."

"Tell me about your family," Sean asked, breaking open a yellow cacao by pounding it against a rock.

"My parents live in New York. They moved there about eight years ago when my father's accounting firm relocated. I have one sister."

"Are you close to each other?" he asked, removing a seed from the cacao and sucking on it. He passed one to Venetta.

"Not particularly. She's just fourteen and right now going through the teenage woes. When I left home she was only four. Then I have my parents-in-law, who live just fifteen minutes from me. I'm closer to them than my own parents."

"Why?" he asked, popping another seed in his mouth.

"MJ and I lived with them for the first three years of our marriage. Then we were the support for each other during his illness and subsequent death."

Sean stood up and skipped a cacao seed on the water. It skipped twice and reached halfway to the middle of the lake. "Top that!" he challenged.

Venetta took her cacao seed and skipped it on the water. It passed his. "Who's the man?" She pumped her fist.

"You know, we use these to make chocolate. My grandmother used to have us suck the flesh off the seeds. Then she'd sun-dry them, roast them, and grind them, before compacting the powder into a stick. We used it to make chocolate tea or, as you guys refer to it, hot chocolate."

He skipped another seed, his arm swinging like a golfer's. It passed Venetta's. "Yeah!" He pumped his fist.

Venetta removed another seed from her mouth and raised her hand. Sean moved behind her, placing his hands on her tiny waist, and kissed the nape of her neck.

"No fair," Venetta protested, leaning into him. "I can't throw this seed with you distracting me like that."

He whispered, his lips lightly brushing her ears, "I never promised to play fairly."

Venetta jabbed him playfully in the stomach. The gesture made him lose his balance on the slippery ground and he fell backward, taking her with him. They rolled toward the lake laughing until they stopped on a grassy verge at the water's edge, with Venetta atop Sean.

Venetta looked down at his large brown eyes crowned by endless lashes and framed by thick arched eyebrows. For a long moment they gazed into each other's eyes.

"That night when I saw you on the beach walking all alone in deep thought, you know what I saw?" Sean whispered, holding her gaze. "Myself. I saw me in you."

Venetta smiled coquettishly. "Literally or figuratively?"

Sean returned her seductive smile. "Both."

He rolled her over, leaving her lying on the damp grassy patch looking up at him. His face drew close to hers as he possessed her lips.

Venetta returned his kiss with fiery passion, aware only of the drumbeat of her heart and the intense heat in her most intimate parts. Tenderly he traced a line along the nape of her neck down to the middle of her back, sending darts of electricity shooting throughout Venetta's body.

Venetta reached up, embracing him, caressing his back and shoulders, feeling the ripple of taut muscle beneath her hands.

He released her lips long enough to send a trail of tiny kisses down her neck and chest between her cleavage. Venetta arched her back, drawing closer to him, feeling his desire grow to match her own. Sean's breathing labored, he tenderly caressed her breast through the thin fabric of her tank top. He kissed her again, his hand wandering beneath her blouse as he unhooked her cotton bra, freeing her full breasts. Slowly he raised her blouse, gently tasting the hard dark buds on her breast.

She gasped, filled with ecstasy. She was on fire and she wanted him more than she had wanted anything else in recent times. A moan escaped her lips as his mouth closed over her breast. She moved her hands over his tight abs and unbuttoned his pants, as he caressed her legs beneath her shorts.

"Oh, Venetta," he breathed as he opened the fly of her pants. "I want you."

Slowly he pulled her pants below her hips. With one hand he removed a condom from his pocket, caressing her with the other. Suddenly he stopped. "Do you hear voices?"

Venetta opened her eyes, her body trembling with desire. She shook her head no, unable to speak for the grapefruit-sized lump stuck in her throat. She groaned.

"Sh," he whispered.

That's when she heard the cracking of twigs and distinct voices approaching. Swiftly they redressed. Venetta had barely straightened her clothes when she saw a small group of hikers atop the basin just above them.

Sean greeted the hikers with a wave, then continued packing his backpack. "Let's go," he said to Venetta.

* * *

They trudged downhill in silence, their bodies still on fire from their passionate encounter. They stopped just before exiting the rain forest.

Sean drew her close to him. "Venetta, Venetta, Venetta," he sighed, a warm feeling enveloping him. He felt alive. It was a heart-throbbing closeness he hadn't felt since Sharon. He wished Venetta didn't have to leave on New Year's Day. What he felt was so much more than physical attraction. He was falling in love with her.

Chapter Thirteen

The warm afternoon sun beat down on the golden sand of Frigate Bay and sparkled off the clear blue waters. Venetta, Kerina, Janelle, and Sheridia, armed with sunshades and sunblock, stretched out on beach chairs, soaking up the sun. They were enjoying a relaxing, lazy day on the beach, something they hadn't done since coming to this island.

The girls had slept in, awakening around noon. They took a long leisurely lunch before dressing in colorful bathing suits and hitting the beach.

"Girl," Janelle said to Venetta, "your phantom can sure sing. I did not realize he was so talented." Yesterday evening, the four friends had attended a beauty pageant with Deborah, where they saw Sean, handsomely dressed in slacks and sport coat, serenading the contestants. He sang "You are so beautiful to me" in a deep clear baritone, melting the audience and shattering Venetta's heart into tiny pieces.

"Not to mention hot," Sheridia added, making Venetta blush instantly. "Did you see when he removed his sport coat how the crowd went wild? Girl, if you hadn't discover him first, I'd put my hooks in him and never let go!"

Venetta rolled her eyes, thankful she was wearing dark glasses. Despite her calmness, her heart raced at the very thought of Sean. After the pageant Sean joined the four friends and his sister at Sprat Net, a waterfront hangout five miles west of the capital city. When they finally returned to the Frigate Bay area, it was almost dawn. Instead of returning to the hotel, Venetta and Sean walked along the beach where they'd first met. Hand in hand, they walked and talked about everything. They discussed their hopes, their dreams, their desires, revealing themselves to each other in a most intimate way. And then they shared long leisurely kisses, because time did not exist when they were together. Venetta only returned to the hotel after witnessing the lovely sunrise over the Southeast Peninsula. By then Venetta knew she was in love with Sean and it scared her half to death.

Kerina responded to Sheridia dismissively, "You'll put your hooks in anything as long as it has male organs and breath."

"Breath is optional," Janelle joined in. The girls erupted with laughter.

"So tell me," Sheridia persisted, "is he a good kisser?"

Venetta smiled coyly. "I don't kiss and tell," she said, eliciting chuckles from her friends.

Sheridia got up from her chair, her red lowrider bikini barely covering her coffee-cream bottom. Raising her sunglasses, she looked over the waters of the calm Caribbean Sea intermittently disturbed by a Jet Ski or water skiers. "Hanging out with you guys is boring, especially when Venetta is withholding all the juicy details of her steamy romance," she complained. "I want to do that." She pointed at some windsurfers.

Janelle rifled through her green-print tote bag that matched her one-piece bathing suit and sarong and removed a schedule of activities. "There's a boat leaving at two for deep-sea diving and snorkeling."

"It's past two," Kerina responded lazily.

"There's a windsurfing demonstration in fifteen minutes and a water skiing class in half an hour."

Sheridia started packing up her stuff. "What are you waiting for, let's go."

Janelle joined her. They looked at Venetta and Kerina, who remained immobile. "Aren't you coming?"

"Hell no," Kerina responded, adjusting the strap on her white string bikini and lying back on the lounge chair. "I am going to take all the rest and relaxation I can from now till I go back home. I have two rowdy kids and a sex-starved husband waiting for me when I get back."

"Couch potato," Sheridia teased.

"Adrenaline junkie," Kerina shot back as the girls headed off.

With Janelle and Sheridia gone, Kerina and Venetta lay back enjoying the quiet tranquility of the beach. A few kids ran by excitedly collecting shells. Several teenagers frolicked in the waters while a couple of honeymooners kissed romantically. Brown pelicans swooped overhead, diving into the warm waters for an occasional meal.

Venetta looked over at Kerina. "I love this island. I'm glad you bullied me into coming."

"I guess I won't have to bully you next time." Kerina grinned knowingly. "We should make it an annual thing. But next time, I'm bringing Mark and the kids with me. I miss them so much."

"I can't afford it. This hotel is outrageously expensive."

"All you need is the plane ticket. Mrs. Bryan and Debbie already invited us to stay with them. And I'm sure your phantom wouldn't mind a warm body in his bed," she teased.

Venetta thought of the conversations they'd had last night and Sean's gentle urging to move to St. Kitts. She knew she felt more than just physical attraction to him.

"Is it possible to fall in love with a man you know only a few days?"

Kerina regarded her pensively. "You know why Mark's mother hates me?"

Venetta shook her head wondering how it related to her question.

"Mark and I met on an internship in Ohio. We met June first, we were married the twenty-second. I knew from the first day Mark was the person I wanted to spend my life with. Unfortunately, his mother told me I robbed her of her only son and vowed to make my life a living hell. But, Venetta, I don't regret for one minute marrying him. So, are you in love with Sean or just in lust?"

Venetta sighed. "I'm feeling things that I haven't felt since MJ. With MJ, everything took time. We dated four years before becoming intimate and that was on our wedding night. And to be honest, I was more excited about the wedding than the consummation. But with Sean I find myself desiring things I never imagined. And it's not just the physical attraction, but we have this connection. We understand each other and I can tell him everything and anything. Kerina, I think I'm in love with him and I don't know what to do. When we're together, I feel like anything we do is right, but when he leaves I begin to feel guilty, like I shouldn't have these feelings."

Kerina teased, "Personally I don't go for the dreadlocks look, but I have to admit, when it comes to sex appeal he beats MJ hands down. I mean, this guy is ripped. MJ was kind of on the scrawny side. . . ."

"MJ was ill," Venetta defended. "He couldn't help being pale and thin."

Kerina chuckled. "I was just trying to get you to lighten up a bit. The point is, Venetta, sometimes love comes once in a lifetime, but on rare occasions, some people are lucky and find it twice or more. Maybe you're one of the lucky ones. It doesn't take anything from what you had or what you felt for MJ. So if it's meant to be, let it be. And if not, then enjoy the time of your life."

Venetta sighed, silently trying to make sense of Kerina's advice. "We kind of have an agreement to just have fun now with no real commitment after I leave."

"You're not Sheridia. I don't see you having a noncommittal love affair and leaving unscathed. But then, an indefinite long-distance relationship doesn't make much sense either. If it is serious one of you may have to relocate."

"He's been subtly urging me to move to St. Kitts," Venetta admitted.

"Is that what you want?"

"I don't know. I love the island. I like the people and I like his family. But my whole family is back in the States."

"Let's put things into perspective. Your parents live in New York and even though it's only a four-hour drive, you guys rarely visit—telephone calls mostly. Your little sister only calls you when she wants to complain—not that she doesn't love you. Your family will be fine."

"MJ's parents need me."

Kerina clucked her tongue. "Or is it the other way around, you're keeping MJ alive through them?"

Venetta silently contemplated Kerina's advice.

"Look who's here . . ." Kerina said.

Venetta looked out onto the waters. There, wearing only baggy swim shorts, his wet locks flying in the wind, was Sean riding on a Jet Ski. He was the embodiment of virility.

Sean cut the engine on the Jet Ski and pulled it to the water's edge.

"Go enjoy yourself," Kerina urged.

Venetta strolled toward the water's edge, her aqua tankini emphasizing her curvaceous body. "Hi."

He returned her smile. "I have this for half an hour," he said. "Where would you like to go?"

Without a word, she donned the life vest from the storage compartment on the Jet Ski and got on behind him, pointing to the cliffs of the Southeast Peninsula. He revved the engine and they cut through the waters of the calm sea. They moved swiftly around the long peninsula, past cliffs and concealed beaches, and into the open waters where the Caribbean Sea met the Atlantic Ocean. Finally he pulled into a deserted cove and cut the engine. They floated on the water in the shelter of a mangrove swamp. On either side of them were hills and salt ponds.

Sean spoke for the first time since beginning the ride. "This is also one of my favorite places. On the other side of those hills is the village of Conaree. But here there is nothing but beach and salt ponds and mangrove swamps."

"It's peaceful."

"I know. It's not easily accessible by land." He pulled up onto the deserted beach and they walked around collecting shells. "You remember that soup I told you about? I'm making it this afternoon. Care to join me?"

Venetta teased, "Sure. I won't miss the opportunity to see you cook the only thing you're good at."

"Hey, I'm good at other things."

"Like what?"

"Music, singing, and some things I'd prefer to show you than tell you," he replied with a wink.

Venetta chuckled and dove into the shallow waters protected by a coral reef. "You know, I never realized the Caribbean would be so much fun."

Sean followed her lead, diving under the water and breaking the surface with a loud splash. "It's hard to believe in all your travels you never came to the Caribbean."

"We always went to Europe," she said, swimming toward him. "MJ liked museums and old castles, snow and skiing."

"What did you like?" he asked, shaking his wet locks like a dog after a bath.

Venetta shrugged. "I guess whatever MJ liked. I never really explored what I wanted. But I know now I love the Caribbean, I love St. Kitts, I love the beach and I love . . ." Venetta stopped short, realizing what she was about to say. "Don't you have to turn in this Jet Ski soon?"

Sean looked at his watch. "You're right. I should have booked it for an hour instead."

They remounted the Jet Ski and raced back to the hotel, where he waited in her suite for her to shower and change before going off to his home.

Chapter Fourteen

"How many starches are you putting into this soup?" Venetta questioned as she watched Sean peel numerous vegetables, then measure out flour to make dumplings.

"It's a big man's meal," he responded, playfully putting flour on her nose.

The soup had everything. Chunks of beef, smoked turkey necks, and red beans cooked in the pressure cooker, while Sean and Venetta peeled vegetables. "Most people use pig tail or pig snout or the bone from their Christmas ham in this soup. I don't eat pork, so smoked turkey will have to do," Sean explained.

He removed an enormous silver pot, filled it with water, and added chopped-up whole chicken, the pressurized meat and beans, all the vegetables, and numerous green seasonings. He let it simmer while rolling the dumplings.

"I thought we were only cooking for us?" Venetta questioned, looking at the size of the pot.

"My soup is like the Pied Piper's flute. When the smell goes wafting on the air, people come from far and wide," he joked, placing the dumplings in the now boiling pot.

Venetta moved to the kitchen sink to wash her hands. She looked out of the large bay window that gave an unobstructed view of the Southeast Peninsula and the beach below. The window was opened, letting in sounds of birds chirping outside in the garden. She saw a hummingbird flit from flower to flower, its wings a blur of flutter as it sampled the sweet nectar of the hibiscus.

Sean moved behind her, putting his floury hands around her and into the stream of running water. His nearness caused her heart to flutter like the hummingbird's wings and her body to throb in excitement. She leaned into him. He turned off the tap and nibbled lightly on her ears.

Drawing her to his chest, Sean whispered into her ears, "You never finished your sentence at the beach."

"What sentence?" Venetta asked breathlessly.

"You love St. Kitts, you love the beach, and you love . . . What else?" He turned her around to face him.

Venetta felt her face flush. She kept her eyes averted. "It doesn't matter, does it?"

"Yes, it does, Venetta. You matter to me. Your feelings matter to me. And I hope mine matter to you."

"Sean, in two days I leave this country and—"

"V, what we have does not have to end when you get on that plane. If this is just a vacation fling, fine. But we both know that it's more than that, regardless of what agreement we made."

Venetta closed her eyes. The only person who had ever called her V before was MJ. Trying not to let sentiment get in the way of good sense, she said firmly "Long-distance relationships don't work, Sean, especially when you have permanent dwellings thousands of miles away."

"Then stay. I got you some application forms from the Ministry of Education."

"Sean, don't do this to me."

"I don't mean to pressure you, but, V, I want us to be together. Before I met you, I felt like I was barely existing. You make me want to embrace life again, write songs, laugh, be happy. I don't want it to end with a plane ride."

"Then you move to the States," Venetta challenged. "You can find employment as a chemical engineer."

Sean placed his chin on her head. "Migrating to the U.S., getting a work permit or, God forbid, a green card, is a lot more difficult and complicated than moving to St. Kitts. Gosh, even obtaining a visitor's visa is hard."

Venetta looked into Sean's eyes. She could see the emotions there. She could see he had deep feelings for her. "What's my incentive for wanting to stay?"

Sean's mouth curled into a smile. "Me," he whispered, and his lips possessed hers. He kissed her passionately, every emotion wrapped into that one expression of love and affection. Her heart throbbed, her knees felt weak as he pressed her against the sink.

They heard the gate opened and voices outside. "They're here," Sean whispered breathlessly, reluctantly releasing her.

Venetta looked puzzled. "Who?"

"My folks. Every year I cook soup sometime during the season and invite everyone over. I was hoping to reintroduce you, not as Debbie's guest but as my—"

Venetta extricated herself from his embrace. "Stop it Sean. We're taking things way too fast."

Before they could leave the kitchen, the front door opened and Mr. and Mrs. Bryan and several of their sons entered without knocking. Mrs. Bryan hugged Venetta. "Hey, our newest daughter-in-law is here," she announced.

Venetta self-consciously greeted the others. It seemed a foregone conclusion that she was Sean's girl and that their relationship would outlast her vacation.

Sean's brothers joked around playfully as they dished out the food while his father told old-time stories. A few

minutes later, Deborah and her family showed up. To
Venetta the soup was delicious but on the spicy side. And
Sean was absolutely right; it was a man's meal. When she
was finished, she needed a nap.

It was a calm gathering until Darren showed up with a
case of beer. "Okay, Sean," Darren called loudly. "Break
out that CSR you have hoarding."

In a few minutes the liquor came out and the laughter
got louder, the teasing rowdier, and the jokes raunchier.

"Don't mind my brothers," Sean whispered to Venetta
loudly enough so that everyone could hear. "They're half
crazy."

"I'll clean up for you, Sean," Mrs. Bryan volunteered
while the brothers horsed around.

"I'll help you," Deborah said, eager to escape the teasing and riling.

"That won't be necessary," Mrs. Bryan responded, smiling at Venetta. "My new daughter-in-law will help me."

Deborah looked at Venetta and mouthed, "Uh-oh!"
giving Venetta a twinge of fear for the first time since
meeting this warm, welcoming family.

Venetta remained silent, uncertain what Mrs. Bryan
wanted to say. She looked out at the red dusk sky and its
reflection on the smooth blanket of water in the distance.
Flocks of birds were flying to roost. A few people walked
by and stopped at a house at the bottom of the hill, calling loudly to the tenants. Some children were playing
unsupervised in the yard a few houses down the hill.

"Nice scenery, isn't it?" Mrs. Bryan asked.

"Yes, it is. I love this place."

"Does that mean you won't mind moving here sometime in the future?" Mrs. Bryan asked sweetly.

"You know I do have a home in Maryland and a job
that I love," Venetta countered politely.

Mrs. Bryan said softly, "Debbie told me about your late husband. I guess that's why you and Sean connected so easily. He told you about Sharon?"

Venetta nodded in response.

"I don't usually get into my kids' love lives. But Sean is different. Of my sons, he's the most talented and sensitive. His brothers would brag about their athletic prowess, even their women. Not Sean. He's always been a very private, introspective person. But I remember a time when he was outgoing, when he talked happily about the future. He was into athletics, music, the arts. All that ended when Sharon died. He turned inward and shut everyone out. He gave up songwriting and athletics and spent almost all his time in his workshop or wandering the beach. He only continued playing in the band because Darren would not let him give it up. Most importantly, he'd lost that sparkle in his eyes. But since you came around, Venetta, he's got that sparkle again. I have never seen him this happy or content in years. So I just want to know that you're not going to hurt him. I couldn't bear to see him suffer again."

Venetta didn't know how to respond. She looked out of the window at the darkening skies. Finally she turned to Mrs. Bryan. "I don't know what to say, Mrs. Bryan. We've only just met and I don't know for certain if there's even a future. We live worlds apart."

Mrs. Bryan smiled. "I'm sure if this is meant to be, you guys will find a way to work out the distance."

Chapter Fifteen

It was their last night on St. Kitts, New Year's Eve, or as the locals dubbed it, "Old Year's Night." While the girls prepared to attend a ball, Venetta, wearing a simple dress, paced anxiously waiting for Sean. They were attending Old Year's Night service at the Zion Moravian Church. Sean was late.

"If he doesn't show, you can come to the ball with us," Sheridia suggested.

Just then they heard a knock on the door and Venetta breathed a sigh of relief. She opened the door to Sean, handsomely dressed in a dark gray button-down shirt and black slacks. His dreadlocks were pulled back neatly in an elastic band, highlighting his high cheekbones and generous lips. She invited him into the sitting room.

"You ladies are absolutely beautiful," he complimented the girls before they left. He then turned to Venetta. "And you look divine. But I must warn you, your beautiful hair may not survive the wind off the motorcycle."

Venetta laughed and touched her delicate curls, "My hair can stand up to anything."

By the time they got to the church, the wind along with a slight drizzle of rain had removed every curl from her hair and it lay limp and flat on her head.

"I told you," Sean laughed. "Motorcycle rides are not curl-friendly."

Venetta gave him a playful shove as they walked into

the packed stone church building, where the service was already under way.

It was a nice service done almost entirely in candle-light. As they rang in the new year with meditative prayer and singing, Venetta couldn't be happier, or more thankful. Yet she felt a shadow of loss. She was leaving tomorrow and leaving behind a man she knew she loved. Every bit of uncertainty seemed to come crashing down on her as she followed him through the wrought-iron gate of his home and up the flight of stone steps.

She sat on the balcony, staring forlornly at the silver moon high in the sky, painting the smooth water down below with brushstrokes of silver.

Sean brought out two glasses of champagne. Soft music played on the stereo. He raised his glass and toasted. "To a new year, to new beginnings, to us. Happy New Year, Venetta."

"Happy New Year, Sean."

They slow-danced under the light of the moon. "We're having our own New Year's ball," he whispered in her ears, drawing her closer to him. "I wish I could hold you like this forever."

Venetta sighed. "Oh, Sean, I wish things were different. I wish that it was less complicated. That I didn't have to leave."

Sean held on to her tight. "It doesn't have to be this complicated, V."

"When I came here, I never expected this. I never expected to meet you or to have these feelings."

Sean showered her with tiny kisses, from her temples to her cheeks to her chin, whispering between kisses. "We can't control everything in our lives. We don't know what the future holds or what tomorrow will bring. But we've got tonight, Venetta. Stay with me."

He kissed her passionately, his tongue darting into her mouth, exploring every hidden crevice. Venetta returned his kiss with fiery passion, feeling every fiber of her being come alive. He ran his hands tenderly, tantalizingly down her back, coming to rest on her round bottom. Sean sent a trail of little kisses down her neck, setting her on fire, then kissed her again.

He scooped her up in his arms, his lips never leaving hers as their tongues tangoed. Pushing the front door open with his shoulders, he entered the house, taking her to the bedroom. He laid Venetta down on the queen-sized bed. Venetta looked around the bedroom and smiled, realizing he had cleaned it especially for her.

He smiled down at her, his eyes filled with desire, his heart with love. He slowly undressed her, his hands shaking slightly with a mixture of desire and nervousness. As he looked down at her lying naked in his bed, her breasts standing pert like two Egyptian pyramids, her narrow waist and wide hips inviting him to be one with her, he could barely contain himself. "You are beautiful," he breathed.

Venetta kneeled at the edge of the bed, using one finger to signal for him to come closer. Slowly, tantalizingly, she unbuttoned his shirt, kissing his hairless chest and nibbling at his nipples. He moaned softly, caressing her creamy breasts as she slipped her hands beneath his fly, slowly unbuttoning his pants. She slipped them down his long, lean, muscular legs, until he stood like a Nubian god, completely naked before her.

The sight made Venetta's head reel and her most intimate parts moist with desire. "Oh, Sean," she whispered, cupping his firm buns in her hands.

He lowered her onto the bed, taking her breast into his mouth while tantalizingly caressing her legs. Venetta felt as if she would burst with desire. His fingers explored her most intimate places. Venetta, breathing labored, writhed in pleasure, arching her back invitingly as he sent her into a frenzy of ecstasy. "Make love to me," she gasped, succumbing to the intense waves of pleasure that washed over her.

He removed a condom from the nightstand, placing it in her hands. She stared at it, confused. She had never used one before. He smiled, and like the teacher he was, carefully guided her hands, showing her what to do.

Then ever so slowly he entered her, filling her completely. Venetta moaned with pleasure as they moved together, slowly, tenderly, to the rhythm of the love songs still playing softly on the stereo. Venetta felt herself rise to heights of ecstasy, causing her to move faster. Her movements excited Sean even more, making him thrust deeper into her. With every thrust, every motion, Venetta climbed higher and higher, her body reacting on its own until waves of orgasm washed over her, again and again. Her enjoyment sent Sean over the edge, causing him to climax violently, shuddering against her as he whispered her name over and over again.

They lay in each other's arms, spent and satiated. Venetta felt tears trickle down the side of her eyes. Sean tenderly wiped her tears. "Venetta, are you okay?"

"Oh yes," Venetta whispered, smiling through her tears. "I'm just so happy. I've never experienced anything like this."

Sean drew her into his arms, holding her tight against him. "You want me to tell you a secret?"

She nodded.

"You're the only person besides Sharon that I've ever made love to."

Venetta's heart swelled with love. She knew what they

shared was much more than a tryst of desire, but an expression of love. Love that she knew was mutually felt. She held on to him tightly and again they made slow, passionate love, expressing their feelings for each other in a way words could not describe. And again Sean brought her to a place of fulfillment, greater than any she'd ever before experienced.

As she listened to his soft snoring next to her, she whispered almost inaudibly, "I love you, Sean Kevin Bryan."

Chapter Sixteen

A rooster crowing in the distance awoke Venetta. She looked around the room slightly disoriented, for a fleeting moment wondering where she was. Then she remembered she was in Sean's bed and the magical night they'd had. She glanced at the alarm clock on the nightstand: 4:55. She looked over at Sean snoring peacefully, his legs and arms wrapped protectively around her, his breathing even. Venetta smiled and closed her eyes, attempting to go back to sleep, but sleep eluded her. Her mind was a jumble of anxious thoughts.

Half an hour later she gave up, pulled on Sean's shirt abandoned carelessly at the foot of the bed, and slipped through the French doors onto the balcony. Wrapping the shirt around her naked body, she sniffed the masculine odor that she'd come to associate with Sean and smiled. Venetta inhaled the dew-kissed predawn air. There was so much to think about. She didn't want to leave, but she had no choice. Over and over her mind replayed her conversations with Kerina, Mrs. Bryan, and Sean. She recalled their passionate lovemaking and the wonderful fulfillment she had. She thought of how happy and complete he made her feel. She didn't want the beautiful passionate relationship she had with Sean to end, yet she felt powerless to stop it.

She closed her eyes, listening to the whistle of a teakettle and smelling the aroma of bush tea. Sean was awake.

The door squeaked and Sean, dressed only in his boxers, joined her on the dimly lit balcony.

"Good morning, sweetie," he greeted softly, a contented smile on his face. His lean, muscular frame stood tall and stately like a Greek god against the dim light of dawn. "Why are you up so early?"

"Couldn't sleep," Venetta responded, hugging the shirt close to her body as a chill ran down her spine.

"I made you breakfast," he said. "The corned beef is from a can. I hope you don't mind."

He placed a tray of corned beef hash, scrambled eggs, and fresh baguettes on the concrete railing of the balcony as the sun began its slow ascent over the Southeast Peninsula. The sky was a picturesque canvas of orange, red, and gray strokes that could never be replicated by a painter's brush. A cock crowed somewhere in the distance. The quiet lapping of the waves on the beach and the intermittent squawking of a distant brown pelican gave a peaceful surreal feeling.

"You can give me raw fish to eat, I'd still love it," Venetta responded, sipping the cup of bush tea he handed her.

Sean stepped behind her, gently folding his arms around her, lightly kissing her neck. She inhaled deeply, drinking in a mixture of the herb tea, soursop, and apple blossoms from the trees in the yard, and the strong scent of jasmines and roses that draped the front fence.

Wrapped in each other's arms, they witnessed the sun, a bright orange fireball, rise from the depths of the horizon, over the hills, and slowly, tenderly bathing the sky with light. It gently touched the plants and flowers, washing everything in orange and yellow. Rose petals peeled opened, finally receiving the awakening kiss of the sun. Birds flitted through the trees. Crickets closed their eyes and went to bed. It was morning. It was a new year. Venetta was a new woman.

"You know, this is my third sunrise on this island. And I've shared each one with you. What does that say?" Venetta asked, leaning back into Sean's embrace as his hands clasped possessively across her midsection.

"That we're early risers?" Sean quipped playfully, and Venetta gently poked him. He looked out at the distant beach and sighed. "Don't you wish we could do this every day?"

Venetta smiled, closing her eyes, listening to Sean's heartbeat behind her head. Getting on that plane grew less appealing by the minute, but she had responsibilities. She smiled wistfully, leaning her full weight on him, and said dreamily, "And awake next to each other every morning. Make love every day. Hear your rhythmic snoring every night."

"I don't snore."

"Yes, you do. I'll record you next time," Venetta laughed, her light laugh belying the depth of emotions lying just beneath the surface.

Sean breathed a sigh. "So there will be a next time."

"Our breakfast is getting cold." She changed the topic. She moved away from him, sat on the railing, and slowly began eating the corned beef. Her mouth felt dry and her appetite had long gone.

"Venetta," Sean said, striding toward her. "I need to know what happens after you get on that plane today."

Venetta looked silently at the city of Basseterre in the west. "If we decide to pursue this, Sean, we both have to make an enormous sacrifice and one of us has to take a monumental leap of faith. What if I move here and it doesn't work out? What if you move up to Baltimore and find you don't like it there? Or that you don't like me as much as you thought you did? What if this was just an enchanting week and we really have nothing to base this relationship on?"

Sean cupped Venetta's face in his hands. He swallowed the lump in his throat, knowing he was fighting a losing battle. He didn't want to lose Venetta because he was in love with her. But he realized that nothing he said could change her mind unless she wanted it changed. "If ending this relationship when you leave for fear of it failing will make you happy, Venetta, then so be it."

Venetta looked up at him. "Sean," she whispered. "What do you want?"

He closed his eyes, bringing his forehead down to touch hers. "I want whatever makes you happy. If I have brought a little sunshine into your life, then, Venetta, I am happy."

"Oh, Sean," she whispered, clinging to him.

Sean mumbled into her ear. "What time is your flight?"

"Three. Check in at two."

"I have to play for the parade of troupes today, but I'll come to the airport to see you off."

Before she could protest, he spoke. "I want to."

Releasing him, she announced she was taking a shower. He smiled, observing the sway of her hips as she entered the bedroom door. The thought of her naked in the shower was almost more than he could bear. He wanted . . . no, needed Venetta more than anything else right now.

Venetta was soaping herself when the shower door opened and Sean joined her. She smiled seductively.

He returned her smile. "Thought you might need some help," he said, taking the soap from her and soaping her back. Slowly, tantalizingly he soaped her chest, his fingers lingering around her breasts. He soaped her belly, lowering his hands and gently stroking her most secret places. Venetta melted beneath his touch, her breathing deep and labored. She returned the favor, soaping him, caressing him, taking him into her hands, making him want to scream with pleasure.

"Oh, Venetta," he gasped passionately, his mouth hotly coming down on hers. "I need you."

Propped against the shower stall, he lifted her onto him and entered her. Panting, moaning, their wet bodies joined as one, dancing a frenzied dance to imaginary music, they soared to heights of pleasure before climaxing together. They remained in each other's arms, spent, the shower streaming down on them.

Chapter Seventeen

"How many bags will you be checking today?" the uniformed clerk asked lazily. The small airport buzzed with activity as many people prepared to leave the island after a week of nonstop partying.

Venetta looked across the parking lot anxiously, expecting to see Sean riding by on his Ninja any minute now, dreadlocks flying in the wind, that bright smile lighting up his face. But there was no sign of Sean. Disappointed, she turned back to the clerk, distractedly handing over her passport.

The clerk smiled. "Sad to be leaving while all the action's still goin' on, eh?"

Venetta returned her smile and nodded as the clerk checked her passport. She was sad to be leaving all right, but not because of the activities. She was already missing Sean. For the umpteenth time, she gazed across the parking lot expectantly. He had promised to be there at the airport to see her off. She was surprised at how disappointed she was.

"Come on," Janelle urged. "It's almost two. We should proceed through security now."

"One minute," Venetta said softly, searching the parking lot.

Venetta's three friends nodded and wandered around outside, drinking in the bright afternoon sun. Despite

Venetta's calm demeanor, they could see the anxiety in her eyes but they waited patiently.

"Okay," Janelle said impatiently. "We really have to go. Let's head upstairs to security now. I don't want to miss this flight."

As the girls walked toward the stairs, Venetta saw Deborah's Nissan Xtrail pull into the parking lot. "They're here," she announced excitedly, assuming that Sean had gotten a ride with his sister.

She waited anxiously as Deborah, her mother, and her son stepped out and walked toward them. No Sean.

They greeted them with hugs. "I couldn't let you leave without giving you something," Mrs. Bryan said happily.

"And I made you this," Xavier announced, boldly pushing a paper in front of the girls. It was a drawing of a man with long, long legs. "That's a mocojumbie. See, he's dancing."

The girls took turns hugging him.

Deborah gave them CDs of the latest Kittitian carnival music. Then Mrs. Bryan opened her oversized bag. She gave Kerina some local confections: sugar cake and fudge made of coconut, tamarind jam, and guava cheese. "These are some sweets for your kids," she said. "Don't worry, I'm sure they can fit in your hand luggage," she added when she saw Kerina's expression.

"Thank you, Mrs. Bryan. I know the kids will love them. And if they don't, well, that'll just mean more for me," Kerina responded, packing them into her hand luggage.

Mrs. Bryan turned to Sheridia. "I know you love a good time," she said, handing Sheridia a liquor travel box. "This is homemade passion fruit wine and ginger wine. But you know no party is complete without some hard stuff, so I gave you a bottle of CSR and Belmont Estate rum."

"Oh my God, Mrs. B, you are the best," Sheridia shrieked loudly, drawing stares from the other travelers. She grabbed Mrs. Bryan, giving her a tight bear hug.

Mrs. Bryan turned to Janelle. "I got you some salt-fish balls. I remember how much you enjoyed them at Christmas, and a potato pudding."

"Yes!" Janelle pumped her hands and hugged her. "Thank you so much. You were so busy Christmas Day, how did you know the things we liked?"

"I raised seven children. I'm a good observer." She winked.

While the other girls conversed with Deborah, Mrs. Bryan turned to Venetta and smiled, drawing Venetta into an embrace. "Come give your mother-in-law a hug."

Venetta smiled, knowing it was useless correcting her. Whatever she and Sean had shared on this charming island would probably stay on the island, although she wished she'd changed her mind this morning when he'd given her the opportunity. But she had made the decision and now she had to stick with it.

As if reading her mind Mrs. Bryan continued. "No matter what happens between you and Sean, you will always be my daughter-in-law. I have many more daughters-in-law than I have sons."

Finally Venetta understood. For Mrs. Bryan a daughter-in-law wasn't necessarily her son's wife, but anyone who dated her sons that she welcomed. Being the warm, welcoming person she was, there were few people Mrs. Bryan did not embrace.

"Thank you, Mrs. Bryan," Venetta responded.

"You can call me Mother. Everyone else does." Mrs. Bryan sifted through her bag and presented Venetta with a Kittitian cookbook. "This has a lot of the local recipes, including black cake and stewed salt fish." She gave her a black cake and then removed a disposable plastic dish. "Open it," she instructed Venetta, handing the dish to her.

Venetta didn't have to open it. She knew from the aroma just what it was. Tears almost came to her eyes when she saw fried ballahoo and johnnycakes, just as she'd shared with Sean at DuDon Pond. "Oh, Mrs. . . . Mother, thank you. How did you know?"

Mrs. Bryan smiled. "Of my sons, Sean is the closest to me. I know, Venetta, he loves you."

Even though he never vocalized it, Venetta knew he loved her. But she wanted him to be happy. Maybe he'd find himself a beautiful Kittitian and they'd marry and have lovely children. The thought of Sean in the arms of another woman pained Venetta. *She* loved him. She wanted to be with him. She wanted to have his children.

Suddenly Venetta realized she didn't want to end their relationship. She had to tell him she changed her mind. She would make whatever sacrifices she had to make for it to work. She wanted more than a week. She wanted a lifetime.

Venetta's voice was filled with urgency when she spoke. "Do you know where he is? He was supposed to meet us at the airport. There's something I have to tell him."

Mrs. Bryan shook her head. "His band is playing for the carnival parade." She turned to Deborah, who lived just a few blocks from Sean. "Debbie, have you seen Sean today?"

"He's playing for the parade. By now it should have started. Let me call him." She pulled out her cell phone and dialed both his home and cell phones. "He's not picking up."

"Try Darren," Venetta suggested desperately.

Debbie moved a few steps from the girls, covering one ear as she tried to hear Darren on the other end of the line amid the noise of the carnival. A few minutes later she hung up and shook her head. "Darren said he never showed up. They are already lined up. A few of the troupes are already on the road and he hasn't seen Sean yet." Deborah smiled at Venetta reassuringly. "I'm sure he'll show up late as usual. He's probably on his way here now. Anyway, girls, Xavier will never forgive me if he misses the carnival parade, so we've gotta go." She hugged all the girls again. "Have a safe flight. Venetta, if Sean said he'll be here, he will."

Venetta's legs felt like lead as she trudged up the flight of stairs and through security. All the time she kept looking back, expecting to see Sean hustling up the steps at any time. By the time they got through security, their flight had been called and the passengers were lined up at the only departure gate. Through the glass windows the girls could see the small aircraft sitting on the tarmac.

The four girls were last in line as they followed the uniformed airline employee out of the gate.

Halfway to the plane Venetta heard a rumbling over the sound of the plane engine. She looked back and there, locks loose, shirt waving in the wind, was Sean riding his red Ninja full throttle toward them. Venetta stopped, her heart thumping wildly yet warm with happiness. He made it. Sean made it.

Sean rolled to a stop a few feet from Venetta, a huge smile on his face. "Couldn't let you leave without saying bye," he shouted above the roar of the plane engine. He pulled something out of his backpack. "This is for you. Be careful with it, it's not totally dry yet. I worked on it all day."

Venetta stared dumbfounded at the high-gloss wooden plaque with the latex finish. It was a photo of him and Venetta taken by his brother on Christmas Day. They were standing on the veranda of his mother's house, she was looking up into his eyes, and he was looking down at her. The sky in the background was painted with orange yellow, and red strokes of the setting sun. On it was the lyrics to a song he'd written just for her *With Love from S.K.B.*

Venetta smiled gratefully and turned the plaque over. On the back were three letters: SKB. Venetta knew they meant Sean Kevin Bryan, the man she loved.

"I have something to tell you," Venetta said.

"Me, too," Sean responded. "Remember this morning I told you I was okay with your decision to end it when you leave here? I lied. I'm not okay with it, Venetta. I can't do it. I love you and a week with you is not enough. I know asking you to give up everything and move here is a lot, so I'll meet you halfway. If I have to move to Baltimore to be with you, I will. We can make it work. I'll visit for Easter break and we can visit in the summer until we decide what to do permanently. I want to give us a chance, Venetta. Please say this isn't the end."

Venetta threw herself into Sean's arms. "I love you, too, Sean. I don't want us to end any more than you do. That's what I wanted to tell you, Sean. That I changed my mind and I want to give us a chance."

Sean's mouth covered Venetta's in a long emotional kiss. When he released her she said, "You'd better get out of here before the cops get you. I'll miss you," Venetta whispered, kissing him once more.

"Bryan," the airline employee called to Sean as she walked toward the terminal. "Quit de lovey-dovey stuff an' leh de ooman go. You holin' up de flight."

Sean released her, whispering one last time in her ear, "I love you."

As Venetta boarded the small aircraft, she looked back and waved. Sean was still sitting on his Ninja, looking at the plane. She mouthed, "I love you," before entering the narrow confines of the airplane.

Chapter Eighteen

Venetta trotted lightly up the front stairs to her Fells Point town house in the sweltering August heat. Her hair was pulled back into a loose ponytail with stray strands sticking to her forehead. Her navy blue spandex shorts with yellow stripes and matching tank top clung to her skin, a wet circle of perspiration above her breasts the only evidence of her grueling workout at the Downtown Athletic Club.

She carelessly slung her blue gym bag over her shoulder as she inserted the key into her door. A brown package on the top step caught her attention. She bent to pick it up, smiling when she saw the sender. Sean remembered her birthday.

She used her shoulder to push the door open, noticing for the first time her elderly Italian neighbor leering lasciviously at her. She waved to him, observing his pale skin become fiery red with embarrassment. She laughed silently and placed the package on the dining room table before heading upstairs to shower.

Venetta had no real plans for her birthday. The last time she had a party was eight years ago when she was twenty-one. This year she would spend it probably talking to Sean on the telephone. Right now he was in Boston with the steel band playing for the Caribbean carnival there and by the weekend he should be in New York for the steel pan festival and Labor Day Caribbean Parade.

As the warm water cascaded over her head and shoulders, Venetta reminisced about Sean and the lovely relationship they had. When she'd returned from St. Kitts, there was an e-mail waiting for her from Sean. At the end of the e-mail was the first line of a love poem. She replied to the e-mail, tagging a second line to the poem. They did that back and forth for six weeks until Valentine's Day he wired her a bouquet of flowers. On the card was the completed poem.

True to his promise, Sean visited at Easter for two full weeks. That's when he sang their special song to her. He had put music to their poem and recorded it on a CD.

Those two weeks had been wonderful. They visited some of his favorite places where he'd hung out as a college student, toured the Baltimore and Annapolis harbors, and attended the Cherry Blossom Festival in Washington, D.C. Then they drove to New York, where Venetta introduced Sean to her parents. Her parents and in-laws liked him right away and were genuinely happy for her. Even her petulant little sister, who was impossible to please, grew fond of Sean in the three days they spent there.

The nights were filled with bliss. Venetta never thought she could ever feel so loved, so wanted, so desired. When they came together it was as if the world stopped spinning, time ceased to exist, and with every touch, every heart-stopping gaze, Venetta was ablaze with fire. And every time she heard their song, she knew she'd found the person she wanted to spend the rest of her life with. Her only problem was where.

Venetta stepped out of the shower. Wrapped in a towel, she curled and blow-dried her shampooed hair. She thought of this summer and her visit to St. Kitts at the end of June during the intersession before summer school. For three weeks she had the incomparable joy of waking up next to Sean every morning, of looking at the sunrise from the porch. They enjoyed lusciously intimate moments on deserted beaches, and long walks along the water's edge. They talked about everything and anything, baring their souls to each other. She saw him perform at the World Music Festival and quickly realized the local girls were wild about him. But Sean only had eyes for her.

Mrs. Bryan had been as warm and welcoming as she'd been last Christmas, and so had his siblings, especially Deborah. Mrs. Bryan taught her to cook some of Sean's favorite foods and they'd had long talks about life on the island when she grew up compared to now. Venetta was sad to leave and looked forward to seeing him again. But while her summer was taken up with teaching summer school, Sean was busy promoting the new CD that he had released. On it were the songs he'd written for her. By August he'd gone on tour with the band, performing at festivals throughout the Caribbean and the U.S. Right now she was looking forward to returning to St. Kitts for the Christmas break. Venetta, Kerina and her family, Janelle and Sheridia had already booked their flights.

Venetta was removing the curlers from her hair when the phone rang.

"Happy birthday, baby," Sean sang into the receiver, and Venetta's heart soared. "What are you doing for your birthday?"

She walked into the dining room, cradling the phone between her ear and shoulder. "Nothing much. Maybe listen to some music, relax."

"Have you received my gift?"

"Haven't opened it yet," Venetta responded, tearing

open the package. In it was a beautiful homemade card with a poem and a halter-top batik dress. Venetta read the card. "Oh, Sean, it's beautiful."

"Does the dress fit?"

"I haven't tried it yet."

"What are you waiting for, V? Try it and let me know how it looks."

She slipped on the dress. "It's perfect, I love it."

"And I love you," he crooned into the phone. "Did you get the flowers?"

"What flowers?" Venetta asked. Just then her doorbell rang. "I guess that must be them now."

Venetta answered the door to find Sean standing outside, holding a bouquet of two dozen red roses. Venetta gaped speechless as Sean stepped inside, grinning from ear to ear, still holding the cell phone in his hand.

"You're more beautiful than ever," Sean complimented her. "I missed you so much, baby." He drew her into his arms.

When Venetta finally recovered her speech she asked, grinning happily up at him, "What are you doing here, you devious trickster? I thought you were in Boston."

"I was until this morning, but now I've come to take you out for dinner. I couldn't miss your birthday when I was so close by." She now noticed he was dressed in a cream and tan casual shirt and tan cotton slacks.

"When are you going to New York?"

"Friday, and I want you to come with me."

Venetta smiled, wrapping her arms around him. "I wouldn't miss it for the world."

Chapter Nineteen

The atmosphere before the steel pan festival was one of joyous anticipation. The festival was held in an open-air stadium in Brooklyn with multiple steel orchestras side by side. Sean and his band members teased each other playfully as they tested their instruments.

Venetta's mother arrived just before the first band began playing. She'd invited her parents so she didn't have to be alone while Sean played.

"I'm sorry your father couldn't make it. Something to do with work," Viola Amory, Venetta's mother, apologized. "And, Crystal, well you know how teenagers are. She doesn't want to be seen within fifty feet of her 'old' parents. So I gave her my credit card and she went to the mall with some friends."

Different bands from various countries played a balance of calypso, reggae, and pop tunes. Venetta's mother leaned over to her and jokingly shouted over the noise of the pans, "I thought these pans could only play 'Yellow Bird.'"

"That's a thought wasted," Venetta ribbed, laughing with her mother.

Kittitian Pride was the last band to play. Like the other bands, they played a mixture of old and recent calypso medleys, some reggae beats, jazz, and a few American pop mixes. Venetta was pleasantly surprised when they played a syncopated version of "From SKB with Love," the song he'd written for her.

The place emptied out within minutes of the last performance, leaving only Darren and Sean with two lead pans and a smattering of people packing instruments onto large trucks. Venetta was talking to her mother when she heard the lone pans being played. She looked up to see Darren playing the smooth jazzy version of "From SKB with Love." Sean took a microphone and began to sing, his clear baritone giving Venetta goose bumps. Slowly Sean walked toward her, his left hand extended.

Venetta smiled, her heart pounding. Sean's soulful voice almost brought tears to her eyes. He was such a romantic. Sean reached to her, taking her hand in his. He continued singing, sinking to one knee and tacking on a new verse she had never heard:

> My heart's been set on fire
> You're my soul's desire
> With you I'm made complete
> And know I'll never fear defeat
> You are my pride and joy, the love of my life
> Venetta, darling, would you be my wife?

Venetta stood silent, frozen to the ground. The emotions going through her ran the full spectrum. At first there was elation, the kind that sent her heart into a frenzy and brought tears of joy to her eyes. Yes, she wanted to be Sean's wife. She wanted to live with him and love him forever.

Then she looked at Sean and fear crept into her heart. Before her eyes flashed scenes of them together walking the beach, making love on the sands, laughing easily with his family, and goofing off with his band members. She saw the tranquil expression on his face as he welcomed the dawn on his porch, watching the young sun bathe everything with glorious light. She saw him on-stage serenading the girls from the beauty pageant. She saw him working silently in his workshop making delicate crafts of wood. She saw all that and realized she couldn't ask him to give it up. She couldn't ask him to move here. But she was not ready to make that move to St. Kitts.

Venetta slowly exhaled, realizing only then that she was holding her breath. She whispered, "Sean, we've got to talk about this."

Sean got up and for the first time Venetta saw fear and hurt in his eyes. He closed his eyes, inhaling deeply and exhaling through his mouth. "The answer is no, isn't it?"

Venetta cupped his cheeks in both her hands. "Sean, the answer is not no. It is wait awhile. I'm not ready for that kind of commitment or the changes that it would bring. I love you, Sean, and I want to marry you someday. But this is too soon. The changes are too drastic. I just need more time."

"For what, Venetta?"

Venetta swallowed hard. She could no longer look him in the eye. The hurt she saw was too much for her to bear. "To be sure. To know that if one of us has to be uprooted, it is for the right cause. I'm not saying that we have to end our relationship. I'm just saying that I'm not yet ready for that kind of commitment."

A full minute passed before Sean responded. When he spoke his tone was even. There was an almost surreal calm to his voice. "I want a hundred percent of you. And that means we both should be willing to make whatever sacrifices to make our love work. Venetta, if I can't get all of you, then I don't want any."

"Does that mean you're ending our relationship?" Venetta asked, feeling her heart plummet.

Sean nodded. "When you're ready to give one hundred percent, when you're ready to make the kind of commitment that I'm ready to make, then we can talk. Until then I'm afraid there can be no us."

With that Sean walked off to join Darren.

Venetta turned to her mother, who stood speechless while watching the events. She held Venetta in her arms, comforting her as she sobbed uncontrollably.

Darren looked at Sean lumbering dejectedly toward him. "She said no, didn't she?"

Sean nodded. He didn't trust himself to speak. He felt tears sting the back of his eyes, but he refused to cry. Men didn't cry . . . at least not in public.

Darren patted his back comfortingly. "It'll be all right, man." But he knew it wouldn't, at least not soon. He remembered the pain Sean had suffered when he'd asked his sister to marry him and she refused because of her terminal illness. It had broken him even more than losing her had. "You'll find a few women, have a little fun," he suggested, but Darren knew Sean wouldn't. Sean was a one-woman man, and when he loved, he lost himself.

Chapter Twenty

It was a cold December morning. The frigid wind whipped at Venetta's face, forcing her to wrap her wool coat tight around her as she knelt before MJ's grave.

"Oh God, MJ," she cried. "I'm in love with Sean, but I can't seem to let go of you."

Tears ran down her face. She hadn't heard from Sean since he walked out of her life. She was lonely, she was hurt, and she missed him terribly. Everything reminded her of the love she gave up: the cards, the CDs of his songs, the plaque with their photo from Christmas, the goatskin portraits she'd bought on the island. Listening to Kerina, Sheridia, and Janelle plan excitedly for their island trip this Christmas was almost unbearable.

She remembered the painful night three months ago when she turned down his proposal. She couldn't get the hurt in his eyes out of her mind. She returned to Baltimore that same night, driving aimlessly around the city. Finally she stopped at Kerina's house; it was two o'clock in the morning. Kerina came out in her pajamas and comforted her as best she could, but Venetta still cried uncontrollably.

"Why?"

"My life with MJ was here, Kerina. What about my in-laws? I'm the only relative they have left, Kerina. They may need me.

"Venetta, if you hold so tightly to the past, your arms

will be too closed to welcome the future. MJ is your past, Venetta, Sean is your future."

The cold air in the cemetery ended her memory and sent shivers down Venetta's spine. She closed her eyes and cried, "Oh, MJ, just give me a sign, any sign. Let me know what to do."

Venetta heard the windswept voice echoing, it seemed, off the village of tombstones, "Follow your heart, Venetta."

Venetta turned suddenly to see her father-in-law standing behind her, with flowers in his hand. "When you weren't at home, I thought you'd be here."

Venetta wiped the tears from her eyes. "How long have you been standing there?"

"Long enough to know how torn you feel." Michael David placed the flowers on MJ's grave. "Venetta, Angie, and I will never keep you from the man you love, nor would MJ." He handed her two worn diaries held together by rubber bands. "Angie and I decided to foster a child. These were MJ's. We found them while preparing his room for our new foster son."

"Another child?" Venetta asked incredulously, knowing how deeply they loved their only son.

Michael nodded. "This is what MJ wanted. And, Venetta," he said, turning to leave. "If St. Kitts is where the man you love is, for God's sake, move there. The only thing MJ wanted was for you to be happy. You know that's what Angie and I want, too."

Venetta sat on the cold grave leafing through the two volumes of MJ's high school diary. Tears of joy came to her eyes when she read about their first kiss and the butterflies in his stomach. He wrote about their arguments, which for some reason Venetta could not before this remember having. As Venetta read more and more, she realized that she had canonized MJ so much in her mind that her perception of him, his expectations and desires, was far from reality. However, it was clear he loved her.

Her hands were cold and numb when she closed the second book.

Venetta stood up and dusted herself. "Thank you, MJ," she whispered. She knew what she had to do. She just hoped it wasn't too late.

Chapter Twenty-one

The small aircraft approached Robert Bradshaw International Airport, flying low over small hills and colorful housetops. The view below was breathtaking. The gently sloping mountains neatly aligned in the center of the island, the square patches of yellow-green sugarcane fields, the intermittent patches of blue from salt ponds on the southeast side of the island, and the golden strips of the beaches washed by turquoise waters all filled Venetta with nostalgia. Yet she was fearful and anxious. Coming to St. Kitts was a leap of faith. What if he'd found somebody new? What if he was no longer in love with her? What if he couldn't forgive her?

Kerina reached over and touched Venetta's hand reassuringly. Her eyes said everything would be all right, but Venetta was doubtful.

Venetta was quiet when they emerged from customs, her stomach nauseated with butterflies. She said good-bye to Sheridia and Janelle, who took a cab to Mrs. Bryan's house for the group's second Christmas on the island.

"You can ride with us," Kerina and Mark offered, filling out the paperwork for the airport vehicle rental. They were staying with Deborah.

"Thank you, but no. This is something I have to do alone."

Venetta rented a small Suzuki Samurai and headed

onto the narrow main road. She passed through down-town Basseterre with her windows rolled down, watching with fascination as people prepared for Christmas. Shop-pers slipped in and out of decorated shops purchasing gifts, food, and decorations for the holidays, which were a little more than a week away. Christmas carols and local calypsos played loudly. Folks were busy cleaning and painting their bungalows, talking and laughing loudly. The spirit of Christmas was in the air Kittitian style, and Venetta wanted to embrace it, but the fear and anxiety of her impending actions held her hostage.

Finally she arrived at Frigate Bay where the houses were grander and farther apart, the streets were nar-rower and more difficult to navigate, and the beach was just a stone's throw away. She parked in front of Sean's brightly painted house with the right wheels on the curb. She knew he was home because both his Ninja and his Mitsubishi Gallant were parked in the drive-way.

Venetta walked timidly up the stairs to the veranda. Her heart thumped loudly when she knocked on his front door.

Sean, dressed in shorts and a tank top, stepped out and closed the door without a word. His dreadlocks were damp and smelled of his signature herbal shampoo. His expression was unreadable.

Venetta's breath caught in her throat at the sight of him. All the things she'd rehearsed flew from her mind. Her hands shook so much she had to place them in the pockets of her denim skirt to steady them.

Finally he spoke. "This is quite a surprise."

"I know, I . . . I . . . Sean, I'm sorry that I hurt you." Venetta blurted out. It was so easy when she'd rehearsed it, but now words were failing her. "I wasn't ready this summer, but I am now. Ask me again, please, ask me again."

Sean gazed intently at her. "Venetta, I can't ask you again," he said. "I . . ."

Suddenly the door opened and a medium-built girl with braided hair stepped onto the veranda. She acknowledged Venetta with a smile and a nod and spoke directly to Sean in Kittitian dialect. "I see you're busy, so give me the keys, I'll drive myself."

He handed her the keys. Her hands lingered on his. She smiled at him, making Venetta suddenly aware of the special bond they shared.

Venetta's heart sank. She had taken a leap of faith and crashed.

"I'm sorry," she said. "I didn't know you . . . I guess I shouldn't have expected you to wait on me. I . . ." Venetta felt tears coming to her eyes. Her words caught in her throat. Before Sean could react, Venetta turned on her heel and ran toward the gate.

"Wait, Venetta," Sean called as she fumbled with the latch. He was by her side in a flash, his hand over hers on the latch. "Don't go," he said. "That's Sonya, my youngest sister. I don't have anyone else, Venetta, and I still love you. But I can't ask you again until I know that you are ready to give one hundred percent. I won't compete with your loyalties to MJ."

Venetta relaxed a little. "Sean, I am ready to give a hundred percent. I was a fool. I've been holding so much to the past that it impeded my ability to embrace the future. Sean, you are my future and I want to be with you."

Sean smiled for the first time. "What changed your mind?"

"Kerina pound some sense into my head and I read

MJ's diary. When I read it, Sean, I realized I was holding on to something that doesn't exist. MJ loved me but never intended for me to remain in the past forever. Sean, I now know I can have a future of love and that future is with you. I promise to give one hundred percent of myself. So if you will have me, and if you don't think it presumptuous for a woman to propose, will you marry me?"

Sean smiled. "How can I say no to you? Venetta, I love you."

He drew Venetta into a tight embrace. His mouth sought hers. When he released her he was breathless.

"I missed you so much, V," he breathed, his lips millimeters away from hers.

"I missed you, too," Venetta whispered as Sean led her by the hand upstairs and into the living room. "You know what else I missed?" Venetta asked sultrily.

Sean raised his eyebrows innocently, "Why don't you show me?"

Venetta kissed him passionately. She sensually caressed his muscular chest, sending him wild with desire. He moaned, drawing her closer, her soft breast crushed against his chest, setting him on fire. He wanted her.

His mouth hot on hers, Sean kissed her hungrily, tenderly caressing her. A gasp escaped Venetta's throat as she submitted to her passions. Heatedly they undressed each other, leaving a trail of discarded clothing along the way to the bedroom.

In one fluid motion Sean shoved the clothes littering the untidy bed to the floor, and laid her down. He pinned her hands above her head, leaving her body exposed and vulnerable. Slowly he kissed her throat and chest, setting her on fire with his tongue.

Her breathing raspy, her body on fire, Venetta could stand it no more. "Now, Sean," she begged.

He entered her, filling her, completing her. They rode the waves of ecstasy until they exploded, sending shudders throughout their entire bodies. They held each other close as if clinging for dear life.

"I love you, Sean," Venetta whispered.

"I love you, too, V," Sean responded, cradling her possessively in his arms. He reached for her again and slowly, tenderly they made love once more.

Two hours later Sean propped himself up on one elbow and faced Venetta. "Now that we've established that we want to get married, what will we do about living arrangements?"

Venetta smiled, drawing circles on his chest with her index finger. "Let's just say you're going to have to do a better job at keeping this room clean when I move in."

"Does that mean you're moving to St. Kitts?" Sean asked with hope.

Venetta nodded, looking up at him lovingly.

"Are you sure that's what you want to do?"

She ran her fingers lovingly down his neck. "I've already filled out the application for a teaching job and work permit."

"What changed your mind?"

"That night when you proposed, I wanted to say yes. But I looked at the way you related to your band members, I looked at your close-knit family and the life you have carved out here, and I couldn't ask you to give it up and move to the States. This is you, what makes you, and what made me fall in love with you. At that time, though, I didn't think I was ready to take that leap of faith. But, Sean, now I am ready."

"So if I want to get married tomorrow, you'll be ready?"

Venetta smiled and kissed him. "I'm ready to get married today."

Sean held her in his arms and rolled her on top of him. "I love you, Venetta David."

Chapter Twenty-two

Christmas morning, Venetta awoke excited to be the first to wish Sean a merry Christmas. She stretched languorously and reached for Sean, but the space was empty. In his place was a gift bag.

Venetta opened the bag and squealed with delight. In it was a white cotton eyelet off-shoulder dress with a flowing skirt.

As Venetta removed the dress, a card and a pair of coconut-shell earrings with matching necklace and bangles fell out. The card simply read, *Wear these and meet me at the beach*. She knew he was referring to the place where they'd first met.

Venetta showered, combing her hair back into a simple French braid. The dress fit perfectly, seamlessly hugging her bodice and flowing around her ankles. How did he know? With it she wore leather sandals made on the island and the coconut jewelry.

Sean was waiting for her at the beach, sitting on the boat where he'd sat a year ago. He wore cream linen slacks with matching untucked shirt. The first few buttons were undone, accentuating his broad chest. Venetta smiled, noting the symbolism. He silently walked toward her and placed a flower from the poinciana tree, known locally as cock-and-hen, in her hair.

"You are absolutely beautiful," he complimented, taking her hand in his. "I have a surprise for you. Close your eyes."

They walked slowly, hand in hand, toward the beach where they'd shared their first kiss.

"I hear steel pan music and talking," Venetta observed as they walked closer to the sound. Finally they stopped. The fresh ocean breeze and the aroma of spicy food assaulted her nose. The pans beat out the tune "From SKB with Love." "Sean, they're playing our song. Can I open my eyes now?"

"Not yet," he responded, releasing her hand and walking away.

Another person held her hands firmly and walked a few feet toward the music. "You can open your eyes now," she heard a familiar voice say.

Venetta opened her eyes and squealed. "Daddy, what are you doing here?" Her father was standing in front of her holding her hand. She hugged him.

"Wouldn't miss my daughter's wedding for the world," he responded with a smile.

Venetta blanched. "Wedding?" She looked around, mouth agape. She could not believe it. Sean had surprised her with a wedding on the beach just as she had dreamed. The Kittitian Pride steel orchestra was set up under the shade of some coconut palms. A picnic banquet of Christmas breakfast food sat on folding tables set up in a makeshift tent, a tarpaulin stretched across two sea grape trees. Sean, with Darren as his best man and a preacher, stood under an almond tree waiting for her. Venetta felt tears of joy come to her eyes. This was the most wonderful Christmas present ever.

Kerina's two daughters dressed in colorful bathing suits and sarongs with shell necklaces and red hibiscus in their hair served as flower girls. Each girl held a wicker basket of seashells that she scattered on the warm sand. The oldest presented Venetta with a bouquet of locally grown flowers, then went back in line to head the small procession. Janelle, Sheridia, and Venetta's sister, Crystal, were dressed in identical multicolored halter bathing suit tops and matching sarongs with poinciana flowers in their hair. They served as bridesmaids. Kerina in her one-piece bathing suit and matching sarong was the matron of honor.

Mr. and Mrs. Bryan, Venetta's mother, as well as Sean's siblings and their families, were there, all dressed casually in shorts or bathing suits. Sean's parents waved at her and to Venetta's surprise standing next to them were Angela and Michael David smiling approvingly.

Venetta smiled happily as her father guided her down the path between the cheering guests to meet Sean.

With a bow, he handed her over to Sean, who beamed with pride at his new bride. "Merry Christmas," he whispered to her.

"Oh, Sean, this is the best Christmas present ever. How?"

"I had a little help." He nodded to the guests. Venetta saw the happy faces of her best friends and family, everyone waving gleefully.

The young preacher cleared his throat loudly. Sean smiled apologetically.

The preacher announced, "Folks, we are gathered here to join Sean Kevin and Venetta Annette in holy matrimony. Since this ceremony is so untraditional, the couple has decided to recite their own vows."

Sean held both of Venetta's hands and gazed deep into her eyes. He began the poetic prose:

"There was a time when I roamed the beach alone
Wondering if there would ever be someone;
Someone to take the pain away
Someone to wake up with every day
Someone who would make me complete once more
And you showed up on that tranquil shore.
Since then, Venetta, you've become everything to me
You are the calm in the waves of a turbulent sea
You are the song that I hear in the summer breeze
You are the notes of the wind whispering in the trees
You are my sunrise and my sunset
And I promise to love you with every breath.
I promise to protect you, respect you every day, every
*   hour*
Whether life is great, or things grow sour
I will be faithful to you, until my last gasp of breath
And will love you until my eyes shall close in death
Venetta, I gladly take you as my wife
And today, I commit to you my life."

Venetta felt tears come to her eyes. She loved this man, she was so happy. As tears of joy flowed down her face, she looked around and realized she was not alone. Her mother, Kerina, and Sheridia, even Mrs. Bryan and Angie, were all in tears.

Her voice quivering, her hands shaking, Venetta cleared her throat. "You guys know I cannot come up with anything as beautiful and poetic as that. Sean, this is the best surprise, the best gift ever, the gift of love. Sean, when I came to St. Kitts a year ago, I never imagined for one minute that I would have met you and fallen in love with you. Not in my wildest dream did I imagine anything or anyone as romantic and wonderful as this.

For so long I was lost in my own world of grief. But, Sean, your love has opened my eyes and my heart to love. You've made me able to embrace the future and that future is with you. So as of this day, Sean, I promise to love, honor, respect you, whether things be good or bad. I promise to be faithful to you until the day I die, because I love you. You are my lover and you are my best friend. There is no me without you, and there's no you without me, we complete each other. So today, I gladly take you as my husband and I commit my life to you, until the day I die."

The preacher smiled at the newlyweds and announced, "By the powers invested in me, I now pronounce you husband and wife. You may kiss your bride."

Sean took Venetta in his arms and kissed her amid the laughter and cheers of his relatives and friends. As the small gathering ate a huge breakfast of delicious ham, stewed salt fish, eggs, and johnnycakes, Venetta looked up at Sean happy to have found happiness in her life once more, "Sean, you're the best thing that happened to me. Merry Christmas, S.K.B."

He looked down at her and smiled, his heart filled with joy. "Merry Christmas, Mrs. Bryan."

They smiled, gazing into each other's eyes. They knew they'd found a love that would last a lifetime.

No Ordinary Gift

Farrah Rochon

Dedicated to the memories of my grandmothers,
Olga Borne and Joyce Roybiskie.
Two extraordinary gifts from above.

Thanks be to God for his indescribable gift.
—2 Corinthians 9:15

Chapter One

"Well, this is a first."

Kemah Griffin grimaced as she stared at the screen of her sleek BlackBerry Storm.

Breakup by text message.

In the span of one minute, her emotions ran from anger to disappointment to weary acceptance. It's not as if this was the first time she'd been dumped, but it was certainly the trendiest. And the neatest. No crying, no yelling, no accusations hurled across the room. Technology made it way too easy for cowards who were not man enough to break up with a woman face-to-face.

"You didn't like him that much anyway," Kemah muttered under her breath. She grabbed her leather briefcase from the passenger seat, then bumped her car door closed with her hip, pressing the button on her key fob to lock it. This day was starting off badly, and she'd be darned if she gave anyone temptation to help themselves to an early Christmas present. They would be disappointed when they found a bunch of unexecuted contracts inside, but her Dolce & Gabbana briefcase could fetch a nice price on the streets.

Kemah skimmed the other text messages she'd missed as she made her way through the nearly empty parking lot adjacent to the Darolyn Crawford Community Center, deleting those she didn't need anymore—including the high-tech Dear Jane letter—and adding others into the BlackBerry's appointment calendar. The bevy of color-coded blocks underscored the mountain of work that lay ahead of her in the upcoming days. When she had an extra minute, she needed to go through her calendar and reprioritize.

"Yeah, right," she snorted. "As if you ever have an extra minute."

"You talk to yourself all the time?"

Kemah's head popped up at the sound of the rich, deep voice tinted with amusement.

"Tyson," she breathed, holding her chest. "You scared me."

Tyson Crawford stood just outside the doors of the community center that bore his mother's name, his loyal companion, Samson, standing sentry at his side. Kemah waited for the initial flutter she felt in her stomach whenever she saw Tyson. It didn't disappoint, which pissed her off.

She'd told herself her days of quivering at the sight of him had ended the day he'd reached inside her chest and crushed her heart with his bare hand.

Okay, so it wasn't as graphic as all that, but still, her breakup with Tyson had devastated her. Her insides should vibrate with anger when she was around him, not tremble with this desperate wanting she could hardly control.

But it's not as if she had an off-switch for her reaction to him. Her body had responded to Tyson the moment he'd walked onto the construction site of the high-end outlet shopping mall where she'd been project manager.

The subtly sculpted muscles filling out his well over six-foot frame told at least a partial story of what he did on the days he wasn't at the community center, and it wasn't sitting around watching television. A couch potato didn't earn the abs Kemah had ran her fingers over more times than she ever wanted to remember, but couldn't help but recall.

Keeping a tight lid on those feelings that constantly wanted to surface had become her own private battle, because despite the way he'd broken her heart, Tyson was still one of the most compassionate people she'd ever known. Case in point, the boxer at his side, Samson. Tyson had rescued the dog from the pound only moments before he was to be euthanized.

"Good morning," Kemah said, bending to give Samson a scratch behind the ear. She missed this dog almost as much as she missed Tyson.

"Morning," Tyson greeted with a smile. He nodded at the device in her hand. "That phone will get you in trouble one day. With all the potholes in these sidewalks, you're going to walk right into one if you're not paying attention."

"Ah, that's right, you weren't here when I came in last Saturday. I've already starred in that show. Ruined the heel of my new shoe."

"Sorry I missed it," he said with a sly version of that same smile. Her stomach flitters went into overdrive. "If we can't get the city to fix the sidewalk, I'm going to bring in a contractor and get it done on my own. Know of any good ones?"

"Ha, ha," Kemah said with sufficient sarcasm. "Holmes Construction happens to be swamped at the moment, thanks to the reigning king of commercial real estate."

"You're welcome." Tyson sketched a slight bow. "Happy to throw a little business your way. Come on in." He motioned with his head as he tightened his hold on Samson's leash. "We're about to start the meeting."

Kemah ducked into the door he held open for her,

catching an intoxicating whiff of the musk cologne he wore. It wasn't overpowering, just enough to tickle her senses. Kind of like Tyson himself.

He'd never break up with a woman via text message. No, Tyson was way too much of a gentleman to do something so spineless. Kemah doubted Tyson had any idea she was still nursing the broken heart he'd left her with when he ended their yearlong relationship six months ago. She was growing weary of the pretense that working with him at the center wasn't eating her up inside.

But what choice did she have? Give up the center? That wasn't even an option. The kids who showed up faithfully to this center every Saturday morning had become a crucial part of her life. These kids, this center; they reminded her of who she was, and made certain she didn't forget where she came from.

Yes, she was a successful project manager who'd overseen the construction of multimillion-dollar buildings, who drove a luxury car and lived in a nice neighborhood. But she would never let herself forget little Kemah Griffin who grew up in the housing projects with a single mother who, more often than not, Kemah had to take care of instead of the other way around. Remembering where she came from made the fruits of her labor that much sweeter to enjoy.

Kemah followed Tyson up the short hallway that led to the main area of the center. The once dilapidated school gymnasium had been transformed into a brightly lit den of learning and recreation. The walls were dotted with glittery Christmas scenes, finger-painted Santas with cotton-ball beards, and garland made out of loops of red and green construction paper.

The left side of the community center was Kemah's

home—the dance area. A portion was lined with mirrored panels and a ballet bar that ran the length of them.

In the center of the gymnasium was a full-length basketball court that was transformed into a dining room, an exercise floor, or a double-dutch jump rope competition area, based on what was needed at the time.

Kemah walked ahead of Tyson to the community center's kitchen, where the weekly meeting was held every Saturday morning. Before he'd taken over the operation of the center, there were no weekly meetings. All the volunteers came in and did their own thing. Kemah reluctantly admitted that she liked the structure Tyson had brought to the center.

For a selfish moment, she'd hoped he would crash and burn so she wouldn't have to work with him. Thankfully, her wish had not come true. Not only had Tyson *not* failed, but he'd come in and given the center the shot in the arm it had needed.

The last director, Mrs. Johnston—a woman Kemah knew only by her last name even though they'd worked together for nearly a year—had spent ninety percent of her time huddled in the back office instead of with the kids. As they had learned later, she had been mismanaging center funds.

"Good morning," Kemah greeted as she entered the kitchen. The room was filled with the usual suspects.

Gladys Baker, the Crawford family's former cook who'd moved into the role as the center's cook two months after Darolyn Crawford's death from cancer. Ashanti Taylor, computer genius extraordinaire who could get a job anywhere she wanted, yet chose to teach at one of New Orleans's roughest high schools. And, lastly, there was Pamela Harris. Kemah still wasn't sure what Pam did when she was away from the center, but she was a jill-of-all-trades here, teaching the girls arts and crafts one minute, and playing dodgeball with the boys the next.

"This morning's meeting will be short," Tyson started, grabbing an apple from a cardboard crate on the counter and receiving a stern look from Gladys. He winked at the cook as he leaned back against the counter and continued. "Since the kids get the entire week off between Christmas and New Year's, I've decided to keep the center open from six a.m. till six p.m. over their winter break. Ashanti has some of her high school students who need community service hours to help staff, but I've also hired a couple of people as well."

"Where exactly will their pay come from?" Pamela asked. She also functioned as the bookkeeper.

"I'm covering it," Tyson replied. "I don't want these kids running the streets the entire time they're out of school."

His selfless gesture reminded Kemah of why she'd fallen so hard, so extremely fast, for Tyson. He played the role of a hard-hitting businessman with aplomb, but deep in the crevices of that heart was a soul as generous as his mother's. How many people would go into their own pocket to make sure the center had enough people to keep the neighborhood kids occupied during their Christmas break?

"Where do we stand on the Christmas Eve dinner and toy drive?" Tyson asked.

"You don't worry about the dinner," Gladys said. "I've got that taken care of."

"It's gonna be a lot of people," Tyson said around a bite of his apple. "We've invited the entire neighborhood."

"I told you I've got it," Gladys reiterated. "I've got a

bunch of the ladies from my church helping out with the food. We'll have enough to feed an army."

"Okay, then." Tyson smiled. "Check Christmas Eve dinner off the list."

"The toy drive is going well," Ashanti said. "Have you peeked in that back office lately? There are bags of toys everywhere."

"We need to separate them by age group," Pamela said.

Kemah heard three finger snaps, followed by "What's wrong with you?"

"What?" She looked over at Pam, who was staring at her with a frown.

"We've been going on and on about the Christmas plans and you haven't said a thing yet. What's up with you?"

"Nothing," Kemah said.

"No, nothing is what's come out of your mouth in the last ten minutes, which means that *something* is wrong. You usually can't wait to add your two cents."

"Haven't you heard? We're in a recession. I'm holding on to my two cents," Kemah returned.

"And I thought the kids were sassy," Pam grunted.

"I'm sorry," Kemah said with a sheepish grin. She ran her fingers through her supershort hair, and sighed, "I'm fine. Just got a lot on my mind today."

"Don't tell me it has to do with the guy you met on that dating Web site?" Pam said with an exasperated eye roll, and Kemah wished she could melt right into the floor.

She shot Pam a severe glare, but the woman just continued to stare with that same, expectant look. She knew Pam would not let the issue rest. Kemah stifled another sigh. One cat was already out of the bag. Might as well bring out the entire litter.

She waved her BlackBerry in the air. "He dumped me via text message. Thank you *so* much for forcing me to broadcast it in front of everyone," she finished with a saccharine smile.

Pam waved her off. "He wasn't all that anyway. You can do better."

Kemah rolled her eyes at Pam, then looked up to find Tyson staring at her, a curious look on his face. *Oh, God, just let me disappear right now. Please.* That's exactly what she did *not* need: Tyson's pity.

"Can we please get back to the business at hand?" Kemah encouraged, making a *move on* motion with her hand.

"We've covered everything on my agenda," Tyson said. "Does anyone have anything else to add?"

"I do have something," Kemah said. "I want to include a Kwanzaa celebration in the festivities this year. I was talking to a few of the girls in my dance class last week, and not one of them even knew what Kwanzaa was. That's just sad for a neighborhood that's almost one hundred percent African-American."

"We'd have to make it interesting enough," Ashanti chimed in. "The kids grumble every time someone even mentions them having to learn something."

"I think Kemah can handle that," Tyson said. "You're gonna head it up, right?"

"Yes," she answered with a nod.

"Great. Just let me know what you need."

That was a loaded statement.

"Is that it?" she asked, wanting to end the meeting before she uttered anything that could heap even more humiliation over her head. "It's almost eight o'clock. The kids will start trickling in any time now."

"Yeah, that's it," Tyson said, clamping his hands on his jean-clad thighs. "Let's have a good day, ladies."

* * *

Tyson stood just inside the archway that led to the back offices, looking out over the swarm of activity buzzing around the community center. There was a Christmas fair going on at one of the neighborhood churches this afternoon, so the kids were trying to pack a day's worth of fun into a few hours.

Most of the older boys he mentored were helping out at the church, giving Tyson time to tackle the mountain of paperwork he'd had no idea he would face when he took over as the center's director. He'd been pecking away at his keyboard for the past hour and needed a break in the worst way.

The proposal he'd been working on this week was not nearly good enough to convince the board of the Crawford Foundation to allot more money to the community center. He had to be more persuasive in laying out his plans for next year. As much as he hated to admit it, he needed help to whip the proposal into shape.

Tyson shoved the paperwork into a back corner in his mind as he focused on the activity in the center. A group of younger boys had started a pickup game of basketball at the goal farthest from the gymnasium's front door. He glanced over at the computer room's Plexiglas walls to find it packed with kids, Ashanti leaning over one of the computer stations, instructing a child.

He lasted all of ten seconds before his eyes zeroed in on the dance area and the person he knew he would find there.

Tyson welcomed the rush of heat that sluiced down his spine and settled low in the pit of his stomach. It had become automatic just at the sight of Kemah. She'd changed into dark blue tights and an oversized blue and white Dillard University T-shirt, and was surrounded by a half dozen little girls who looked up to her as if she were a queen. He could relate.

Tyson sucked in a deep, calming breath as he watched Kemah gracefully arch her back and spread her arms wide. She stepped forward with one leg, and swooped into a low bow. He slowly let out the breath he'd taken, willing his blood to back off its race to high boil.

God, this woman had him tied in so many knots he wasn't sure he'd ever find his way out. It had been that way from the first day he saw her. He remembered thinking how much she didn't belong on a dusty construction site, yet being blown away by how she commanded the respect of the seasoned construction workers. She had been a sight to behold.

Something about her had grabbed hold of him that day, and had yet to let go. Despite the months they'd been apart—also known as the toughest months of his entire life—Kemah had never been far from his mind.

Maybe it was her dedication to doing good that appealed to him? Even though she was swamped with work—Tyson knew she was overseeing at least three projects for his company alone—she was loyal to the center and showed up faithfully every Saturday.

Tyson had been sure after their breakup that she would cut all ties to his family, but Kemah had developed a special bond with his mother—something he still didn't fully understand. They'd known each other for such a short amount of time, yet had forged the type of relationship it took years for people to develop. As he thought about it, it shouldn't have been a surprise that she'd remained a volunteer at the center.

He had never paid much attention to his family's charitable work. His interests had lain in bringing more money to the coffers, not spending it. But that had changed upon his mother's death. Tyson knew how much she loved giving back to the community, and after hearing the kids and young adults who'd spoken at her memorial service about how Darolyn Crawford had changed their lives, Tyson knew he had to get more involved. He wanted to carry on his mother's legacy.

And then, of course, there was Kemah.

Early on he'd acknowledged that just the chance to be in the same space she occupied again had played a huge part in getting him out of bed at seven every Saturday morning. Kemah's body had always mesmerized him. He wasn't completely shallow when it came to women, but he was a guy, and like any other guy, that first zing of attraction was purely physical.

It was more than just that beautiful face and killer body, though. It was *her*. There was something about Kemah as a person that had caused him to fall harder for her than any other woman he'd ever dated, and Tyson found himself falling deeper and deeper every second he was around her.

He couldn't think of a single thing he regretted more than the day he'd ended things with her. It had been an on-the-spot decision, partly because he'd been in the midst of grieving the death of his mother, but also because the feelings he'd felt for Kemah had grown so strong, and so fast, they had started to scare him.

It was a piercing, heartrending love that consumed everything, completely took over your life. The kind of love that, if you ever lost it, the hurt was so bad that recovery wasn't even an option. He'd suffered through that kind of lost with the death of both of his parents, but it didn't take death to feel the sting of that loss. All it would have taken was Kemah deciding she didn't love him.

In one irrational moment, he had decided it would be

easier to end things on his own terms, instead of losing yet another person he loved without having any control over the matter.

It hadn't taken Tyson long to realize that he'd made the biggest mistake of his life. Like a lost soul wandering through a thick, hazy fog, he'd spent months trying to figure out how to fill the gaping hole Kemah's absence caused in his heart. The truth, when it finally hit, was like a Mack truck against a concrete wall: there was no other substitute.

He had to get Kemah back.

When the opportunity to work at the center had surfaced, the chance to see Kemah again had been one of the main draws. It had been two months since he'd started here, and Tyson still wasn't certain which approach he should take.

She was harder to read than a wall of ancient hieroglyphics. She said she'd be okay with him taking over as director of the center, and not once had she tried to start any drama about their breakup. But at this point Tyson *wanted* her to bring it up. He was over the polite chitchat mode they'd fallen into. He didn't want the same relationship with Kemah that he had with the other volunteers. He wanted what they used to have together, but this time, he wanted to do it right.

He'd noticed the embarrassment tinting her cheeks today when she'd admitted to being dumped. She'd glanced at him, then quickly looked away. Tyson didn't know what fool was dumb enough to let a woman like Kemah slip through his fingers, but he'd been that same fool once.

Now he was ready to take action. He'd been holding back from pursuing her because he thought she was in a relationship. She wasn't in one anymore, and he wasn't going to sit back while she found another man on some dating Web site—what the hell was she doing resorting to a dating Web site anyway?

He was going to get her back. He just had to figure out the best way to go about it.

Tyson leaned a shoulder against the wall and crossed his arms over his chest as he settled in to watch her with the kids. They all clamored around her, but she quickly got them in line and within a few minutes the six little girls were following her fluid motions with ease. He heard Kemah counting out loud over her shoulder as she guided the girls through one step after another, her body swaying side to side like a gentle wave upon water.

She was hypnotic. Like a mythical siren who'd woven her spell around him, not with her sweet singing, but with her sexy, swaying body.

She turned to face the girls and looked straight at him.

Tyson's first instinct was to retreat, but that would look as if he were running—something he was not doing where Kemah was concerned. He had no reason to back down; he wasn't stepping on another man's territory anymore. Instead, Tyson pushed away from the wall and stooped down to unhook Samson's leash from his collar. He sent the dog to the back offices with a pat on his brindle-patterned rump; then Tyson walked over to the dance area.

Kemah stood there with a curious look on her face, a hand on her hip and her chest moving in and out with every breath she took.

"Girls, why don't you all get some water? Remember you should always—"

"Stay hydrated," the girls sang.

"That's right," Kemah laughed, pulling the ponytail of one of the girls as she scampered away. Kemah looked up as he approached, a delicate frown creasing her forehead as she stared at him with the same questioning look.

"I'm sorry. I didn't mean to interrupt your lesson," Tyson started.

"That's okay," she said, waving him off. "What's up?"

He needed to come up with some reason for getting caught staring at her like a low-rate stalker. He couldn't just spring his hastily laid plan to win her back, partly because he didn't even have a hastily laid plan, just an overwhelming sense of purpose.

Tyson had to bite back a smile as the perfect excuse popped into his head. "I was hoping you could help me with a proposal I've been working on. I've been struggling over it for the past week, but I think what it needs is a fresh pair of eyes."

"Uh, sure." She hesitated only a second as she grabbed a towel from the ballet bar and passed it over her face. "Does it have to be right now? I'm scheduled to teach the twelve- to fourteen-year-olds their liturgical dance at ten," she said, gesturing toward the huge clock that sat high up on the gymnasium's wall, protected by an iron grate.

"Well," Tyson said, "actually, there is a bit of a rush. I need to turn the proposal in by the end of next week in order for my additions to be budgeted for the next fiscal year. If they're accepted by the board, that is."

"Maybe after my class?"

Tyson grimaced. "I promised some of the boys we'd play one last game of touch football before the cold front that's moving in gets here. You know New Orleans weather, in the seventies one minute, and the thirties the next." He paused for only a second before he said, "Can we hash out some ideas over lunch."

If he was going to go for it, he was doing it with both feet. No tipping his toes in to test the waters.

The uncertainty that flashed over Kemah's face made him pause. A part of him knew that her seemingly blasé attitude about them working together had been a front, and for the first time since he'd started as the director here, he'd caught a glimpse of her discomfort. But she quickly recovered, pasting on a hesitant smile.

"Okay." She nodded.

Not the most enthusiastic acceptance, but he'd take it.

"Good," Tyson said. "I'll see you at lunch."

Getting her to agree to meet with him alone, away from the center, was the first step in his plan. Now all he had to do was develop the rest of it.

Chapter Two

"Miss Kemah, this is too hard," Sasha Lewis whined in her ear.

"It's only hard if you allow it to be. Now, come on, Sasha. I had less lip from the five- and six-year-olds."

"That's because their dance routine is easy."

Kemah rolled her eyes as she shielded them from the sun streaking through the clouds. A second basketball to the middle of her back had forced her to take the girls out of the center and onto a portion of the narrow, fenced-in lawn that ran the length of the building.

It wasn't the first time a rogue piece of athletic equipment had sent her dance class running for the hills, but Kemah knew they had to share the space with all the kids, and the boys had done a good job of keeping their basketball game confined to only one area of the court for most of the morning. It wasn't fair that her dance class keep an entire side of the gymnasium occupied. The touch football game taking place at the other end of the lawn had yet to make its way toward the back fence where they practiced their dance routine.

Even though they were yards away, Kemah could still make out the muscles displayed underneath Tyson's sweat-stained T-shirt. She knew if it wasn't out of respect for the highly impressionable young girls she had brought out here, that shirt would have been off already. The knowledge was enough to make her want to send the girls back inside the center.

They were having lunch this afternoon. How had that happened? Kemah struggled to recall the conversation, but she'd spent most of it trying to get her heart rate under control. All she remembered was Tyson inviting her to lunch, and herself accepting. Her stomach started rolling again, and she couldn't tell if it was from queasiness or excitement.

From the moment their eyes had met over the stack of papers he'd knocked out of her hands when he'd bumped into her on his construction site, Kemah knew the connection between them had been stronger than anything she'd ever felt with another man. She'd fallen into bed with him that same night—something else she'd never done with another man. She'd lived her life by the three-date rule. It wasn't until the third date that she even considered getting physical with a man. But after one afternoon of pouring over blueprints with Tyson, then sharing a cup of coffee that turned into four hours of chatting about everything from movies to demonstrating aikido techniques—that had drawn a few stares—Kemah had been done for. She'd quickly handed herself over to him, body and soul.

If only she'd known that a year later he would so casually end what they'd had together, Kemah wasn't sure she would have ever allowed it to start.

No, that was a lie. The time she'd spent with Tyson had been one of the brightest years of her decidedly dark life. Being immersed in his world, where people treated each other with respect, and mothers loved their children unconditionally, had been what Kemah had needed to restore her faith in humanity. Not every mother was like the one who'd given birth to her. Kemah wasn't ashamed to admit that she'd cried more at Darolyn Crawford's funeral than at her own mother's. In the year that she'd known Darolyn, the woman had been more of a mother to Kemah than her own had ever been.

The loss had been doubly hard when Tyson had ended their relationship just two days after his mother's funeral. Even though he'd tried to explain in the simplest terms possible why he thought they just wouldn't work—they were going in different directions, he needed time away to figure things out in his own head, he wasn't ready to make a commitment—Kemah was still trying to figure out exactly what had caused the shift in their relationship. They had been going along fine; then all of a sudden he'd handed her the girlfriend pink slip.

Kemah had not even tried masking her surprise the day he'd walked in and introduced himself as the center's new director. She'd been a volunteer from the first day the center's doors opened a year and a half ago—not long after they'd begun dating—but Tyson had been content to just sign his name on the dotted line when asked. He'd never shown interest in the center.

The only acknowledgment that he had considered her feelings at all was the softly spoken "Are you okay with this?" he'd asked the first day he'd taken over as director. Apparently, her quick nod had been all he'd needed to shove the time they'd been together to the side and treat Kemah like every other volunteer at the center.

There was an awkwardness between them that they both tried—unsuccessfully—to deny. Several times she'd caught him shooting curious looks her way, but they'd been so fleeting, Kemah wasn't sure it was not all in her imagination. Putting on a brave face and pretending his being here didn't affect her on the most visceral level was a constant battle.

"Miss Kemah, tell Armani that we're supposed to dip before we pirouette."

"What?" Kemah asked, shaking her head to try and clear it. "Yes," she said. "Dip, then pirouette, before ending in a bow."

A couple of the girls stood to the side snickering and pointing toward the fence. Kemah clapped her hands together. "Hello, you two want to pay attention?"

They both rolled their eyes and nodded, but continued to smirk.

Kemah looked over to where they had been pointing and spotted the young girl standing just beyond the fence, hands crossed over her chest, her chin up in the air. She stared Kemah right in the eye and held her gaze for long, charged moments.

"You know her?" she asked Ladasha and Bethany, the two girls who'd been pointing and snickering.

"That's Janelle," Bethany answered.

"Does she go to your school?"

They both nodded.

"I've never seen her at the center," Kemah said.

"You don't want her here," Ladasha said, thick with innuendo. A couple of the other girls laughed and nodded.

"Okay, enough," Kemah said. "You all don't have a minute to waste, unless you want the younger girls to show you up on the dance floor."

"Yeah, right," Bethany said. "There ain't no way those little girls gonna make me look bad. Come on, ya'll," she called to her dance mates.

Kemah looked back to where the other girl, Janelle, had been standing, but she'd disappeared from the spot. She squinted and caught a glimpse of a pink shirt moving farther and farther down Terpsichore Street.

It wasn't as if every girl in the neighborhood was a

regular at the center, but there had been enough community-wide functions—like the huge Christmas Eve dinner they would hold in just two days—that brought nearly everyone to the center. Throughout the year and a half that she'd been a volunteer, Kemah was sure she'd come in contact with every girl under the age of fourteen who lived within ten blocks of this place. This was the first time she'd ever seen Janelle, and the haunted, far-away look in the girl's eyes hit closer to home than Kemah wanted to admit.

"Miss Kemah, how many more times do we have to practice this part?" one of the girls asked.

Kemah gave her head a shake, trying to bring herself back into focus. She looked at her watch. "Actually, we should probably wrap it up for today, but you girls will have to practice on your own tomorrow. I want you all sticking every move when you dance at the Christmas Eve dinner on Monday."

"Yes, Miss Kemah," they said in unison.

"Good." She winked at them. "Now let's get inside. It looks like rain." Kemah stared up at the thick clouds that had quickly gathered overhead, blocking out the sun.

As they made their way along the side of the building, the girls giggled and pointed at the boys who tried their hardest to impress them by making rougher tackles than their game of touch football warranted.

"Finished so soon?" Tyson called as he threw out a short pass.

"You will be, too." Kemah pointed to the sky.

"We won't let a little rain stop us," he said as Kemah felt the first fat drop of rain upon her arm.

"Man, my dreads will shrink up," the boy standing next to Tyson complained. His turquoise and white Chris Paul Hornets jersey reached his knees.

"I guess we *will* let a little ran stop us," Tyson returned. He quickly wrangled the boys in, cutting their game short. Kemah stood just inside the front door, holding it open as the line of sweaty little boys and gossiping little girls made their way into the center.

"Dang," Tyson said, shucking off the raindrops that clung to his close-cut hair. "Wasn't the sun shining just a minute ago?"

"How long have you lived in New Orleans?" Kemah asked.

"All my life," he said with a grin. "And, yes, I know the weather can change at the drop of a hat."

"Before the hat even touches the ground," she emphasized.

"Which means it'll probably be sunny in no time. Those storm clouds should move out as quickly as they came in."

Just as Tyson had predicted, twenty minutes later the downpour had subsided, leaving shallow puddles in the street and the sidewalk's potholes. The sun didn't make a reappearance, however, and a brisk wind had started to blow.

The church fair kicked off at noon, and the kids were all antsy to get to the Space Walk, Ferris wheel, and Tilt-a-Whirl occupying the church parking lot.

Kemah stood just outside the door this time, waiting for the last of the children to leave the community center. Ashanti and Pam had tidied up while she and Tyson had been outside with the kids. All that had been left to do was to hand each child a parting snack—an apple, cheese crackers, and a juice box in a brown paper sack. Kemah knew it would be the only thing some of them had to eat for the rest of the day.

Her mind instantly conjured the image of the young

girl in the pink shirt. Janelle. Would she have anything to eat tonight?

It was foolish of her to assume anything about the girl. She didn't know her; had no clue as to her situation. But Kemah could not get the look she'd seen in Janelle's eyes out of her head. That blank look of longing and lost hope, as if she wanted to belong to the group, but didn't think she was worthy. God, how many times had she felt that way herself?

She had to find out more about her. Monday, when the kids came back to the community center, Kemah vowed to learn Janelle's story.

She had a strange feeling it mimicked her own.

"Thanks for joining me," Tyson said. He waited for her to slide into the booth before taking a seat across from her.

"It's no problem," Kemah lied, spreading the cloth napkin in her lap. "You said you needed an extra pair of eyes to look over your proposal. I just want to help."

"Is that the only reason?" he asked.

The low pitch of his voice brought her head up. Kemah was about to ask what he meant by the question, but the table attendant interrupted her.

They both ordered unsweetened iced tea and chips with salsa to share. Not your normal holiday fare, but the cold front hadn't pushed all the way through just yet, and temperatures in the low seventies called for iced tea.

"So, how much have you gotten done on the proposal?" Kemah asked after the server had left them.

"Before we get to that, can I ask you a question?"

"Okay." Kemah hesitated. The look on his face was serious, and she wasn't so sure she was prepared for his question.

He brought both elbows up on the table—so not the

manners she expected of a Crawford—and clasped his hands together. His deep brown eyes stared so intently at her Kemah had to fight the urge not to squirm.

"What are you doing using a Web site to find dates?"

Okay, she definitely wasn't prepared for *that* question.

This was the first time since he'd started at the center that the subject of dating had come up between them. Kemah knew it would surface eventually; she was just annoyed that it was her humiliating breakup by text message that had been the catalyst. And she was *more* than annoyed that Tyson would bring it up so casually.

"What's wrong with online dating? People do it all the time," Kemah said defensively, though she felt the hypocrisy wash over her as the words left her mouth. Even though it *was* commonplace these days, even she had felt resorting to the Internet seemed a bit desperate. From the skeptical look Tyson leveled at her across the table, Kemah could tell he'd read through her like a first grade *See Spot Run* book.

She settled back against the booth and crossed her arms over her chest. "Fine," she said, letting her irritation peek out just a bit. "Online dating wasn't my first choice, but after my friend Tara's younger sister married a guy she'd met online, I figured why not? If she could find love that way, why not me?"

"But through a Web site?" he asked.

"Excuse me, but finding someone isn't as easy for some people as it may be for you. Some of us have to work a bit harder."

"Maybe you're looking in the wrong places," he said in a velvety voice that sent instant chills skittering across Kemah's skin.

The clamor of the busy restaurant, combined with the cheesy Beach Boys Christmas song flowing through the speakers, was no match for the sirens Tyson's words had just set off in her head.

"Where should I look?" Kemah asked, the question springing forth from her mouth before her brain had a chance to process it.

Of course, the server picked that moment to return with their drinks and appetizer. Kemah used those few moments to decide if she really wanted an answer to her question.

She'd been attracted to Tyson from the very first minute she'd seen him in a grainy newspaper photo that accompanied a story about his growing commercial real estate company. The day he ran into her—literally—at the construction site had just confirmed what she'd seen in that photograph.

He had classically handsome features. Beautiful deep brown eyes that seemed on the verge of crinkling with laughter more often than not, and a straight nose that flared slightly on those occasions when he allowed his frustration to show.

But it was his mouth that continued to fascinate her. His lips were firm and sensual, his teeth perfect and white against his dark brown skin.

Kemah remembered an article in a magazine years ago that showed how Denzel Washington had the ideal face because of its symmetry. Even though the two looked nothing alike, she'd thought the same of Tyson. His face was ideal.

She'd been floored when he'd asked her for coffee that first day, and even more stunned the next morning when she'd woken in his arms.

After their breakup, Kemah acknowledged that during the entire year they'd been together she had been waiting for the other shoe to drop. Tyson Crawford, with his

Crawford millions resting in the bank, could never seriously think Kemah Griffin, who hailed from a run-down public housing development much like the one that surrounded the community center, could be a match for him. It seemed so preposterous that Kemah had never truly allowed herself the fantasy.

That's why she was still so surprised at how much their breakup had hurt her. She'd been expecting it, had thought it was inevitable. Yet she had been devastated.

During the six months since Tyson had ended things between them, Kemah had come to a sobering conclusion as to why she'd been so wounded. She'd fallen in love with him. She was still in love with him.

The admission was a hard pill to swallow as months, maybe even years, of them working together at the center stretched before her. It was even more frustrating to admit to her feelings when Tyson didn't seem the least bit affected by their working together. How could he be so impervious to this situation? Kemah both condemned him and envied him for it.

Once the server had left with their lunch order, Kemah dove headfirst into the reason they were here. She wanted to steer as clear as possible from their previous conversation. Her dating habits were off the table. After having to admit to the breakup by text message in front of him, Kemah figured she'd suffered enough embarrassment for one day. Or a lifetime.

"The proposal," she started, taking a sip of her tea and gesturing to the folder he'd set at the far end of the table.

Tyson's eyes and mouth tipped up with laughter as he stared at her for a full five seconds longer than was comfortable, and Kemah just knew he was going to go right back to her earlier question. But after another few embarrassingly long moments that she was sure brought a reddish tint to her light, quick to blush skin, he reached over for the folder.

Kemah moved the tortilla chips to the side and made a space for him to lay out the paperwork.

"Here's the deal," he started. "The foundation is given a hundred percent of the interest that has accrued over the previous year to fund projects for the upcoming year. Most of the money allotted is already set in stone, like the scholarships at the local high schools, and the money needed to cover the essential cost of running and maintaining the community center and halfway houses." He looked up. "You with me?"

Kemah nodded.

"Now, here's the thing. There's always a few dollars left, even in an economy like the one we're in now, and it's up to the foundation's board of directors to allocate that money to different projects. What I need to do is lay out a killer plan that will convince them to shuffle some of that money toward the center."

Kemah knew better than to think that he could just demand the money for the simple fact that he was a Crawford. She'd worked with charitable foundations in the past, and knew it was better that a board of outside individuals handle the finances than to leave it up to the family who'd probably bicker over where every cent was spent.

"What did you have in mind?" she asked.

"Well, that's sort of why I asked you to join me for lunch. At least it's one of the reasons," he tacked on, his eyes shifting to and holding hers.

Tyson cleared his throat and continued. "I want to come up with projects for next year that can help the center to grow. When you mentioned the Kwanzaa celebration—definitely a good idea, by the way—I realized that you've probably thought of other things that the center can hold throughout the year."

"Of course I have," Kemah jumped in. "There are so many things that can be implemented to help the kids at the center and others in the neighborhood," she added, thinking of Janelle. "Do you have anything particular in mind?"

"A few ideas I've been mulling over, but I want to hear yours," he said. "Throw out some of your wildest ideas, no matter the cost. Once we've brainstormed a bit we can go through the list and figure out which ideas are feasible and which aren't."

"Well, more computers would be at the top of my list," Kemah said. "There's always a wait for computers, especially during Science Fair time. Oh, and that's another thing, maybe we can bring in some people with a bit more expertise to help the kids with their schoolwork. Ashanti is brilliant with computers and math, and I'm pretty good at writing and grammar, but neither of us are huge science fans."

Tyson scribbled notes on a yellow legal pad, circling some words, drawing double lines under others. The resturant's music had switched from The Beach Boys to "A Chipmunk Christmas," but Kemah hardly registered it. When it came to the center, she was always fully engaged.

"These are good," Tyson said. He tapped his pen against his jaw, then pointed it at her. "You know, I've been contemplating field trips. I know it's a pain in the butt getting permission slips, and there's probably some crap we'd have to go through with the insurance, but I don't care. This is important. Can you believe some of these kids have never left this neighborhood?"

Kemah nodded. She could believe it. Other than the few times her aunt had taken her to City Park and shopping on Canal Street as a kid, she'd been confined to the eight square blocks of her neighborhood, too. Everything was there: her school, her childhood church, the corner grocery store. There had never been an opportunity to venture out.

Kemah was admittedly surprised by Tyson's sympathy toward the neighborhood children's plight. Even though she shared some of her childhood with him, she was convinced Tyson didn't truly understand. It seems she hadn't given him enough credit.

The table server arrived with the matching chicken Caesar salads they'd ordered. Tyson tossed his salad a bit before stabbing the romaine with his fork and stuffing a bunch in his mouth.

"It's pretty depressing when you think about it," he said around a mouthful of salad. "There's so much for the kids to see just in the city, not to mention all the other cool stuff in south Louisiana. Can you imagine those boys on a swamp tour? They've probably never touched a live alligator."

"And you have?" Kemah asked in surprised.

"Yeah," he chuckled. "My dad used to take us fishing down on the bayou when we were younger. I may have been born a city kid, but my dad grew up in the country and in his words, he didn't want his sons to be citified."

"I'm not sure how those boys would take to the swamp, but you never know. They may enjoy it," she said. She pierced a juicy piece of chicken with her fork and popped it in her mouth.

"That's the sad thing about it. They've never had the opportunity to decide whether or not they like it. I want to expose these kids to more than just the guys on the street corners."

She stared at him across the table, contemplating whether or not to say the words hanging on the tip of her tongue. She decided to go for it. He deserved to hear it.

"You've been quite a surprise," Kemah said. The questioning look in his eyes begged for elaboration, so Kemah obliged. "When we heard that a Crawford was taking over the operation of the community center, we didn't really know what to think."

"A Crawford?" he chuckled. "You say that as if my family is some other type of life-form."

Kemah hunched her shoulder. "Well, sorta," she laughed.

"Hey, no fair," he said in mock offense, laughter dancing in his eyes. "We're not that bad, are we?"

"No, you're not," she admitted, "I really like your family."

He nodded. "Especially Mom."

"Yes." Kemah couldn't keep the wistfulness out of her voice. "Your mother was one of the most caring, generous people I'd ever met. She's the reason I'm so dedicated to making sure the center holds true to the vision she had for it."

"She's why I'm there," he said.

"And you're doing a good job, and from the looks of this proposal, you have a lot planned for the future."

"Yeah, but I won't be able to do it alone," Tyson said. "I'll need someone just as dedicated to the center's success to help me see it through."

"I think I can speak on behalf of the rest of the women when I say we're one hundred percent behind you. All the volunteers are just as dedicated, Tyson, and we all work so well together. In fact, that's one of the reasons we were leery of you taking over as director. We were afraid you would come in and change everything around, and in a way, you did, but it's been for the better. You didn't try to implement a bunch of new rules, or anything. You listened to us, and to the kids. You've been really good for the center, Tyson."

He stared at her for so long without saying anything that Kemah started to squirm uncomfortably in the booth.

"I hope you didn't take that the wrong way," she felt the need to say.

"Is there a wrong way to take what you just said?" he asked. "You just validated what I've been doing for the past two months, after I've questioned myself over and over again." He stretched a hand across the table and covered hers. "I really needed to hear that, Kemah. Thank you."

"You're welcome," she answered. Her skin burned hot where he still touched it. God, she didn't want him to let go. It didn't seem as if he wanted to let go either. He kept his hand there, rubbing his thumb lightly back and forth across her fingers.

The memories of what it felt like to have his skin upon her own assaulted her, and just like that, all the tension that had stood as a wall between them began to crumble. She was right back where she'd started, staring into Tyson's chocolate brown eyes, losing herself in their intoxicatingly sensual depths.

That's when Kemah knew she needed to go.

She was smarter than the woman she'd been six months ago. She would not allow herself to be pulled so easily back into Tyson's fold with one simple, sexy look.

"We should—"

"Will you—"

They both grinned, his huge and knowing, hers small and shy. Tyson finally pulled his hand away, and gestured for her to speak first.

"I was just going to say that we should probably wrap this up," Kemah said. "I've got some paperwork I need to get through, and although I love the time I spend at the center, it's nice to have a Saturday afternoon free to myself."

"Yet you're going to spend it doing paperwork?" he asked.

She shrugged.

"But it's the weekend," he said. "You should be going out somewhere, enjoying yourself."

"Well, as you learned earlier today to my extreme mortification, I was dumped."

"I'm sorry," he said. "You deserve better."

This time it was harder to break away from his stare. It was full of meaning, and said everything Kemah needed to hear right now. She needed reassurance; to know she wasn't doomed to be the girl guys felt they could always toss aside without a backward glance.

Tyson signaled for the server to bring their check and handed her a credit card without even looking at the bill. Then he settled his elbows back on the table and resumed the position he'd held when they'd first sat to lunch.

"Earlier, when we were talking about the online dating thing, you asked me where you should look, if not on a Web site."

"Yes," Kemah said, surprised at the hint of breathlessness she heard in her own voice. "Where do you think I should look?"

"Right in front of you," he answered.

The air between them became thick as cotton, cloaking them in a cocoon that drowned out the sounds and smells and people around them. It was just she and Tyson, and the bevy of unanswered questions and emotions and denials the past six months had spawned.

Kemah forced herself to tear her eyes away from the intensity of his gaze, refusing to allow a simple look to draw her so easily under his spell.

"Tyson." She stopped, took a sip of her watered-down iced tea. "Don't do this," she managed to get out.

"Do what? Tell you the truth?"

"You don't have the right to do this to me," Kemah

whispered fiercely, mindful again of the eyes and ears surrounding them despite the overpowering Christmas carols still flowing from the speakers.

"I know I don't have the right," Tyson said. "But I'm hoping you'll give me another chance anyway."

"Another chance?" she asked. "Another chance at what? Breaking my heart?"

The wall of carefully laid cordiality they'd constructed disintegrated like logs in a burning fireplace. She'd never had the chance to speak her mind when they'd broken up, but she was going to do it now.

"You hurt me. At a time when I was hurting just as much as you were."

"I know. I'm sorry."

Kemah asked the one question she'd struggled with for the past six months. "Why?"

He toyed with the edge of the paper napkin. "You won't like the answer," he said.

Kemah's stomach bottomed out.

It was another woman. Had to be. She'd entertained the thought in the weeks—no, months—when she'd tried to figure out just what had caused Tyson to cut things off between them. It had hurt too much to even think of him with another woman.

"Who was she?" Kemah managed to grit past her clenched teeth.

"She?" Tyson's head popped up, his eyes widened. "You think I left you for someone else? No, Kemah." He shook his head vehemently. "There wasn't anyone else." Looking down at the table before looking back up and straight into her eyes, he admitted, "There hasn't been anyone since you."

The words hovered over Kemah's head in a cloud of cautious disbelief. How many nights had she agonized over the thought of him with some other woman? She had not dared to think he would remain single after their breakup.

The significance of the reality underlying his admission meant so much more to her than the simple words he'd uttered. She'd been the only woman in his life, even when she wasn't there.

"Truth is," he continued, "I've been trying to figure out why I ended things myself." He ran a hand down his face, his struggle coming across loud and clear. "It was just a confusing time. I thought I'd prepared myself for losing Mom, but I wasn't ready for her to go. It felt as if everything was closing in on me."

"But I was there," she said, her hands spread out on the table before her. "I could have helped you through it. I *wanted* to help you through it, Tyson, but you never gave me the chance."

"I know. But first I lost my dad and not even two years after that, I lose my mom. I was tired of having no control over when I lost the ones I loved. I just figured it was better to shut you out of my life on my own terms than to be left with that empty feeling if you ever decided to leave."

"If? You threw away what we had on an *if?*" she asked, unable to keep the accusation from her voice. "Instead of talking to me, and telling me what you were feeling? You just assumed I would eventually leave?"

Kemah toed the line between anger at the selfish callowness of his words and heart-wrenching sorrow over the pain she heard in his voice. She pulled in a deep breath, willing her emotions in check.

"That's no way to live, Tyson. You can't just shut people out."

"I know that now," he said. His gaze connected with hers, and Kemah's heart constricted. The pain was so raw; the mask he usually wore so well was nowhere to be found. This was Tyson, still grieving, still broken.

But so was she.

She loved him. She'd never stopped loving him. But he'd hurt her, and Kemah wasn't sure she should open herself up to that kind of pain again.

"I want another chance, Kemah. Please," he pleaded. "Just give me another chance."

Kemah shut her eyes tight, the logical side of her brain warring with the emotions of her heart. She wanted this so badly, but God, how would she survive it if he hurt her again?

"How can I trust you?" Kemah asked. "How do I know you won't just end things again when the going gets tough?"

Tyson stared at her for long, uneasy moments, his fingers toying with the extra straw the waitress had left on the table. He threw the straw to the side and sat back in the booth. "You don't know," he said. "I'll have to earn your trust again."

"Yes, you will," Kemah answered, "because I won't freely give it to you. Not after the way things ended the first time."

Tyson nodded. He stared at a spot on the table, his Adam's apple moving up and down as he swallowed, started to speak, stopped, and started again. Finally, he asked, "Will you at least give me the chance to earn back your trust?"

Kemah stared into the depths of his soulful brown eyes, wondering if she was being the biggest fool in the world. Maybe she was, but between going with her brain and her heart, she chose her heart.

"Yes."

Chapter Three

Tyson rubbed aftershave lotion over the bottom half of his face, then brushed his hair for the third time.

This wasn't his first date, he kept reminding himself, though he couldn't recall being this edgy the night of his actual first date nearly sixteen years ago. At thirty-two, he was ten times more nervous and excited than he'd been back in high school. Those girls had been easy to come by; all he had to do was crook a finger and flash a little cash.

It had been anything but easy to finally get Kemah to agree to go out with him. For a minute there, as they were sitting in that booth this afternoon, Tyson just *knew* she'd been on the verge of reneging on her promise to give him a second chance. It had been the longest minute of his life.

He'd known he'd hurt her that day six months ago. She'd put on a brave front that morning, just a couple of days after his mother's funeral, when she'd woken up in his bed. Tyson couldn't even remember the excuses he'd dished out. He just knew he couldn't shoulder the pain if one day she chose to leave him.

It was more than the threat of her leaving. Kemah had become as close to his mother as any of her own children. She'd sat with her in those final weeks, rubbing her hand, humming softly in her ear as the cancer slowly, painfully stole her life away. She had been in that same spot the moment his mother took her final breath. The picture was seared into his brain.

For days after his mother's death, whenever he saw Kemah, he saw that image. His mother lying on the bed, her body still and finally at peace. But her peace had not taken away his anguish and Kemah had become a constant reminder of the most painful moment of his life. Tyson was convinced he'd never be able to break the link between the two.

But once he'd started to emerge from the fog of grief that had engulfed him after his mother's death, Tyson had realized something was missing. Something he'd come to rely on. Some*one* he'd started to love.

Kemah.

His life had not been the same without her. And finally, after nearly six months of trying to figure out a way to get her back, he was about to go out on his *second* first date with the woman of his dreams.

Unfortunately, when he'd asked her out during their lunch this afternoon, he'd forgotten about the Johnstons' annual Christmas party. He didn't want his second first date with Kemah to be at one of the stuffy Christmas parties he'd been forced to attend since he was in high school.

Tyson tossed the thought out of his mind. It didn't matter where they were, as long as he was with Kemah. Anticipation skirted along his skin at the thought of the night to come.

He finished up in the bathroom and put his toiletries away. Tyson didn't bother with fixing up his bed. He would be the only one to see it tonight after his date. He and Kemah had fallen into bed together the first day they'd met, but this time he was determined to take it slow. He didn't want her thinking the only reason he'd asked her out was to get back into her pants. It was about so much more than the amazing sex they used to have. This was about love.

Tyson filled Samson's bowl with fresh water, and dispensed a cup of dog food from the high-tech Sharper Image dog food dispenser he'd bought on a whim.

"I'll be back later," he called out to Samson, who lifted a sleepy eye at him, puffed out a breath, and rested his chin back on his paws.

His cell phone rang as he locked up the door to his home in the exclusive Audubon Place neighborhood. The picture he'd taken of Kemah in the botanical gardens at City Park last year came up on his iPhone.

Uneasiness clenched his insides. Was she about to cancel on him? The threat had been in the back of his mind from the moment she'd agreed to the date. Tyson's hand shook just a little as he answered.

"Kemah?"

"Yeah, it's me," she answered. "Can you meet me at the center? I left my purse there, of all things. We can just leave my car and you can bring me back to get it after the party."

A relieved breath left Tyson's lungs with a whoosh. "Sure," he answered. "I'll be there in fifteen minutes."

As he exited the gates at Audubon Place and made his way up St. Charles Avenue, he got stuck behind a delivery truck that shouldn't have been traveling along there in the first place. The low-hanging branches of the oak trees that canopied the famous avenue were known for snagging the tops of large trucks.

By the time Tyson pulled up to the center, Kemah's compact sedan was idling in the lot next to the building. Exhaust fumes plumed out of the tailpipe. She no doubt had her heater running. The cold front had finally pushed through, bringing with it a blast of arctic air that had caused the temperature to plummet a good forty degrees since this morning.

Tyson parked next to her car and got out, wondering how long she'd been sitting in this lot by herself. He should have just driven out to her place and brought her back here. He wasn't all that hot on this neighborhood in the middle of the day. Dusk had just fallen and he sure as hell didn't like the thought of her sitting out here by herself.

The driver's-side door swung open before he arrived at her car, and Kemah popped out, wrapped up in a calf-length black coat.

"Thanks for meeting me here," she said, the words forming clouds as they exited her mouth. "I don't know how I forgot my purse."

"Let's get out of this cold," Tyson said, taking hold of her elbow and leading her to the center.

"It's amazing how the weather turns on a dime." Kemah shuddered. "And it looks as if we're going to stay in these temperatures for a while. I was watching the news while getting dressed, and the meteorologist said another arctic front should be arriving in a few days. Who knows, we may have a rare white Christmas in New Orleans."

She grabbed her purse from the pantry in the kitchen where the women all stored their personal belongings, and they quickly made it out of the center and to his car. Tyson opened the passenger-side door for her, but just as she was about to get in, Kemah stopped.

"What?" Tyson asked.

"Over there." She nodded her head toward the fence.

Tyson looked to where she'd nodded, but didn't see anything out of the ordinary, just a couple of people moving with purpose along the sidewalk, probably wanting to get out of the cold as soon as possible.

"The girl sitting on the steps of that house," Kemah said. "She has on a pink shirt."

Tyson squinted, making out the strip of pink. "Who is she?" he asked.

"The girls in my dance class said her name is Janelle. I saw her for the first time today."

"Is she new to the neighborhood?"

Kemah shook her head. "I don't think so. I think she wants to be a part of the center, though. I saw her watching us today, and my heart just broke for her." She turned her eyes up to him. "Do you mind if we go over and talk to her for a bit? I know we're already running late for the Christmas party—"

Tyson cut her off. "I don't care about the Christmas party. I can see this is more important to you."

She graced him with an appreciative smile, which started a warm glow in his chest. They headed toward the other end of the lot and walked through the opening in the fence Tyson had been meaning to get mended. He was sure the young girl would have walked away by the time they arrived, but she was still sitting on the stoop where they'd first spotted her.

The steps leading up to the porch were old and crumbling, the beams shoring up the faded green and gray overhang rusty from years of going paintless in the harsh elements of New Orleans's weather. Tyson was struck by the house's appearance. Not that it looked any different from the rows of structures lining this street. It was the fact that they were all the same that hit him like an elbow to the solar plexus. The house was a metaphor for this entire neighborhood. Ragged. Run-down. Forgotten.

"Hello, Janelle," Kemah started.

"Hello," she said.

Tyson found it strange the girl didn't bother to ask how Kemah knew her name, as if she understood that Kemah knew about her, even though they had never officially met.

"I saw you standing at the fence earlier today."

"I know."

"The gates of the community center are open to everyone in this neighborhood, especially the kids. In fact, it'll be open all week long for the Christmas break. Why don't you join us?"

"I can't dance like those girls," Janelle answered in that same monotone voice. She was slightly plump, with feet that curved in, indicating a bit of bowleggedness. Tyson had suffered with that himself as a child.

"Those girls couldn't dance like that before they were taught either. If you'd like, I'm willing to give you a few lessons one-on-one to catch you up to speed."

Janelle shook her head. "They won't want me there."

"It's not up to the other girls to decide who can be a part of the center," Tyson interjected.

"I'll be back there tomorrow afternoon," Kemah said. "If you want a private lesson, all you have to do is show up. I'll meet you there at noon."

Kemah's statement was met with silence. The girl just stared straight ahead at the doors of the community center. Tyson now understood what Kemah had meant by the look of longing that she'd seen in the girl's eyes. He was witnessing it firsthand.

A gust of cold wind blew, and Janelle pulled the tattered collar of her thin Windbreaker up to her chin.

"You have somewhere to go tonight, don't you?" Tyson felt compelled to ask. He envisioned this young girl hanging out on the streets, and it made his stomach roil.

"Yeah," she answered. "I live here."

She pointed behind her to the left side of the shotgun-style house, and Tyson was once again baffled. She lived directly across the street from the community center and had never been inside? Something wasn't right here.

"Will I see you tomorrow?" Kemah asked.

Janelle hunched her shoulders.

"As I said, the doors will be open."

More silence. More staring.

Kemah tugged on the sleeve of his cashmere coat. Tyson glanced down to where her hand touched him, then back up to her face. She tipped her head to the side, indicating that they should go, but he wasn't so sure about that. What was going to happen to Janelle when they went back to his car and pulled away? Was she going to go inside that house? Was that even her house? What if she had not been telling the truth? What if she really *did* live on these streets?

His muscles tensed with concern, and the rush of cold that poured over him had nothing to do with the weather. When he'd taken over as director of the community center, Tyson had never imagined he'd have to face the questions he now asked himself. The kids here were forced to grow up much too soon.

"I hope I get to see you tomorrow, Janelle," Kemah said. "Come on, Tyson. We need to get going."

Tyson let her lead him away from the curb and across the street to the center's nearly vacant lot. He glanced over his shoulder, finding Janelle still staring at them from her perch on the stoop, her chin still buried in the collar of her frayed Windbreaker.

Tyson opened Kemah's door, waited while she folded herself in, then shut it. He swallowed past a huge lump in his throat as he rounded the car and slid behind the wheel. He started the engine but left the car idling.

"How can we just leave her?" he asked, staring at the shiny hood of his BMW. How many coats could he have bought for the kids in this neighborhood with the eighty thousand dollars he'd spent on this car? Disgust burned like acid in the pit of his stomach.

"We have no choice," Kemah sighed. "It's not as if we can just bring her with us. I'm just hoping she shows up at the center tomorrow. By the way, would it be a problem for you to come by and open up? I know it's a Sunday."

"I'll be there," Tyson said, his gloved fingers clenching the steering wheel.

"Tyson?" Kemah prompted. "We're going to be late for the party if we don't get going."

"Forget the party," Tyson said. "I can't stomach being around those people right now."

"Those people?"

"People like me," he tossed out.

She put a hand on his arm. "Don't let Janelle's situation get to you."

He turned to look at her, shaking his head. "How can I not? She's sitting out there in the cold with nothing but a rag for a jacket and dirty sneakers on her feet. We don't even know if she'll have food to eat tonight. And I'm just supposed to pull away and spend the night partying with a bunch of pretentious people who try to pretend children like Janelle don't exist in this city?"

"I understand how you feel, Tyson, but you're just one person. You can't save every child."

"Yeah, well, I can at least do something for that one," he said, gesturing his head toward Janelle's house. "Are you up for a shopping trip?"

"Uh . . . sure," Kemah answered after a moment's hesitation.

"Good. Let's shop."

Kemah walked alongside the plastic red shopping cart as Tyson maneuvered it around the racks of clothes. Most of the coats and jackets in the Juniors section had been picked over, but Kemah was determined to find one for

Janelle. Every time her eyes fell upon the cart filled with shirts, jeans, underwear, and snack foods, she fell a bit more in love with Tyson.

Even though he'd brushed her off every time she tried telling him how wonderful this gesture was, Kemah couldn't help but say it again.

"It's amazing what you're doing, you know?"

He sent her that same sardonic look he'd adopted since they first started filling the shopping cart. "I'm spending a couple of hundred dollars on a little girl who has absolutely nothing, so I can ease my own guilt. Somebody needs to put me up for sainthood."

"That's not the only reason you're doing this," Kemah said. "You're doing it because you're a good person. There are a lot of people who would have looked at Janelle sitting there in the cold and just walked right past her. Dozens probably did."

"I hate to break it to you, but if you hadn't pointed her out, I would have looked right past her, too," Tyson said.

"You don't know that."

"Face it, Kemah. I've lived my entire life in a bubble. I didn't think about kids like Janelle before I started working at the center."

Kemah knew nothing she said right now could jerk him away from his guilt fest. He might not think what he was doing was special, but Kemah knew firsthand how people could look a lonely, lost child in the face and turn their backs. It had happened to her more than she cared to remember. Even her own mother had done it on a constant basis, too concerned with lamenting over the injustices that had been thrust upon her than to worry about whether her daughter had food to eat. Kemah couldn't suppress the spurt of resentment that surfaced.

Even though Tyson thought this gesture wasn't a big

deal, Kemah suspected it was something Janelle would remember for the rest of her life. Because, for once, she would see that someone cared about her. To a girl like Janelle, that had to mean everything.

"What about shoes?" Tyson asked.

"Huh?" Kemah returned, too wrapped up in her own musing to process his question.

"Shoes?"

"I don't know." She shook her head. "I think we did a good job at guessing her clothes size, but you have to be more exact when it comes to shoes."

He nodded. "We can always get her a few pairs later."

"Yes," Kemah said, acknowledging the tingle that slithered down her spine at his use of *we*. She knew she shouldn't read anything into it, but it caused that tingle all the same. "So, you think we've got enough here?" she asked.

Tyson lowered his eyes to the basket, which was filled with enough to make Janelle's Christmas probably the best she'd ever had. In addition to several outfits, gloves, underwear, and snacks, Tyson had included several young adult books, a handheld video game, and an MP3 player along with a gift card to purchase music from an Internet download site. He'd said he'd use it as incentive to get her to come to the center, since they were both ninety-nine percent sure Janelle didn't have a computer she could use to download music.

"I guess it's enough. For now," he tacked on.

"We should get this to her before it gets too late," Kemah said. "You don't want to go knocking on strange doors in that neighborhood at odd hours of the night."

It was almost nine o'clock by the time they pulled back into the center's parking lot. Thank goodness Janelle had gone inside since the temperature seemed to have dropped another fifteen degrees, but that presented its own problem. Kemah doubted the girl lived where she'd said she lived.

She might not be the most observant person in the world, but Kemah had to believe she'd have seen Janelle before if the young girl lived right across the street from the community center. She had been coming to this place nearly every Saturday for a year and a half. She wasn't so wrapped up in her own life that she would glance right over a girl like Janelle. A girl who reminded her so much of herself at that age.

"You think she's there?" Tyson asked, nodding toward the house where they'd talked to Janelle earlier this evening.

"The truth?" Kemah asked.

"That usually works for me."

"No," she answered. "I would have noticed her before if she'd been living right across the street this entire time."

He nodded. "I figured she wasn't telling the truth. Maybe I should check anyway. The people who live there may know who she is."

He opened his car door, but when Kemah did the same he stopped her with a hand on her left shoulder. "No, you stay in here. God only knows who's behind that door."

Kemah suppressed a smile. She could probably handle herself better in this neighborhood than Tyson could, and he knew it. He'd grown up coddled in a home of loving people and more money than most people saw in five lifetimes. But she found his protectiveness comforting. It had been a rare occasion in her life when anyone sought to protect her.

She spotted Tyson walking back to the car, illuminated by the headlights.

He shook his head as he got closer and as soon as he

opened the door and slid behind the wheel, said, "Not her house. Damn it." He turned the heater up, slid off his gloves, and wiggled his fingers in front of the vents.

"Girls like Janelle don't trust easily," Kemah said. "It figures she wouldn't tell us where she really lives. Let's just hope she takes me up on my offer to meet at the center tomorrow."

Kemah was unsure of how much time passed as they sat in the car, staring at the house across the street, as if the dilapidated structure of weather-worn wooden panels could answer the unspoken questions saturating the air. Where would Janelle lay her head tonight? Was it safe? Would she be warm and fed?

She'd only met the child today. Had anyone asked these same questions about Janelle yesterday? Did anyone care about her at all?

"Well," Tyson finally said, "we have two choices. We can go to the party and spend the night pretending we're interested in boring conversation, or . . ." He brought a hand up and trailed it down her cheek. "I can take you to dinner and we can get reacquainted."

"Reacquainted? In what way?"

He shrugged. "I want to know what's been going on in your life for the past six months. We haven't really talked since I started at the center."

"I talk to you," Kemah defended, though she knew that wasn't the kind of talking Tyson spoke of.

"I want more than a 'Hi, how are you doing?' I want us to *really* talk." His eyes locked with hers and with enough sincerity to steal her breath away, he said, "I miss you, Kemah."

Kemah couldn't speak if she tried. All the emotion she'd bottled up since Tyson's return lodged in her throat. She'd missed him, too. So much more than she'd allowed herself to admit. He'd been her best friend, her lover. She wanted what they had together. She needed that in her life.

"What do you say?" he asked. "A stuffy Christmas party, or dinner in the Quarter?"

"That's a tough choice," Kemah smiled.

"Let me help you make it," he whispered gently. He reached over, grabbed her chin between his fingers, and pressed a delicate kiss upon her lips. It was a sweet reminder of the kisses they'd once shared.

Kemah swallowed a moan as she allowed herself to sink deeper into the memory. But she didn't need her memories anymore, because Tyson was here. Right now. Kissing her again.

It amazed her how quickly she fell back under his spell. Tyson trailed his tongue along the seam of her lips and she quickly surrendered to his subtle prodding, opening her lips and allowing his tongue to delve inside.

A groan echoed inside the confines of the car, but Kemah couldn't tell if it had come from Tyson or herself. He twisted in his seat and brought both hands up to her face, pulling her closer to him as his tongue swiped back and forth inside her mouth. It was warm and tasted like the cinnamon gum she'd seen him pop in his mouth on more than one occasion.

Kemah swallowed the flavor, along with another moan.

Tyson gave her mouth a final thrusting with his tongue before relinquishing and sitting back in his seat. They let out matching deep breaths as they stared straight ahead.

"God, I've missed that," Tyson said.

"So have I," Kemah admitted. "If you want to, we can skip dinner all together," she said before she could stop herself. But she knew what she wanted. Why deny herself?

Did it mean she would allow things to go further? Not

necessarily. She could enjoy spending the night with Tyson and not feel obligated to take it any further if she wasn't ready.

But it was Tyson who shook his head. "We're not going down that road again."

"What?" Kemah's heart stuttered. He didn't want to sleep with her?

"That's how we started the last time, Kemah. We fell into bed that first night."

He didn't have to remind her of that. The memory had helped her through many lonely nights these past six months.

"So you're saying you don't want to sleep with me?"

"Not tonight," Tyson said, and then he quickly added, "Tomorrow, yes. And the day after, and the day after. But I want to take it slow tonight." He looked over at her and blinded her with one of his amazing smiles. "As my dad used to say, I need to court you before trying to get fresh with you."

Kemah couldn't hold in her laugh. "I like the sound of that," she said. "Now, are you going to feed me, or was that kiss dinner?"

"I remember you would always eat dessert first, just in case you get hit by a meteor before the meal was over."

"I still do," Kemah said.

"Well, that . . ." He leaned over and placed another kiss on her lips. ". . . was dessert."

Chapter Four

Fake snowflakes rained down upon their heads as Christmas carols piped through discreetly hidden speakers along the small alleyway that had been converted into a winter wonderland. Every year Fulton Street, in the heart of downtown New Orleans, underwent this transformation into a scene straight out of a Dickens classic. A white tent arched over the pathway, with hundreds of shimmering fleur-de-lis in different sizes hanging overhead.

The enchanting display was usually the only taste of winter natives experienced, but with the cold snap that had brought the temperatures down into the low thirties, it felt more as though they were steps away from Lake Michigan than the southern end of the great Mississippi River.

Tyson wasn't complaining about the cold. It had become his ally as the night moved on. With each drop of the thermometer, Kemah had snuggled closer and closer to him. As they strolled under the canopy of glittering foam snowflakes and fleur-de-lis along Fulton Street, Tyson tucked her deeper into the cradle of his arm, his body relishing the heat just being near her had created within him.

"You remember when we were here last year?" Kemah asked.

Tyson grinned. "How can I forget? I'm surprised they don't have our pictures on the wall like those Wanted posters in the post office."

"Hey, it's not my fault we got caught," Kemah said with a sexy little giggle that brought back more vivid memories of the slow, sweet kiss that had turned into an explosion of lips, tongues, and hands. God, they'd been hot for each other.

"We were lucky we were only escorted out," Tyson said. "The only time that kind of display is tolerated on the streets of New Orleans is during Mardi Gras."

Kemah's laugh at his quip turned into a deep sigh. "We couldn't get enough of each other back then."

Tyson pulled her even closer to his side and pressed his lips to the crown of her cottony knit hat.

They walked along the wide boulevard that was lined with sparkling, lighted Christmas trees and pots over-flowing with pungent poinsettias. Like clockwork, well-hidden bubble machines emitted a gentle dusting of fluffy bubbles that looked remarkably like snow.

Kemah extracted her hand from inside her coat and held it out. A small cluster of bubbles landed on her gloved palm, quickly dissipating.

"I think this closes at eleven," she said after a moment.

Tyson glanced at his watch. It was ten minutes till, but he had no intention of letting her go so soon. "Are you up for a cup of coffee?" he asked.

"Oh yeah." Kemah nodded. "Anything to warm me up."

If that was the case, he had something a lot better than coffee that would warm them both up. The thought had jumped to the forefront of his mind every time he felt the softness of her breast rubbing against his side. Tyson had struggled against the urge to slip his hand around her waist and bring her into full-frontal contact with his body.

But he couldn't go there. After all, *he* was the one who'd instituted the no-sex-on-their-second-first-date rule.

What the hell had he been thinking?

Kemah pointed to the hotel across the street. "It looks like the hotel bar is still open. Maybe they have coffee."

Tyson kept her close to his side as they crossed the street and walked into the hotel. The lounge was almost empty, and they were seated on a plush love seat moments later.

"This is gorgeous," Kemah said, her face lifted up to the ceiling that was covered in gold leaf. Huge ornate mirrors adorned the walls, draped in lighted garland and red and gold ribbons. A Christmas tree at least twelve feet high stood in one corner with a miniature ceramic village scene nestled underneath its lower branches.

There were more of the comfortable loveseats and sofas arranged in semiprivate seating areas, each with its own coffee table decorated with clusters of candles that cast a warm, subtle glow throughout the bar. The place invited intimate conversation, which was exactly what Tyson was going for. He couldn't have chosen a better place for coffee.

A server came to their table and Kemah ordered a mocha latte with a shot of Baileys Irish Cream.

"That any good?" Tyson asked.

"Oh yeah," Kemah laughed, and the server nodded in agreement. "It'll warm you up pretty quickly." The laughter that sparkled in her eyes did more to light up the room than those candles on the table ever could.

"Then make it two," he told the server. He sat back on the love seat and draped an arm over the back.

Kemah followed, settling into the plush seating. "What a night, huh?"

"It's been interesting," Tyson said. "Not exactly what I'd planned, but I wouldn't have it any other way. My eyes were opened tonight, thanks in part to you."

Kemah shook her head. "You don't give yourself enough credit, Tyson. Look at what you did for Janelle."

"Spent a few hundred dollars on clothes? Big deal."

"It *is* a big deal, especially to a girl like Janelle. I know, Tyson, I was that girl once. That little bit of kindness goes a long way. I just hope she shows up tomorrow so you can give her all the things you bought. Lord knows she needs them."

The server returned with their drinks. They sipped at the same time, and Kemah let out a soft moan. She put her drink on the table and turned to him.

"What's wrong?" she asked.

The side of his mouth tipped up in a self-deprecating grin. "You could always tell when something was bothering me," he murmured, shaking his head. "I just can't imagine what it's like. I've always gotten everything I ever wanted."

"Just because you grew up rich, it doesn't mean you don't understand what these kids are going through. I've seen you interact with them. You give them the respect they deserve. I promise you, not everyone does." She reached over and covered his clenched fist with her hand. "You are a good man, Tyson."

"Despite how I hurt you?" he asked.

Her gaze met his and he held it, willing what he felt for her to show through his eyes. Kemah was the first to break eye contact, tearing her gaze away and looking to the side.

Tyson reached over with his other hand and captured her chin between his fingers, turning her head so he could look into her eyes once more.

"I'm sorry, Kemah."

She cast her eyes downward, but Tyson dipped his head low, needing her to look at him as he said the words he should have said six months ago. "I know that I'll never truly understand how much I hurt you, because you would never tell me, but I need you to know how sorry I am. I've regretted the way I ended things from the moment it happened."

"Is it the *way* you ended it that you regret?" Kemah asked in a reedy whisper. She lifted her gaze and looked him dead-on. "Or that you ended it at all?"

"Both," Tyson admitted without hesitation. "It was the worst decision I've ever made."

She continued to stare at him, confusion and resentment mingling in her soft brown eyes. "I asked you earlier why you broke things off with me, and your answer was bull. I want the *real* answer this time, Tyson. Why did you push me away?"

Tyson knew the question would eventually surface, knew she'd wanted to ask it since the moment he started working at the center two months ago. He just wished he had an answer that didn't make him look like the selfish jerk he knew himself to be.

"Because it hurt to look at you," he answered. Then, because that answer sounded weak even to his ears, Tyson explained, "During the last few months of my mother's life, you were there for her more than just about anyone."

"I loved your mother."

"I know you did, and she loved you. You made it easier for her, Kemah. You sat by her side for hours, reading to her, talking with her, just holding her hand."

"And you had a problem with that?" she asked, her voice gaining a bit of indignation.

"No, no, of course not. I loved you even more because of it."

"So why did you end things between us? What changed?"

"My mom died," he answered simply. "For those last two weeks I watched her get weaker and weaker as the life slowly drained out of her."

"I know," Kemah said. "I was there."

"Yeah, that was part of the problem," Tyson answered. "When I looked at you, I saw her, sickly and pale and dying. I heard that sound, Kemah. That low, steady moan that she couldn't control because the pain was too bad."

Tyson shut his eyes tight against the memory, swallowing past the thick lump in his throat. "Watching her die was the hardest thing I've ever done, and every time I looked at you it was a constant reminder. I couldn't break the connection. I thought it would be easier to handle if I didn't have to look at you anymore."

"Was it?"

Tyson nodded. "For the first couple of days after the funeral, yeah. But then this other ache started in my chest, and I couldn't shake it. I walked around in a daze, trying to figure out just what the hell was wrong with me. Then I realized what it was. You were gone."

She started to speak, then stopped. She needed a breath. Finally, she asked, "Why didn't you call me?"

"Would you have listened to me?"

"Yes," she answered. "I would have listened because I was in love with you, and I was hurting just as much as you were. I was angry, Tyson, but I'm not foolish enough to put my pride above my heart."

Her voice broke on the last word. It felt as if a hand had reached into his chest and crushed his heart.

"I'm sorry," he said again. He could say the words a million times, and it would never be enough.

"I am, too," Kemah answered.

Tyson took a slow, deep breath before asking his next

question. The answer would affect every facet of his world from this point on.

"Is it too late for us?" he managed to push past the lump in his throat. He held his breath as he waited for her response.

Kemah looked him in the eye, and with one simple word, changed his life forever.

"No."

Chapter Five

Kemah unlocked the door to her condo in the Cotton Mill, an old mill in the city's warehouse district that had been converted into condos. She'd loved this neighborhood as a child, when she and her aunt would pass through on their way to the riverfront. Owning her own home here had been a dream she'd worked hard to make a reality.

Another dream walked steps behind her, following her into the condo. For months she'd fantasized about this very thing, welcoming Tyson back into her home, into her life. She was a long way from fully trusting him with her heart again, but she was ready to give him another chance.

"I told myself this wouldn't happen tonight," Tyson said as he closed and locked the door behind him.

"Do you need me to change your mind?" Kemah asked, turning to him and bringing her hands up to his neck, lacing them behind his head.

"No," he answered. He clutched her hips in his hands and pulled her close. Lowering his head, he took her mouth in a slow, mocha-flavored kiss. Kemah moaned, sinking into his kiss, enjoying the taste of him ten times more than the drink she'd had at the bar.

Tyson pushed her coat from her shoulders, letting it fall to the floor. He fingered the hem of her sweater and pushed it up her stomach, his hands smoothing along her skin. Kemah helped him out, breaking contact with his mouth only long enough to pull the sweater over her head.

They traveled to her bedroom in a slow stroll of loud, wet kisses and fumbling hands, leaving a trail of discarded clothing in their wake. By the time they made it to her bed, Kemah was clad only in the lacy black underwear she'd donned while getting dressed for the Christmas party.

Tyson pulled back far enough to look her body up and down.

"I can't even begin to tell you how much I've missed this," he said.

Kemah's eyes traveled down his chest, to his waist, and a bit below. "I can tell," she said, unable to stop the crooked smile from tipping up the corner of her lips.

Tyson's smile mirrored her own as he hooked his thumbs in the waistband of his boxers and pushed them down his legs. He did the same to her panties, catching them at her waist and slowly pushing them over her hips. Kemah reclined on the bed so he could roll the lacy garment down her legs. Then she opened her arms wide and welcomed him back into her bed.

Into her heart.

Tyson crawled from the foot of the bed, planting hot, wet kisses along the way. He kissed her knee, her hip. Dipped his tongue into her belly button and swirled it up the plane of her stomach. He placed a featherlight kiss upon each of her breasts before pulling a nipple in and sucking hard. Kemah's body bowed, her head pushing into the pillow.

Tyson continued his trek up her body, finally reaching her mouth, capturing it in a lazy, delicious kiss as he used his knee to wedge her thighs apart.

He pulled his mouth from hers and asked, "Are they still in the top drawer?"

Kemah nodded, her breathing coming too hard to allow coherent speech.

Tyson reached over and slid the top drawer of the nightstand open, retrieving a box of condoms. He emptied the box on the nightstand and took one of the foil packets, ripping it open with his teeth and rolling it over himself with one hand.

Then he was back. Back to kissing her, nuzzling her neck, sucking on her skin. Back to the spot between her legs that craved him more than anything in the world.

Kemah's entire body clenched tight in anticipation, then slowly relaxed in decadent remembrance as Tyson pushed his way into her body. Their mutual groans rumbled throughout the room as his pace quickened with each thrust. Over and over he moved within her, inviting memories of the countless times they'd done this, reminding her of how much she'd missed it. How much she'd missed *him*.

Tyson increased his pace, burying his head in the shallow dip between her shoulder and neck. He reached down with one hand to rub that spot he knew from experience would send her over the edge. Kemah exploded in a haze of white-hot light, her body shivering from the pleasure cascading through her bloodstream.

Tyson plowed into her with harder, more intense thrusts before throwing his head back, his eyes shut tight, the muscles in his arms straining against his taut skin as he released a groan of pleasure. He rolled off her and onto his back, the breath rushing out of his mouth.

"That was way better than a Christmas party," he said.

"I'd have to agree with you on that one," Kemah returned with a breathless laugh.

After several long, comfortable minutes where the only sounds were their contented sighs filling the room, Tyson turned to her.

"Kemah?" He waited until she looked over at him before continuing. "Tell me something about yourself that I don't already know."

"You know just about everything about me. I haven't changed much over the past six months."

"Not everything," he said. "Tell me something fun, like the best Christmas present you've ever received."

A smile broke out across her lips. "That's easy," Kemah said. She turned and snuggled her back against his chest. "It was a set of My Little Pony figurines. I was obsessed with them as a kid, and my dad bought me the purple, yellow, and light blue one. I can't even remember their names," she said wistfully.

"I hope you don't hold this against me, but I have no idea what the hell a My Little Pony is."

"I doubted you would," she laughed. "You know, now that I think about it, I had the green and the pink one, too, but I don't remember how I got them. I think I loved the ones I got for Christmas so much because they were from my dad."

Tyson draped an arm around her and pulled her tighter. She'd shared the story of her dad with him before, so Kemah knew she didn't have to elaborate, but maybe it was the holiday spirit in the air that had her wanting to talk about him.

"He was such a rock star, Tyson. At least in my eyes. Of course, my mom talked about him all the time, about how great he was, and how much she wanted him with us. I think that's why he seemed larger than life on the rare occasions that he did come around."

"But he had his other family," Tyson said.

"Yeah, those one-night-stands really do come back to haunt you." She tried for a light laugh, but it fell flat. "He never made me feel like he resented me, though. It was my mom who took care of that."

"I'm sorry, baby," Tyson whispered against her shoulder before planting a comforting kiss there.

"It's okay. As I grew older, I understood my dad's point of view. I really was his one mistake. I never expected him to give up his family for me. And even though he didn't come around often he still sent me a card every birthday."

Kemah smiled, remembering how excited she would be when that card came in the mail, always a day or two early. She would force herself to wait until her birthday to open it, not wanting to invite bad luck by celebrating her birthday early.

"You got presents from him. Why were the ponies he bought you so special?" Tyson asked.

"Because he brought them to me *himself* on Christmas Eve. It was one of the rare occasions I got to see him. I guess that's what made them so special."

Tyson rubbed his hand slowly back and forth over her forearm, knowing it wasn't much in the way of the comforting she needed right now, but hoping it would help all the same.

"How about you?" Kemah asked a little too brightly to convince him that she was really okay.

Damn. He hadn't meant for his question to bring up those memories. He was going for light and fun, not heavy and melancholy. He needed to bring a bit more levity to the conversation.

"I'm not sure it's appropriate to talk about my favorite Christmas present," Tyson said.

"Do I even want to know this?" Kemah laughed.

"Probably not." He grinned even wider. "It was the

type of present a boy of fifteen never forgets. Courtesy of my first girlfriend, Yvette Mitchell."

She snorted. "My Little Pony can't compete with that."

"Not unless that pony did some really cool tricks," Tyson said.

"They didn't," Kemah said wistfully. "But I was good at pretending." She turned around in his arms to face him. "I would stay up way past my bedtime. The curtains in my room were so threadbare that the moon shone through them, and I used to just play by the light of the moon, pretending the purple and blue ponies were my mom and dad, and that we all lived together, in a huge house, and not in a run-down development. That was before I really understood why he couldn't live with us."

She looked up at him. "It wasn't easy, Tyson, growing up that way. And unlike the kids we see every Saturday, I didn't have a safe haven I could turn to. That's why the center is so important to that community. You have no idea how many lives you're completely turning around."

"That's why you're so dedicated to it, aren't you?"

"Yeah," she answered. "And because it's just the right thing to do. I'm happy I'm a part of it." She kissed the tops of his fingers. "I hope I can be a part of it for many years to come."

"So do I," he said, dipping his head down to capture her lips. "So do I."

As they waited at a traffic light on their way to the center Sunday morning, Tyson glanced over at Kemah sitting in the passenger seat of the car, hope and anticipation radiating from every part of her. When they'd awoken this morning, wrapped in each other's arms in her bed, one of the first things she mentioned was getting to the center to meet up with Janelle.

Tyson couldn't ignore the sinking feeling in his gut that told him Janelle wasn't showing up. He'd seen it in the girl's untrusting eyes yesterday, in how wary she'd appeared when they'd tried to talk to her. But Kemah seemed to have turned a blind eye to the vibes he'd picked up on during yesterday's encounter.

Tyson knew he would never fully understand this burning need she had to help Janelle. Discussions about Kemah's childhood had surfaced several times over the course of the year they'd spent together. Growing up the way she did had affected her on a level Tyson struggled to comprehend. He wouldn't question her need to help other kids, even when those kids weren't ready to be helped.

He pulled into the center's parking lot, edging his car next to Kemah's.

"I know the chances are slim that she'll show up," Kemah said, her eyes darting from left to right. "I wanted to be here just in case."

"We'll give her some time," Tyson replied, thankful she wasn't getting her hopes up too much.

They remained in the car with the heater running for more than a half hour, until Kemah finally said, "She's not coming."

Tyson reached over to her lap and captured one of her gloved hands, giving it a reassuring squeeze. "You'll see the other girls at the Christmas Eve dinner tomorrow. You can ask them about Janelle. Maybe they know where she lives."

Kemah nodded, still peering up and down the street. "I hope so." She looked over at him. "The thought of that little girl spending Christmas on the street makes me sick to my stomach."

Tyson squeezed her hand again. He knew just how she felt.

Chapter Six

Kemah leaned against the doorjamb leading from the computer lab, looking out over the sea of people who had gathered for the community center's second annual Christmas Eve dinner. She recognized most of the mothers of the kids who attended the center. Many of them had shown up to volunteer a time or two throughout the year. Most had admitted to Kemah that it was their first time volunteering for anything, but if she could find time in her busy life to help their children, they could do so as well.

The thought that the time and energy she'd sacrificed for the center had affected so many others started a warm glow burning in Kemah's stomach. If another person inspired another person who inspired another person, maybe the words of her favorite song, John Lennon's "Imagine," could be more than just lyrics.

As she scanned the crowd, her eyes fell upon Tyson. He was crouched at the end of one of the tables, looking completely helpless as he tried to put together a toy figurine for a toddler who sat patiently waiting in his mother's lap. Even though the minimum age requirement to attend the center was five, many of their regular attendees had younger siblings. It would be tragic for any of them to go without a present on Christmas morning. Kemah had to remember to address the thank-you notes for the businesses they'd solicited to help in their toy drive.

Tyson finally found success with the toy. He handed it over to the little boy, both of them sharing wide smiles. Then he looked over at her and their gazes held. His smile grew even wider.

He stood up from his crouch and was standing before her after just a few long strides.

"Why are you here in no-man's land? Everybody's been served their dinner. Why don't you come over and get something to eat?"

"Not yet." Kemah gestured her head toward the restrooms to her right. "My girls are in there getting ready for their dance."

"Oh yeah. I forgot this was dinner and a show," Tyson said. "That seems to be your specialty." He lowered his head, swooping in for a kiss, but Kemah stopped him.

"Not here," she chastised. "Too many eyes. I don't want any of the ladies suspecting anything."

"Kemah, this morning when I walked in, Gladys took one look at me and gave me a hug."

"Why?"

"She told me it was about time I came to my senses and got you back."

"Oh God," Kemah groaned. "I should have known we wouldn't be able to hide it, especially from Gladys. She saw us together when we really *were* together."

His head reared back. "Are you saying we're not together now?"

"What?" Kemah looked up at him.

"These past two nights have not been for old times' sake, Kemah. Please don't tell me that's what this has been for you."

"I—I don't know, Tyson. I'm not sure what to make of this weekend."

"This weekend was me, trying to win you back." He

took her chin in his hand and brought her head up so he could look in her eyes. "It's still me, right here, trying to win you back. I don't want just a couple of nights with you, Kemah. I want all of it. Everything. I have to know if that's what you want, too."

Just as she was about to speak, her girls came running out of the bathroom dressed in their black leotards with the red- gold- and green-striped capes tied around their necks.

"Miss Kemah, is it time?" Sasha Lewis asked.

"Yes," Kemah answered, and then she looked up at Tyson and nodded, answering his question. "Yes."

Tyson's nerves were so on edge he was moments from jumping out of his skin. He hadn't had a chance to get Kemah alone since she left him to go and direct her girls in their dance routine. The center's Christmas Eve dinner was over, and nearly all of the families had cleared out with their gifts and extra food to take home, but still no Kemah.

Tyson wasn't arrogant enough to think that one weekend spent in her bed would be enough to wipe away the hurt he'd caused her six months ago, but he'd hoped it was a start. With the way Kemah was avoiding him right now, it felt as if they were back to square one.

He couldn't let that happen. The plan was to get Kemah back, not let her slip further away from him. Tyson refused to give her a chance to shut him out again.

Tyson hung the folding chair he'd collapsed onto the storing rack, and dusted his hands on his jeans. He spotted Ashanti over at the buffet table.

"Have you seen Kemah?" he called out to her.

"I think she's in the kitchen," she answered. "Come here for a sec." She motioned with her head.

Tyson took off on a slight jog across the gymnasium,

dodging the folding tables that had yet to be put away. When he arrived at the tables they'd set up as a buffet, Ashanti handed him a stack of aluminum pans.

"Bring these in the kitchen while you're going. Kemah's in there helping Gladys with the dishes."

Tyson carried the pans across the gymnasium floor, being careful not to let the leftover turkey gravy drip onto the floor. He backed his way into the kitchen and spotted Kemah at the sink bin, using the elongated hose to rinse soap suds off of a sink full of pots.

She looked up and graced him with a smile that melted his anxiety away.

"Just what I needed, more pans to scrub."

"Don't worry about those," Gladys said, coming in from the back pantry. "I told you to get out of this kitchen. I'm happy you came to drag her out of here." She winked at Tyson.

"He didn't come to drag me away," Kemah said. "He came to help."

"Girl, that boy wouldn't know what to do with a soap sponge. He never washed a dish in his life."

"That's not true," Tyson said. "I used to wash my cereal bowl in the mornings."

"Only because you were afraid someone would break it," Gladys said, sticking her cheek out for a kiss, which Tyson happily gave her. "Now you two get out of here. It's Christmas Eve."

"You're going to be here day after tomorrow for the Kwanzaa celebration, right?" Kemah asked.

"Of course," Gladys said. She winked at Tyson again. "I wouldn't miss it for the world."

Tyson couldn't contain his smile. Gladys Baker was one smart woman, and the type of ally every man on a mission should have.

"Let me get my coat and purse," Kemah said. She wiped her hands on a dish towel and went into the pantry for her things.

"You really going through with this?" Gladys whispered to him with raised eyebrows once Kemah left the room.

Tyson nodded. Earlier that day, he'd hinted at the special gift he had in store for Kemah for the first day of Kwanzaa. It was a tradition to share gifts on the last day of the celebration, but not this time. Everything about the gift he had in mind was embodied in the Kwanzaa principal of umoja. Unity.

Perfect.

With Gladys's help, Tyson knew he'd be able to pull this off. The only unknown factor was Kemah. Would he be able to convince *her* to accept his gift? He had tonight and tomorrow—Christmas Day—to make it happen.

"Gladys, we're running low on pudding cups," Kemah said as she exited the pantry, already donning her coat.

"Marcus Graham," Gladys said in explanation. "I sent him in there to get a bag of sugar, and he came out with his pockets bulging. Let me go see what else is missing."

"He stole them?" Tyson asked.

"Yep," came Gladys's voice from within the storage room. "A few packs of peanut butter crackers are gone, too."

Kemah put a hand on his arm. "She sent him in there knowing he'd take stuff," she explained. "We've tried to give him extra to take home with him, but he's too proud to admit his family needs it. We know allowing him to steal isn't encouraging the right behavior, but we've been at a loss. It's either that or watch him lose more and more weight. In that proposal you're about to submit, having the money to bring in someone who knows how to better handle these issues would be a nice thing, too."

Tyson closed his eyes, wishing he could blot out just a small portion of the things he'd learned about these kids over the past two months. He'd never expected the life-altering affect they would have on him, but how could his life not change when they had a six-year-old stealing pudding cups because he didn't have food to eat?

"Don't go there," Kemah said in a soft voice. Tyson opened his eyes and found her shaking her head. "I know it's hard, especially to think about a kid like Marcus on Christmas Eve, but you did what you could for him and his family. Not one of them is going to bed hungry tonight. You can feel good about that."

Tyson stared at the strip of light peeking out from the closed storage room where Gladys was still taking inventory. He looked up at Kemah. "I never thought it would be this hard," he admitted.

"It is hard, but you do what you can, and you think about how much harder it would be for those kids if you weren't here," she said. "Now, come on. It's Christmas Eve."

Tyson pulled her in and wrapped his arms around her, kissing the top of her head. He knew he still had a long way to go before he was the man Kemah made him out to be, but she had this way of making him feel as if he were already that better man.

"I love you," he whispered into her hair. "I never stopped."

"Neither did I," Kemah answered against his chest. She lifted her head, and the love pouring from her eyes was like a salve to his aching heart. "I love you, too, Tyson."

Tyson dipped his head and kissed her, tasting her lips slowly, thoroughly.

"You two still here?" Gladys asked, making them jump apart.

"We were just leaving," Tyson answered with a rueful

smile. He stepped over to her and gave her a hug and kiss. "Merry Christmas. Give my love to that houseful of grandchildren for me."

"They've probably set my house on fire by now," Gladys laughed.

He and Kemah followed Gladys out of the center. Tyson locked up behind them, and pocketed the huge ring of keys.

Kemah had walked Gladys to her car. Tyson waited while they hugged good-bye. Standing at the driver's-side door of her car, which she'd parked next to his, he considered saying to hell with his Kwanzaa plans and popping the question right here and now. But the shabby community center parking lot was not the ideal setting he had in mind when he asked Kemah to spend the rest of her life with him. Besides, Tyson figured he still had some work to do before he could convince Kemah to say yes.

Knowing she still loved him and had never stopped gave him a huge advantage. He would get her to say yes. After tonight, Tyson was more determined than ever. He needed her. They needed each other.

She walked over to him, a huge smile on her face.

"What are you grinning about?" he asked her.

She hunched her shoulders. "It's Christmas Eve. Can't a girl be happy about that?" She stretched her arms up and over his shoulders, clasping them behind his neck. "Especially when I'm going to spend it the way I plan to spend it."

"Mmm . . ." Tyson murmured. "Can I get a preview?"

He zeroed in on the spot on her neck that he knew would make her toes curl, but before he could take the first bite, he felt Kemah's body tense.

She tapped him on the shoulder, and whispered, "Tyson, look."

He turned to see Janelle getting shoved into a car she obviously didn't want to get into. The driver rounded the car, got in, and it took off down the street.

"We've got to follow them," Kemah said.

Tyson was way ahead of her. He took the car keys out of her hands and got behind the wheel, and had the car started before Kemah could get in on the passenger side.

They took off down Terpsichore Street, heading toward the central business district. The late-model Oldsmobile Cutlass Janelle had been shoved into hadn't gotten very far. Tyson caught up to the car in less than five minutes, but now that he was there, he wasn't sure what they should do.

"So, what's the plan?" he asked Kemah. "It's not as if we can demand they pull over."

"I just want to see what they're up to. Janelle didn't want to get into that car. If it looks like whoever took her is forcing her to stay with him, I think we should call the cops."

Calling the cops didn't seem like a bad idea; *waiting* to call them did. Tyson had seen with his own eyes the way Janelle had been shoved into the backseat of that car.

The car slowed and the brake lights illuminated as it pulled up to the curb of a house on Clio Street. Two boys were sitting on the porch. They couldn't be older than sixteen. The driver got out and rounded the back of the car, holding up a pair of jeans that were at least three sizes too big for his lanky frame with one hand. He opened the back door and pulled a pouting Janelle out of the car by her arm.

Leaving Kemah's car running, Tyson opened the door and got out.

"Tyson!"

"Stay in there," he called to Kemah when he heard the car door opening.

He was at the Oldsmobile in an instant, his heart beating like a drum in his chest. He didn't know who these boys were, but there wasn't a chance in hell he'd leave Janelle with them.

"What's going on here?" Tyson asked, making sure to keep all three boys in his sights. He hunched his chin into the collar of his coat. The cold wind howled like a banshee as it blew through the narrow alleyway between the houses. Tyson saw Janelle shiver, and took off his coat. He pulled her from the grip of the car driver and wrapped the coat around her shoulders. "Did he hurt you?" Tyson asked.

"Man, what you doing?"

"Did you hurt her?" Tyson roared.

"Hell no. You think I'd hurt my sister?"

Tyson jerked his gaze to Janelle. "Is this your brother?"

She remained silent, looking at the crumbling concrete sidewalk.

"Man, you better get out of here. This ain't none of yo business."

"Is everything okay?" came Kemah's voice behind him.

Tyson turned and shot her an irritated look. Didn't he tell her to stay in the damn car?

"Janelle, are you okay?" she asked, ignoring Tyson's glare and walking over to Janelle, putting her arms around her.

"She's fine," the driver answered. "Who the hell are ya'll?"

"We're two people who are concerned about Janelle, that's who we are," Kemah answered. "And she is not fine. You forced her to come with you."

"I didn't force nobody."

"If she really wanted to come with you, you wouldn't have had to yank her into the car."

"We don't have time for this, D.," one of the boys from the porch yelled. "Just leave her."

"I'm not leaving my little sister with these people," the driver said.

"Is this really your brother?" Tyson asked again.

Janelle nodded. "But I don't want to go with him," she said, staring her brother down with cautious defiance.

"Forget her," the other guy from the porch said. "I didn't want her dragging behind us anyway."

Janelle's brother looked at her, then at his friends. "You betta be home when I get back," he said. Then he got into the car along with the other two guys from the porch and took off.

Tyson saw the relief wash over Janelle's face as she watched the car speed away. Kemah held her by the shoulders and looked her in the eyes.

"Janelle, please tell me the truth, was that really your brother?" Kemah asked.

"Yeah," Janelle answered.

"Is it just the two of you?" Kemah asked.

She nodded.

"He can't be more than twenty years old."

"Nineteen. Our mama died last year. So it's just me and Daron."

Another gust of wind blew, cutting through Tyson's sweater. "Let's get in the car," he said.

In the five yards it took to get back to Kemah's car, Tyson's hands had turned numb from the cold. He turned the heat up and held his hands to the vents on the dashboard.

"Where was your brother taking you?" Tyson asked Janelle. Kemah had gotten into the backseat with her.

"He said they were going to some party, but I didn't want to go. Daron's friends start acting stupid when they get drunk." She turned her head to look out the window. "I knew he didn't want me with him anyway."

"Janelle?" Tyson knew the question Kemah was going to ask before she asked it. "Your brother and his friends, they've never hurt you, have they?"

"You mean touch me?" Janelle asked. "No. Daron would kill 'em. He wouldn't let anybody hurt me. He don't always act stupid the way he did tonight. Just sometimes."

"Do you have somewhere to go for Christmas?" Tyson asked. She shook her head. "Do you mind spending it with us? I think you'll enjoy it," Tyson said, thinking of the bags of gifts they'd bought for Janelle a couple of days ago. They were still in the trunk of his car.

"Ya'll not like crazy people, huh?"

"I know you've seen us both at the center, and nothing has happened to any of the kids there," Kemah said. "You can trust us. I would love it if you would spend Christmas with us, Janelle. And the day after tomorrow, you can join us at the center for our Kwanzaa celebration. Does that sound okay with you?"

"Yes," Janelle answered. "That sounds good."

Tyson caught Kemah's eyes in the review mirror and smiled. At least one of the items on his agenda was working out as planned.

Chapter Seven

"That's the worst guessing I've ever seen in my life," Kemah laughed, throwing a fistful of popcorn that was left over from trimming the Christmas tree at Tyson's head.

"Hey, not my fault," he defended. "She's giving you better clues."

"No, I'm not," Janelle said, shuffling the cards from the board game.

"Yes, you are. I think you're cheating for Ms. Kemah because she promised to teach you ballet." Tyson stood and stretched.

"Don't pay him any mind, Janelle. He's just upset because I'm winning," Kemah laughed. "It's time to wrap this up anyway. The food should be warm by now."

"I can help," Janelle offered, looking expectantly at her, as if she wanted nothing more than to be needed. Kemah's heart swelled with understanding sympathy.

"I would love that," she answered. "Why don't you pick up the game and put everything back in the box? Then maybe you can help Tyson set the table while I get dinner together."

Kemah stood and followed Tyson into the kitchen, Samson trailing behind her. She went for the oven, opening it to check on the spiral-cut ham that had come with the packaged meal they'd bought from a local restaurant that was probably making a killing selling precooked

Christmas dinner. The ham looked as if it could use a few more minutes.

She broke off a small piece and tossed it at Samson, who caught it between his teeth and walked lazily to his spot next to the baker's rack.

Kemah closed the oven and looked over to the glass-fronted cabinets where Tyson was retrieving china and stemware. This was probably the first time he'd used those dishes since . . . the dinner he'd cooked for her this past Valentine's Day. He admitted there had been no one else since her. It was unbelievable how good that made her feel.

She walked up to him and put her arms around his waist, resting her cheek on his back. "Janelle is a sweet girl, isn't she?"

"Yeah. She's not as tough as she let on. I think she's having a good time."

"You saw how quick she was to call her brother and wish him a merry Christmas this morning? I think they're just two kids struggling. At first, I thought maybe we should call Protective Services, but it sounds as if her brother is really trying."

"I thought about that, too," Tyson said, turning around and wrapping his arms around her waist. He dipped his head to give her a kiss on the tip of her nose before continuing. "Maybe I can talk to him, find out exactly what their situation is. It can't be easy for a nineteen-year-old to take care of his eleven-year-old sister by himself . . ." Tyson shrugged.

"What right do we have to split them up?" Kemah finished for him.

When Janelle's brother called his sister's cell phone after midnight, Tyson had answered, and told the teen Janelle was safe sleeping there, at his place, with him and

Kemah to watch over her. Daron had hesitated only a second before he thanked Tyson and apologized for not calling earlier for his little sister.

Janelle had assured Daron that she was safe, and said Tyson had invited him to join them for Christmas dinner. But Daron explained that he got double time if he worked on Christmas. Tyson took back the phone and he and Daron had come to an agreement that he and Kemah would keep Janelle until after Daron clocked off the job later tonight.

"Something tells me he's going to buck at the idea, but when Daron comes to pick her up tonight, I'm going to offer to help him out. Financially."

Kemah shook her head. "Too much pride."

"I know, but I just want to put it out there. I know he can use the help."

She patted his chest. "You are a good man, Tyson Crawford."

"I'm even better when you're around, Kemah Griffin."

Kemah laughed and accepted his slow, languid kiss. It was the type of Christmas present that rivaled her My Little Ponies.

As they sat around the black-lacquered table in Tyson's sleekly designed dining room, Kemah couldn't remember a more enjoyable Christmas. Of course, she'd had few as a child, but after she'd started out on her own and made her own friends, she'd come to love the holidays. Sitting at the table, listening to Janelle, who had become little miss chatterbox as the day wore on, and sharing those special glances with Tyson, Kemah felt a contentment that was hard to deny.

She wanted this. Not just for today, but every day. She wanted to come home to a house filled with family. A house filled with meals at the dinner table where they talked about their day. She wanted a home with Tyson and children of their own.

Kemah caught his gaze and held it, pleading that he see what was in her eyes, in her heart.

Please want this.

The corner of Tyson's mouth tipped up in a slight grin. Kemah returned it, refusing to ruin her Christmas with questions of *what if?*

In her heart, it felt as if they were back together again. He didn't have to ask, and she didn't have to answer. The sense of how right this felt was all the answer that was needed.

She and Tyson belonged together. Like a tinsel-draped tree and carols of hope and joy. A holiday feast and shouts of laughter. A young girl with ponytails and smiles on Christmas morning.

For the remainder of her Christmas, Kemah wanted nothing more than to rest in the peaceful joy of belonging.

"A bit more to the right. Right. There."

Kemah ran a hand across the green table runner, smoothing out the bunching caused by the red and black tablecloths underneath.

"What goes on the table?" Janelle asked, her eyes bright and eager.

"Remember the office where Tyson brought Samson this morning?" Janelle nodded. "Well, in the office next door, there's a box with wooden bowls, candles, and a candleholder that looks like a boat on a stand."

"A boat on a stand?" Janelle's forehead crinkled in a frown.

"Trust me, you'll know it when you see it," Kemah

laughed. "I'll get the fruits and vegetables out of the kitchen."

"But you'll wait until I'm back before you put them on the table, right? I wanna help."

"Don't worry, I won't do anything else without you."

As she took off for the back office, Janelle's smile was as wide as the kinara Kemah had sent her to retrieve.

Kemah couldn't contain the grin brought on by Janelle's enthusiasm. It had only taken someone showing they cared to bring the girl out of her shell. She'd been waiting on the porch this morning when they picked her up from her brother's, who Janelle said would be stopping in for today's Kwanzaa celebration on his lunch break.

Kemah admitted both she and Tyson had judged Daron too harshly, basing their opinions on his outward appearance instead of taking a moment to learn what was on the inside. He was trying his hardest to keep him and his sister together. But like any young man, he wanted a life of his own, too. That shoving they'd witnessed on Christmas Eve was Daron's frustration at having to drag Janelle along to the party he wanted to attend.

Yesterday, they'd hashed out a plan everyone could live with. Janelle would come to the center on Saturdays and after school for the new program Tyson was implementing, and if Daron ever needed someone to watch her, all he had to do was call Kemah or Tyson and they would be there to pick her up. Kemah was already thinking of places they could take Janelle for New Year's Eve.

They?

When had she become a *they* again? She and Tyson had yet to fully discuss this new thing that had developed between them. Yes, they'd had an amazing couple of days together. With what they'd both done for Janelle, combined with the holiday spirit that continued to suffuse the air, this Christmas had turned out to be absolutely magical.

But Kemah wouldn't allow that magic to cloud her common sense. As much as she'd hoped they could just fall back into the *before* they'd shared, too much had happened *after* to just sweep it all under the table.

She knew Tyson had started to feel something for her again. And God knows she wanted it more than just about anything. But Tyson was the one who'd said he wanted to take things slower. Kemah wouldn't push.

"What's up with that face?" Tyson's voice broke through her hazy musings.

"I'm . . . I'm fine," Kemah answered.

"This is the big Kwanzaa celebration you wanted. You're supposed to be filled with all these positive vibes."

"I'm positive, I'm positive," Kemah lamented. "You can be so annoying sometimes," she said with a smile to take the edge off.

"But you love it."

She did.

She loved his teasing, his smile. She loved *him*.

As they decorated the table with the traditional Kwanzaa symbols, a strong, straw mat or mkeka for the foundation, a kinara, the traditional candleholder with three red, three green, and one black candle in the center, and an arrangement of harvest fruits and vegetables, the anxiety over the state of her relationship with Tyson lifted.

Whatever the future had in store for them, she would accept it. No, she would do more than just accept it; she would embrace it. They had been given a second chance. Kemah knew she'd found love again. Whether the road led Tyson's heart to that same place, only time would tell. She'd enjoy every moment of what she'd been given.

Kemah surveyed the table, admiring the spread. They

were ready for an all-out feast. Traditionally, the celebration they were holding today was not done until the sixth day of Kwanzaa, but she'd decided to use this celebration as a learning tool for the kids. Today, they would go through all seven principles of Kwanzaa with the children from the center, with instructions for them to go to their homes and have their own seven-day Kwanzaa celebrations with their families.

"Where's the unity cup?" she asked, realizing it wasn't on the table.

"It's in the kitchen," Tyson answered. "Gladys is still putting the finishing touches on it.

Kemah was about to ask what kind of finishing touches the cup needed, but Tyson had already taken off to help Pamela drape colorful African-print fabric across the top of the doorway leading from the entryway into the gymnasium.

To incorporate kuumba, or creativity, into their celebration, Ashanti had set up tables with paper and crayons for the younger kids to draw pictures representing the Kwanzaa principles. They would teach the third principle, ujima, collective work and responsibility, by getting the older kids to help with the drawings.

The children started trickling into the gymnasium around 10:00 a.m. Many were accompanied by their mothers, siblings, and even a few fathers, Kemah was happy to see. The string of oohs and ahhs as they entered the center and set their eyes upon the decorations brought a smile to Kemah's lips and a fullness to her heart that she had expected yet, in a way, still surprised her.

She remembered when she'd first celebrated Kwanzaa, back as a freshman in college. She had known nothing of the holiday, and since Christmas had never been the most joyful time in the Griffin household, she thought Kwanzaa would just be an extension of that loneliness.

But the sense of community and belonging she'd felt during that first Kwanzaa celebration had been unlike anything she'd ever experienced. It had given her a sense of purpose, and was one of the reasons she felt the need to give back by volunteering at the community center. The principles of the holiday had helped to mold her into the woman she had become: strong, self-sufficient, and constantly humbled by those who continued to teach her more and more about herself.

Like Janelle.

Kemah sought her out in what had quickly become a rather crowded center. She spotted Janelle over by the table that held an additional collection of all the items they would use in today's celebration. Tyson had brought them so the kids could see and touch the symbols of Kwanzaa.

Janelle had been joined by LaDasha and Bethany, the same two girls who'd been snickering at her a couple of days ago. Kemah could see the tension in Janelle's face; her eyes were downcast and that bright smile she'd worn since yesterday had faded.

Kemah dropped the stalk of corn she'd been arranging on the feast table, determined to rescue Janelle, but she was stopped by a hand on her shoulder.

"Didn't you tell me you had to fight your own battles?"

She turned and stared at Tyson, wondering when he'd even crossed the gymnasium to get to her side.

His eyebrows rose in question. "Well, didn't you?" he asked.

"Yes," Kemah answered.

"You know as well as I do, if you go over there trying to

stick up for her, things will only get worse. She has to deal with them on her own."

"I know how mean little girls can be. But you're right," Kemah sighed. "She has to earn their respect, even if they don't deserve hers."

Kemah's heartbeat stuttered for several moments as she watched the girls interact. LaDasha pointed at the wide-mouth kikombe cha umoja, the unity cup, and Janelle picked it up and showed it to her. Janelle put the cup on her head like a hat and all three girls started to giggle.

And just like that, the tension was broken.

Kemah let out a huge breath she hadn't realized she'd been holding as the girls examined the rest of the Kwanzaa symbols on the table. They were joined by a couple of boys who, of course, took over the role of acting out crazy characters with the trinkets. Kemah watched as Janelle's eyes brightened with laughter. Her entire demeanor had changed. She looked like a girl who belonged.

"You're crying."

"What?" Kemah asked, turning to Tyson. He brought a thumb to her cheek. Kemah was stunned when it came away damp. She *was* crying.

"It's okay," Tyson said. He wrapped his arms around her and squeezed. "It feels good knowing you helped to make that happen, doesn't it?"

Kemah nodded, her chin tucked into the curve of his neck. She pulled back and wiped even more tears from her eyes. God, she must look a mess.

"For so long I felt as if I didn't belong, and it was pure hell. Janelle doesn't have to be that lonely girl on the outside looking in. She may not know it yet, but it's a gift more precious than any of the clothes or electronics we bought her."

"She knows it," Tyson said, nodding toward where an

even bigger group had gathered, including a few parents. Janelle stood center stage, and held her audience captive as she held up the kinara, pointing out its features. "Maybe we should let her guide the celebration."

Kemah just stood back, marveling at the transformation. What a difference two days had made. All it had taken was showing Janelle that someone cared, and in return, the girl had shown Kemah the power she held. By giving just a bit of herself, by taking the time to pay just a little attention, she'd changed Janelle's life.

It was a gift Kemah didn't realize she'd needed.

Chapter Eight

The activities leading up to the karamu—their Kwanzaa feast—had gone off without a hitch.

Dozens of families now surrounded the feast table in a wide arc, humming the traditional African hymn Pamela had taught them earlier as Tyson poured grape juice into the unity cup for the libation ceremony.

"We're ready to begin the first celebration," Kemah started. "Who can tell me what umoja means?"

Dozens of hands flew up in the air, and several of the kids shouted, "Unity," before she had a chance to call on anyone.

"Kemah," Tyson interrupted. "Before we get started, there's something I'd like to ask you."

"Now?" Kemah asked, motioning to the large group of people gathered around.

"Actually, this is the perfect place and time," he answered. Tyson took her hand, then lowered himself to one knee. A rumble of excited whispers and gasps rolled around the center.

The significance of his posture hit Kemah with full force and her knees instantly weakened. She stared down at him, a confusing mixture of elation, apprehension, and outright shock causing her heart to beat like mad. It felt as if a lump the size of a golf ball had lodged in her throat.

"Tyson?"

"Shhh," he said with a grin. He reached into his pocket

with his free hand and came out with a small velvet-covered ring box.

"Since umoja is a celebration of unity," Tyson started. "I'm hoping you will agree to unite your life with mine. Forever." He slid the ring onto her trembling finger, then stared into her eyes. "Will you marry me, Kemah?"

The crowd erupted in shouts and applause, but Kemah could hear nothing past the blood pumping through her veins. "Oh my God," she whispered.

Tyson rose, and clasped his palms around both of her hands. "Is that 'oh my God, yes' or 'oh my God, no'?" he asked in a slightly strained voice.

"Yes," Kemah cried. "Oh my God, yes." She threw her arms around his neck as tears flooded her cheeks.

Tyson's shoulders sank with relief.

Kemah tilted her head back, and looked into Tyson's eyes, praying every ounce of the love she was feeling shone through.

"I love you," she said.

"It can't compare to how much I love you," Tyson answered.

"You wanna bet?"

He lowered his head and mumbled against her lips, "Only if I get to pick the prize." Then he kissed her.

For the second time in two days, Tyson marveled at how at home he felt sharing a meal with the people from this neighborhood. He was the outsider here. He was the one who never had to struggle to pay a bill, or choose between keeping the lights on and putting food on the table. Everyone here should resent him for the easy life he'd led.

But as Tyson listened to the talk around the tables, he heard very few complaints. These people were grateful. Grateful to God, grateful to him, and Kemah and the rest of the volunteers for the work they did at the center. Grateful for this meal of traditional African foods they were able to share with each other.

Kemah had been right. He couldn't save the world, but what they had done here today, what they were doing every Saturday, and hopefully soon, every evening during the week here at the center, was making a difference. He was doing some good in this world.

Just as he'd done for the Christmas Eve dinner, Tyson was making his rounds to every table. He graciously accepted thanks and congratulations from just about every adult, and even many of the kids from the center, who were so excited to know he and Miss Kemah were getting married. Nearly all of them asked if they were going to have a baby, and if they would bring the baby with them to the center.

"I hope so," was his pat answer, and a true one. He couldn't wait to have babies with Kemah. Seeing how good she was with these children, and how she was falling in love with Janelle already, showed him how much she would cherish their child.

The thought brought a smile to Tyson's lips. As he looked over and saw her surrounded by a group of little ones, guiding them through some kind of African dance, his smile broadened. He couldn't wait to start a family with this woman. *His* woman.

He took a sip from the unity cup, smiling at the words Gladys had written on the inside rim on his behalf, so that Kemah could see it when she drank. *Thank you for saying yes!* They were going to use this cup for many Kwanzaa celebrations to come.

Kemah caught his eye and motioned him over with a wave.

Tyson shook his head. No way was she getting him to

dance. But then she sent the cavalry after him, and he found himself being pulled by the tiny hands of three- and four-year-olds who would eventually become a part of the center.

"You know I don't dance," Tyson said.

"This doesn't require any skill," Kemah returned.

"Ah, so I should be perfect."

"You said it, I didn't," she laughed. "Come on, you'll like this one. It's a special gift we're giving to the parents. Which principle are we demonstrating with our dance?" Kemah asked the children.

"Kuumba," they shouted.

"That's right. Kuumba means honoring your creativity, and we are going to honor our creativity with—dance." She took Tyson by the hand, love and laughter dancing in her eyes. "Don't worry. I'll teach you everything you need to know."

A half hour later, Tyson joined the three- and four-year-olds—the future generation of the Darolyn Crawford Community Center—as they ended the Kwanzaa celebration in the anyako atsia, a traditional West African social dance. Pretty soon, everyone was out of their chairs, joining them in the dance.

Tyson caught Kemah by the back of her shirt and tugged.

"What are you doing?" she laughed.

"Shhh," he said with a finger to her lips. He pulled her a few steps into the hallway that led toward the back offices.

"Tyson, what are you—"

He broke her words off with the kind of kiss that vibrated throughout his body and made him want to scream for more. Only after his lungs started burning in protest did he release her.

"I couldn't look at you another second and not kiss you," Tyson said. "I have a feeling it's going to be that way for a long, long time."

Kemah tilted her head back, her light, teasing smile the best gift Tyson could ever ask for. "I wouldn't have it any other way."

HeavenSent.com

Stefanie Worth

To all those angels—earthly and above—keeping watch over me and mine.

Chapter One

"In Sunday school, heaven was all cherubs and choirs," Kay muttered. "Now they tell me there's more work?"

Certainly grateful to pass the Life Inspection Application Process, Kay wasn't sure she liked the unexpected promotion that resulted. If they'd asked, she would have declined this job and opted for a role more appropriate.

"I would've figured that a life—albeit, short—of faithful service, daily prayer, and eager witnessing deserved more than being appointed Official Babysitter of Fickle Grown Folks." Miffed and disappointed, Kay lamented her plight. "At least it's only for twelve days."

"Maybe it's my profile picture." At the end of the year, in less than two weeks, Brenna Campbell's online match guarantee would expire and no one would be able to view the photo no one seemed to want anyway. "HeavenSent-dot-com, can't you find one single man to send my way?"

She stared at happily hitched couples proclaiming their finds and contemplated revising her Perfect Mate criteria. When Brenna first joined the site, she'd spent so much time agonizing over the questionnaire, the thought of reworking her heart's desires in order to snag a suitor was unbearable.

A dialogue box appeared at the center of her screen: YOUR FREE MEMBERSHIP EXPIRES ON DECEMBER 31ST. CLICK HERE TO SUBSCRIBE.

"So does that mean you think there's hope for me yet, or that I need a full year of rejection to prove my lack of compatibility?" She asked the laptop its opinion since none of her family, friends, or coworkers knew she'd reached the online dating level of desperation.

To Brenna, a goal was a goal. Five years of failing to achieve marriage meant she needed a change in strategy. That's why, as another year wound itself to a fitful close, she found herself assessing her life list of things-to-do:

Spiritual life: check.

Healthy eating, regular exercise: check, check.

Job, savings, good credit rating: check, check, check.

But no matches to her personality profile meant she kept falling short of one particular aim, signaling a personal low that she had no tactics to address: Brenna still hadn't managed to find a man.

"Nobody wants *me*." She clicked on a video featuring a man supposedly searching for his soul mate. "Or could it be that they don't know I *am* what they're looking for?"

A split-second pause in thought let the background sounds of Sunday night television news seep to the forefront of her consciousness. According to recent reports, she heard, about half of all African-American women had never married, nor would ever.

"Oh, please let me be on the other side of that unwed half," Brenna begged the universe, suddenly even more motivated to find her perfect someone among the profiles of HeavenSent.com.

Not as though she hadn't tried this exercise before; skimming the pictures, searching for the optimum mix of rugged features—gentle smile, mysterious eyes, touchable hair—and then reviewing the selected faces' profiles to see what they claimed to be about. Lastly, she looked at the qualities of the women they professed to want.

Most of them had entered few choices other than *No preference.*

"You don't care what my religious, political, or relationship philosophies are?" *Hmmm.* "No man is that easygoing."

Yet Brenna extended Nods—quick "I'm interested, are you?" notes—to five men in their late thirties, telling herself they were more likely to be ready to settle down than twenty-somethings. Last time she took this approach, no one Nodded back.

She could hardly wait to see who appeared in her results this time.

"I just don't get this," she whined to the laptop. "Maybe five-ten is too tall or they don't like layered bobs. I'm brown-haired, my full lips and well-placed curves are original factory equipment, so to speak. So why is it that HeavenSent makes me feel outdated and used up?"

She tapped the SIGN OUT link and shut down her computer.

The chances of landing the man who made her heart flutter and let her check off the last item on her to-do list seemed dismally slim this close to the end of the year.

Singsong tones on her computer indicated the laptop was going to sleep and she probably should, too. She closed its lid, turned off her desk lamp, and swept her hand across the desk's mahogany surface to shovel a palmful of the day's dust and paper crumbs into the waiting wastebasket below. She picked up her PDA in time to catch an incoming text message.

The note from HeavenSent proclaimed *Mr. Decent Nodded back! Log in to meet up.*

"Why not?" she whispered. A quick glance at the desktop digital clock let her know she'd be just shy of her eight hours of beauty sleep if she started tinkering around online once more. But she did it anyway, opening the laptop, signing on, and pulling up HeavenSent.com to read the message from the self-proclaimed Mr. Decent.

A face she wouldn't notice if it passed her on the street messaged, *Hi! You're beautiful!! When can we hook up??!!!*

Her stomach flipped. "The profile says he's thirty-eight, but he's using teenage jargon. Maybe he's trying to be cool. Maybe he thinks this is the booty call site." She stared at his ordinary face, devoid of facial hair or personality. Her stomach flopped.

"It is your first nibble, girlfriend," she argued with herself. "Bite back."

His real name, he said, was Ron. They exchanged a flurry of polite electronic niceties and decided they'd meet for lunch on Tuesday at a spot of her choosing. Brenna opted for a familiar downtown eatery, public and escapable, in case he turned out to be a psychopath.

Tuesday at 2, she typed in confirmation, trying not to read more into the line than the words on the screen said.

Evan Shephard sensed his serial dating days were ending. Possibly tonight.

Thirty-seven, he'd been told he could be a model with his looks, an athlete with his tall, stocky build, or a politician with his charm. None of the above, he still considered himself one of Detroit's most eligible bachelors, though lately he'd started to question the title's so-called perks.

In reality, with forty no longer far away, stranger sex had long ago become boring and Evan caught himself admitting the unthinkable: what he wanted was a real woman, an honest relationship, and maybe even marriage.

"I used to feel differently," he said to the ebony-hued woman across the table from him, rating her cute-kid-producing potential. "But I don't think it's right to bring children into the world without two parents and a stable home. What about you?"

"What's that option on the HeavenSent.com questionnaire? 'Not for me.'" She laughed, sealing the statement with a smoky gaze that implied dinner was in the way of her true plans for the evening. Her gray eyes sparkled above a sultry smile of perfectly shaped, bleached-white, soldier-straight teeth that could only be veneers.

Evan tried not to frown at the fakeness that explained the extra-long lashes. He wondered if her pupils were colored by contacts, how much of the hair bouncing on her shoulders was a high-priced weave, and whether or not he'd be able to feel her scalp if he ran his fingers through her hair. Some fellas liked that stuff. He preferred the real thing.

"What did you say you do for a living?" he asked just to make conversation—and see if tonight's answer matched the job in her profile.

"I'm an automotive engineer. At least for now," she giggled, and tossed her hair.

He laughed along with her, sympathetic to the nervous insight that represented Detroit's uncertain economy, particularly its crumbling automotive sector. "Will you stay local if things don't work out?"

"Not so sure. Depends on how they let me go." She shrugged. Her nonchalant demeanor took on a sullen cast. "That's one good thing about being single *with no kids*. If I need to move on, I just can pick up and go."

He wasn't so sure she painted the best future scenario at a first-date outing, though he appreciated her candor. "How's your dinner?" he asked, changing the topic from work and thoughts of a tomorrow that wouldn't be shared with the woman across the table.

"It's wonderful. Never met a lobster I didn't like." She stabbed the last forkful and washed it down with a final swig of wine. "What time's the show?"

Evan glanced at his watch: 7:13. "Eight o'clock, but it's right around the corner. We have plenty of time."

"I can always have a cup or two of coffee while we wait for the cab."

Evan had no intention of hailing a cab. She expected him to pay for parking and cover a cab to ride two blocks away? "Think I'll have that caramel apple flan. Dessert for you?"

He could see she'd already staked out the tiny sweets menu, but asked out of courtesy.

They ordered the meal's last course and then sat in silence for a minute or two.

"So you like the theater?" she asked him.

"Season ticket holder," he said proudly. The kind of woman he wanted appreciated a cultured man.

"Seems odd for a technical guy to like soft, fluffy, creative undertakings." She raised her eyebrows.

Was she trying to feel out any Down Low tendencies? Evan ignored the probe. "It's all about the intricacy."

"You mean in-ti-ma-cy."

"I meant a sense of complexity, so-phi-sti-ca-tion." He mimicked the way she'd drawn out her statement to him, hoping to impart a small dig. "Weaving a plot and pulling together the elements of a production is a lot like building a computer network. Theater uses songs and situations to connect people. I use wires."

"Never thought about it that way." She looked at him with wide-eyed awe, as if she'd just discovered he had a brain. "How long have you been doing installation?"

"I don't." Evan ran a mental check of his HeavenSent .com profile, knowing full well he'd listed himself as an IT Administrator. He'd even spelled out Internet Technology on his page to simplify the explanation. She still didn't get it. Or him. "I manage my company's computer systems."

"Oh, like when my screen freezes at work. I'd call you, right?" She giggled excitedly.

"You got it!" His employers didn't. They seemed to think stuck software, lost passwords, and deleted files were all he was good for. He couldn't wait for the day he'd be able to exercise his real abilities for creating complex security interfaces.

At the moment he was biding his time workwise until the recession let up. The way he was biding his time with tonight's date until the curtain went down on this play they were about to see. Evan raised a forefinger to signal the waiter.

"Check please," he called, flashing his own fake smile.

Chapter Two

Kay peered down at the earth below her feet. She wasn't afraid of heights, per se, but being able to see the entire world from her slot in the sky was a heady experience.

"Kay, it's me," a tentative voice called out.

She turned to see the man she thought she would be with forever. "Jay?"

"Welcome," he said, opening his arms.

She ran toward him and wrapped him in a hug. "I wasn't sure how this afterlife worked, I was so afraid I'd have to miss you for eternity."

"I'd say we have catching up to do, but you must know that I've been watching over you anyway," said Jay.

"I have babysitting duty, too," Kay said sourly.

"There's much more to it than that," Jay laughed. "I'll help you through it."

"So there's no policy against us working together?" asked Kay.

"Not that I'm aware of," said Jay.

"Good. Because I want off this detail as soon as possible."

"You haven't changed."

Jay smiled, but Kay couldn't tell whether it was from happiness or irritation.

Early, as always, Brenna sat at her corner office mahogany desk watching the sun crest in the morning sky outside her wall of windows. The clouds seemed to huddle for warmth around the solar bulb, allowing only a horizon-wide sheen to escape and kindle the day.

Though Brenna wasn't one to waste time gazing longingly over the Detroit River, the approaching holidays had somehow shrunk her usual to-do list, leaving her a rare moment to dawdle. Several people she worked with at Sandstone Personnel Services were already taking sporadic vacation days in order to attend their children's school festivities, finish last-minute shopping, or ready their homes for incoming out-of-town guests.

Brenna the Faithful, as she was jokingly dubbed, could always be counted on to fill in the gaps while everyone else was off living their lives.

Her solitude would end soon. Within the hour, others at the modest-sized company would hunker down in their cubicles, pretending to wrap up year-end reports or detail month-by-month plans for the upcoming year. Really, she knew, they'd be drawing up holiday shopping lists and furtively surfing the Internet for online sales, biding their time until the company's ten-day shutdown just two weeks away.

What kind of human resources manager would Brenna be if she didn't know such things?

Yet insights into this type of employee activity made her glad she worked in an informal corporate structure; one prone to ignoring on-the-job technology pursuits as long as the Net surfing didn't involve pornography or gambling Web sites. Around here, management only cared about recruiting companies that needed staffing help, placing those temps, and keeping their hiring organizations happy.

Unfortunately, business for a business specializing in placing auto-related temporary employees was scant in a marketplace plagued with cutbacks and shutdowns. So, at the moment, Brenna felt bored.

She wasn't in the mood for interviewing one more laid-off hopeful desperately seeking any paying position. She didn't want to analyze any more client surveys to see what she could be doing better with fewer resources. And, yet, she couldn't allow Sandstone's shortcomings to impact her overall life view.

"The company's failing. I'm not."

In the stillness, though, Brenna found it hard to ignore the one unspoken expectation she couldn't seem to check off her life list.

Soul mate. Lover. Husband.

"One of these days, I'm going to beat you into the office."

Brenna jumped as Evan Shephard's voice tainted her air space. He'd caught her daydreaming. She'd hear about it for months.

One, two, three, be calm. She spun her chair toward the doorway and another surprise: Evan dressed in black slacks and a matching muscle-grazing turtleneck instead of his usual crinkled khakis and sky-blue button-down oxford shirt. Black dress shoes—were those Cole Haans?—replaced the Timberland boots she kept telling him he was too old to be wearing.

Of course he'd sparkle on the day she'd opted for Fat Day clothes; faded dark denims and a stretched-out Christmas sweater. She even wore a ponytail because she fell asleep without wrapping her hair last night. Did he have the nerve to sport a fresh shave? And new cologne? On a Tuesday?

He could've slapped her with a "Gotcha!" All he did was smile.

"What'd you do? Hit the lottery?" Brenna couldn't think of any other explanation for the makeover.

"Nope. Lunch date." Now he beamed, forcing her to notice how perfect his teeth were and wonder if he'd ever worn braces. She hoped he got broccoli stuck right there in the front of that grin. And that nobody told him.

Brenna smirked. "What desperate soul wants to eat with you?"

He pointed at her. "You're not doing anything. I already checked your calendar. And I need to run a piece of information by HR. One o'clock?"

She felt so frumpy. And this whole ambush tactic was quite unlike the Evan she knew. Maybe he'd found another job.

The idea upset Brenna more than she wanted to admit. Not just because she'd have to recruit a new information technology manager, but more so because at midthirty-ish, they were Sandstone Personnel's oldest employees. As much as he annoyed her, he was the only person she could really relate to at the office—even if she was technically his superior.

I'll miss his uppity behind. Brenna laughed at the thought. She pictured him settling into new surroundings, making new nine-to-five friends, hanging out at someone else's door the way he did hers every day.

The thought ended, leaving her staring at Evan in a semidazed state. He winked. Brenna winced. Too late to hide the wistfulness he no doubt saw, she snatched her gaze back to the present and scampered into her I'm-in-charge-here persona to mask her growing embarrassment.

"Let's do one thirty," she suggested, straightening in her seat and returning to her practiced straight face. Evan had upstaged her once today; Brenna wouldn't give him

an encore. She'd go home and change first, making sure
the memories he walked off the job with were not only
pleasant, but platonic.

Brenna will flip when I tell her. Evan could hardly wait to
feel out her thoughts about online dating. He'd debated
the move all year, listening to his friends telling him
which sites were strictly for hit-it-and-quit-it hookups and
which ones would get a brother caught up.

Evan picked his first based on how fast he could get a
decent date. That was six months ago and he'd since
changed his definition of "decent." Now, based on his recent string of bad dates, he figured he shouldn't listen to
the fellas any longer. A change of venue—Web site—was
certainly in order. He just wouldn't tell them.

*If all I want is one night with a no name shorty, I can get
that at the bar. No password required.* He could even scroll
through his cell phone's contact list and come up with a
cutie who'd sleep with him for old times' sake. But then
what? *Evan Shepard, I do believe you've developed standards.*

"No, Brenna's not going to flip. She won't believe I actually acted on her 'get a life' sarcasm after all this time."

Peering inside the cubicle he passed to ensure that it
was empty, he hurried into his own space and logged on
to the HeavenSent.com matchmaking site. The name
was corny, okay, but those commercials had him sold on
finding just the right woman.

Even though he was confident in his choice of Web
site, he wasn't so sure about his selection criteria anymore.
That's where he hoped Brenna could help. Until now,
theirs was a work-based relationship that leaned toward
personal from time to time. He wasn't sure which details
he could share yet.

"Jeez! They've got a million questions on here." A little

overwhelmed, he faltered at the sight of the HeavenSent. com's twenty-plus categories of coupledom. "She better not lie on her questionnaire."

Once he started his own question-and-answer session on the site, Evan realized he never thought deeply about what he wanted in a future mate. He'd also never put much thought into how much personal space he required in a relationship, how many books he read the previous year or what his parents' marriage taught him about commitment.

Long after the cubicles around him began filling with employees and buzzing with their workday activities, Evan continued, answering the online interrogation as completely—and honestly—as he could. He would save his file and come back to it later if he needed to step away from his desk.

But Evan was riveted to his own screen by the possibility that a tallish, medium-built, confident, and intelligent woman would find his life perspective a perfect match for hers.

"What woman would want a man who loves sushi, old-school music, and unusual sports? Makes him sound mixed up." Jay shook his head. His wings shuddered in agreement.

"Brenna," declared Kay.

"I can see the possibilities, but maybe you should exercise a little more caution. She seems fragile."

"I always loved your sensitivity, Jay, but all she needs is a check mark for her list."

Jay shook his head. "I'd hope you want her to have more, though."

"Look, we all have a goal here," said Kay. "In business terms, it'd be a win-win joint venture." Kay smiled.

"Like combining two valuable portfolios to create one incredible deal." Jay seemed to agree.

"Perfect. Then we have eleven days to get final approval." Kay finally settled into the idea of herself as someone's guardian angel.

Shaken out of her lull by Evan's look, secret, and lunch invitation, Brenna became hyperproductive after he left her office. His resignation would create more work at the worst time of the year. Handling new tasks meant clearing away the old ones she'd prefer to ignore—end-of-year reports, client satisfaction surveys, and performance reviews. Duly prodded, she dove into the items clamoring from her desktop files.

Focusing helped the morning hours pass so quickly that Brenna barely left herself enough time to drive from her downtown parking garage to her town house just five minutes away. Still, short on time or not, she had to change. She'd been criticizing her wardrobe choice ever since Evan walked out of her office.

How dare he toss an extra stride of confidence in his step as he left! His footsteps still echoed in her mind; the sound of a friend walking out of her life?

At home, she sprinted the steep stairs to the cramped second floor that topped her tiny mid-'50s house. Its all-brick exterior cuddled a renovated interior that mixed plaster ceilings with drywalled rooms and click-in-place hardwood floors with arched doorways. Few squeaks remained after her pre-move-in renovation, but plush white carpet covered the hallway floor she hurried across and the bedroom she entered breathlessly.

Today's lunch with Evan excited her in a way their get-togethers usually didn't. As colleagues, they were close but not confidant-close. So why was she feeling offended because he forgot to tell her he was job-hunting? Better yet, why care how she looked over salad and panini sandwiches?

Why was she treating his new job like a personal affront?

Brenna wished away her thudding heart and the dampness of anxiety threatening her breasts. She chose a seldom-worn beige knit pantsuit from her collection of navy, gray, and black suits. Her closet looked the part of a high-powered human resources executive, the role she hoped to one day assume at a bigger company and better salary.

Evan hadn't seen this outfit. With the help of a pair of gold hoop earrings and brown boots, she improvised a casual prepared-for-anything-look fitting their usual buddy banter but proper enough to deliver her HR exit steps spiel. She slid the elastic holder from her ponytail and brushed her hair back from her forehead, letting its layered ends hang behind her shoulders.

It was 1:20. She'd be late, but cute.

She skipped down the steps, grabbed her fur-lined shearling coat, cued the house alarm, and ran out the front door to her haphazardly parked car. Two minutes later, her cell phone rang as she fussed at the lights on Jefferson to hurry up and change. Her wireless earpiece picked up the call from Evan.

"I'm on my way." She cut off his complaining before he started.

"No problem," he answered coolly. "Wouldn't be Brenna if you showed up on time. Just meet me at the restaurant by the rink."

"It's cold over there."

"They have heaters. You'll be fine. Trust me."

Oh, she hated that phrase. Men and employees who

used it generally did so to hide their dishonesty. But she obliged him anyway, parking at a nearby meter, and walking two windy blocks to the eatery.

Evan greeted her with a wave from an outdoor bench shrouded by short pines. In summer, giant planters with flowers of all colors decorated the area. A band shell occupied the rink space and a rainbow of music enthusiasts enjoyed free concerts, good food, and Detroit's short-lived hot weather season.

"You said there were heaters." Brenna saw no infrared lamps overhead or warming tents nearby.

Evan scooted over. "Sit here. It's nice and toasty." He patted the spot of concrete he'd just freed.

"Have you lost your mind?" She huffed and spun toward the restaurant behind them. "I'm going inside to get something to eat. If you're staying out here, I'll see you back at the office."

Got all dressed up to sit outside . . . Brenna restrained herself from growling aloud—or running back to cuss him out.

A sensation of self-consciousness rose from the pit of her stomach, scratched her throat, and scorched her cheeks. Like the hunch she harbored that his leaving was somehow about *her*, she now suspected that ruining her meager lunch hour was yet another game Evan was playing in the Wonderful World of Brenna.

Embarrassed by the ordeal, she hoisted her chin and continued her most poised and practiced sashay into the overcrowded eatery. Dismay attacked head-on. The register line wrapped halfway through the cramped space. A dozen or so patrons milled around farther back, awaiting their orders. Bodies occupied every wooden seat at each tiny café table.

Ordinarily—especially if she was with Evan—they wouldn't even consider staying. Downtown was riddled with places to eat, from hot dogs to haute cuisine, but pride glued her feet to the path of dirty footprints before her and led her farther from her expectations of the outing.

"How in the world did this happen?" she muttered quietly to herself.

Evan placed a hand on her back and whispered into her ear, "Because you're afraid to let go."

Startled, Brenna jumped and swung her shoulder backward, into his chest. "I am so through with you."

"So you'd rather stand in this long line—alone—than test the ice with me?"

"What are you talking about?" *Surely he doesn't mean anything romantic—*

"The rink." He answered as if she ought to know. "I rented skates and everything."

Flustered, she took a calming breath. "All you had to do was ask." She covered her misjudgment by blaming him for the misunderstanding.

"Then you definitely would've said no." He laughed and nudged her forward to fill a gap in the slow winding trail of diners. "We do have different ideas of fun."

"Falling all over myself in public, out in the cold, no, is not on my list of private joys."

"Like I'm going to ask you to hang out with me and let you hurt yourself." He shook his head in mock disgust. "I told you to trust me."

He had. "As if you know what you're doing any more than me."

"That I do. Call it a prep school leftover. Hockey was mandatory at Northridge Academy. Either you learned how to skate or spent every gym class of every winter for four years getting flattened. I can skate my butt off, thank you."

"You never mentioned it."

"And I probably wouldn't have if they hadn't built that outdoor rink this year. I look at it through the coffee room window every time I go in there for a refill. Guess it finally got to me."

"Well, then. It was nice of you to think of me for your little expedition."

"Cashier's open." He nodded.

Brenna did not believe in wasting time. Wasted moments were a sinful expense and she now owed the universe for an entire morning's worth of misspent energy.

He walked just ahead of her as they left the sandwich shop; the way men do when they don't want other women to think you're their woman. She didn't bother catching up. Instead, she kept staring at his feet, hoping one of his shiny black shoes would catch on a crack in the sidewalk and send him tumbling onto his ego.

That was mean, but she was mad. Mostly, she'd angered herself by letting him distract her from work—for no reason.

Evan walked faster to beat the DON'T WALK light at the corner across from their office building. Brenna stopped, watching him run through the intersection and arrive at the opposite side alone.

Parallel lanes of traffic proceeded to separate them. They might as well have been distanced by a bridgeless river at evening tide. She could not reach him now. He turned to eye her with a steely gaze accented with a smirk that made her feel silly and inept.

The air around him seemed to tease her: *can't skate, can't keep up, won't trust enough to try either.*

She waved her hand to shoo him on his way, wishing for her ponytail, sweater, and jeans. His back grew smaller and smaller and eventually disappeared into the crowd. The WALK light beckoned and Brenna stepped boldly off the curb, into the street. Holiday banners billowed from towering lampposts lining the city blocks surrounding the building housing Sandstone's offices. HAPPY HOLIDAY. MERRY CHRISTMAS. HAPPY NEW YEAR. Brenna read, walked, and suddenly realized her problem.

It was the New Year's resolution—the one about not turning another life page alone. She was subconsciously eyeing Evan Shephard as a possible write-in for her unchecked objective.

Desperation had slunk its way in.

Chapter Three

"What's going on?" Evan greeted Brenna with furrowed brows as she stepped off the elevator.

"You took off—"

"Not that." He shook his head as if she should know what he meant. "Here. Them." He pointed at the office doorway several feet ahead. "Reps from corporate are here. How come you didn't tell me? I would've fixed those two computers before we left."

"What reps?" Brenna ignored the barely veiled accusation he leveled and addressed her own worry. "How long have they been here? Why didn't they call?"

Impromptu executive visits were never a surprise to her. Managing human resources meant she needed to know more than most staff relegated to need-to-know informational status. She sat in on higher-level meetings where changes were discussed and decisions were made. Brenna had never been caught off guard in her three years with the company until now.

"Nobody's saying much," Evan reported, "but the temp at the desk said they got here right after I left."

They started back toward the glass double doors declaring Sandstone's mission to provide the highest quality staffing in metro Detroit. The wide-eyed receptionist greeted them with a quivering lip. "They're laying people off!" she whispered.

This time, Brenna left Evan as she rushed through the

inner office door. She murmured as she scanned the floor for faces of Chicago-based executives she knew only from photographs on the company Web site. "No e-mail. No meeting. No warning at all."

"You didn't know either?" Evan's steps nipped at her heels. His query pricked her nerves.

"No," she hissed.

Veering to the right, down the row of cubicles that led to her office, Brenna noticed a silent computer and empty walls in a space that had been filled with quaint framed quotes and a data-entry clerk earlier in the day. Brenna heaved a guilty sigh as she thought of the young man she'd hired into the post only six months before. *Last hired, first fired*, she thought.

"What do you think's going on? How does she know he got laid off? Maybe he did something and got fired. Or quit." Evan's speculation raced Brenna's mental analysis.

"Well, if it was that urgent—like a physical or verbal assault—I would have been notified." Knowing nothing left Brenna anxious and worried.

"Excuse me, Miss Campbell?" A petite woman with oversized, pastel glasses and a mop of auburn hair entered her office alongside a matching man, barely taller, with a bad toupee.

Neither of them looked like anyone Brenna recognized from the Sandstone Web site. Evan peered over their heads, motioning with a thumb and pinky gesture at his ear and mouthing for Brenna to call him. She blinked a yes in reply and addressed her guests.

"Yes, I'm Brenna Campbell. How can I help you?" She extended a hand, which the female shook.

"Keeley Gates and this is Joel Goodman." Keeley closed the door.

Joel moved to the opposite corner of Brenna's desk and

removed a sealed white envelope from a leather portfolio that seemed to be empty of anything else. Brenna plunked into her seat.

This cannot be happening, she thought. She clenched her lips, unable to speak because she knew this drill: she'd performed it before for other employees.

Keeley spoke slowly, evenly, above the whispery strains of smooth jazz wafting softly from Brenna's radio. "Due to forces beyond our control, Sandstone has been forced to take drastic measures to maintain its financial solvency."

Brenna began sinking into the muck of disbelief. She knew Keeley's surreal start led to an ending she didn't want to hear.

"We've decided at this time to consolidate our HR operations." Joel continued Keeley's devastation. He handed his envelope to Brenna. "Sandstone Personnel appreciates your tenure and dedication. However, at this point we are laying you off indefinitely."

"Today will be your last day in the office but you will be paid through the thirty-first of this month. That letter explains your severance and options for continuing company benefits," said Keeley.

"Please sign and leave a copy acknowledging receipt. Someone will be available to escort you from the building in half an hour," Joel finished.

She imagined that the small, soft-spoken pair were probably very nice people in other circumstances, but in this situation, she found their kindness condescending, their patience patronizing. She ripped open the envelope and scrawled her signature across the bottom, completing it with today's date. No need to read a document she'd worked with the legal department to develop.

"Will that be all?" She stood and spoke as steadily as she could while flinging the paper at Joel. "I have greatly enjoyed my time with Sandstone and am very disappointed to depart this way. But I do appreciate your graciousness in this difficult matter."

"Take care of yourself," Keeley said as she waited for Joel to open and close the door behind her.

The instant it clicked shut, Brenna sank into her chair and dropped her head onto her desk. She burst into sobs, drowning amid the thoughts flooding her mind: car, mortgage, and utility payments, holiday bills and finding a new job.

She reached for the handy quips she doled out to pink-slipped colleagues who called her for job leads, advice, or consolation. "When a door closes, a window opens." "All things in divine order." "Never look back."

Does that stuff sound as fake to other people as it feels to me right now? she wondered. *If the situation wore a window, it must be stuck shut. How could shattering my world be God's ordered life step? And what do I have to look forward to?*

Evan rapped at her door, his signature *tap-tap-tip-tip-tap* drumming that he used when he wanted to sit awhile and chat about nothing.

I can't, she thought. Semihumiliated, fully devastated, Brenna couldn't muster small talk for an unscathed co-worker. She sniffled and wiped at her bleary eyes hoping he couldn't hear her.

The knob jiggled. An opening appeared. Evan's head slid through.

His eyes widened as they focused on her face. His wordless jaw fell, then clamped shut. He pushed the rest of himself through the door and pushed it quietly closed, leaning against it as if he were keeping out intruders—as if he was an invited guest.

"Are you okay?" He turned the lock on her doorknob. "Who were those people? What's going on?"

"A Keeley and Joel Somebody and Somebody." She swallowed hard, but burst into tears again. "Evan, they're letting me go!"

"No way. How? Why?"

"Consolidating HR." Syllables escaped between sobs. "So Sandstone doesn't need me anymore."

Evan's shoulders sagged. He hung his head and ran a hand across his thick low-cut curls. He raised his gaze and murmured, "I am so sorry, Brenna."

More than the several feet between them, awkward silence separated the pair with palpable questions of how to respond and what to do now.

"I'll be okay. Just want to hurry up and get out of here."

Fresh tears flowed. This time, Evan acted, surprising Brenna for the second time that day by crossing the room and offering her a hug she so needed. She fell against his warmth and let him shroud her in his arms.

"Figure you'll take advantage of the fact that I can't get you for harassment?" She tried to laugh. He squeezed her tighter.

"Let me know what I can do for you. Anything."

Brenna swore the air between them changed.

Warning: Man Zone Ahead. Love-starved women should exercise caution before viewing, speaking, touching . . .

Falling.

Evan smelled Brenna's perfume every day. Now he *noticed* it: a head-turning fragrance, heavily oriental, slightly floral, and—this close—absolutely intoxicating. He bowed to the temptation to inhale a little bit deeper, drew in his breath, and felt her tremble against his body.

Uh-oh.

Would now be a good time to tell her that an e-mail

from corporate actually sent him running down the hall? That he hoped the notification that she'd been barred from accessing the company's network was an error?

Why add to her insult by spilling useless details? Especially right now when she smelled, and felt, so incredible. Who knew there was a real woman behind that executive exterior she flaunted?

"They only gave me thirty minutes to get my things together." Brenna's muffled words rose above their embrace. "How do you pack three years' accumulation in half an hour?"

The last statement bore a bitter edge uncommon to Brenna's even-keeled demeanor. With a final squeeze, Evan extracted himself from the embrace he started. He stepped back a pace or two—just enough to wonder if he should have let her go. The smooth move and his racing mind tripped over each other.

For a second, he faltered, and reached for words she'd use in this kind of situation before deciding that offering to be a reference was a hollow promise even he wouldn't want to hear.

"Let me help." What else was he good for right now?

"Sure, why not?" She dabbed at the mascara smears below her eyes. "Can you grab some boxes from the copy room?"

A conflicting combination of pride and shame lurched beneath his navel. *Evan Shephard is a friend of the victim,* news reports might say. *Sandstone Personnel is as heartless as some of the companies they staffed, laying off hard workers right before the holidays,* he thought.

"Be right back." Not wanting to refuel the accidental gaze they'd stumbled into before the hug, Evan glanced quickly at Brenna, just long enough to look apologetic, before backing away a few steps farther and turning toward her office door. He took a deep breath, turned the knob, and let himself out into the world where nothing much had happened.

Closing the door with a quiet click he wondered if anyone else knew.

All this and he didn't even get to pick her brain about the online dating idea.

"I hear there's layoffs today," whispered a red-haired colleague known for her fashion, not her discretion. She'd popped out of her cubicle and into his path like a spring-wired toy. "Bet Brenna's taking it hard having to let people go this time of year."

Evan stopped thinking and walking and tried not to scowl at her. "Yeah, she's taking things hard."

Hopefully, his answer didn't betray Brenna's trust and gave Miss Curious something to investigate somewhere else. He stood in place for a moment.

The boxes would definitely give the secret away.

He spun back toward Brenna's office. Did she care who knew? Did she want her things later? He could drop them off at her home.

Knocking just for formality, he opened the door to find her clearing bookshelves, stacking personal reference guides and manuals in neat stacks on the floor. Her desk appeared to be emptied, its surface covered with highlighters and Post-it notes she'd picked up for herself on one lunch outing or another. Spare shoes she kept beneath the desk now lay piled at its side, probably waiting for the box he didn't have.

"Brenna, what about them?" He pointed his thumb and fisted fingers toward the door.

"Part of me wants to make it a show, you know? Strut out of here with my head high like I don't give a hoot." Without looking up or slowing down, she slammed a book atop her growing stack. "The other side wants to throw that computer out the window." She heaved a sigh. "I don't care, Evan. Really. It's okay to bring the boxes."

Moments later, he'd passed the place where he'd turned around before. Once inside the copy room, he studied the boxes. After being emptied of printer paper and envelopes, staff set them aside in a corner for recycling.

He picked two large and one small. That's all he could carry at once. And as he retraced his path, his colleagues' typing slowed then stopped as he passed. He ignored the eyes boring his thoughts as he strode by in silence, hiding Brenna's secret for just a few minutes more.

"Here you go." Unsure how she wanted to organize her haul, he tried shoving his hands into the tight pants pockets—nervous habit. He felt as though he'd lost his usefulness. Maybe the way she felt about now. "How about I go get your car and pull it up in front of the building?"

Brenna raised her head and jammed her eyebrows together. "I parked over by the restaurant."

Now wasn't the time to tease her about trusting him; his attempted lunchtime surprise already proved her doubt. "That's a long walk with your arms full."

She pursed her lips at the comment—making him sure he'd picked the wrong words—and began dropping books in boxes. "Don't mess up my car, Evan. Keys are in my purse. Top right drawer."

"Woman, please." He clicked his tongue and rolled his eyes. "I haven't had an accident in months."

"Exactly." Brenna snickered.

Evan left with a grin.

This is what you get for wishing he'd get broccoli stuck in his teeth at lunch, Brenna thought wryly. Karma, they called it—though this payback must be for *all* the snide things she'd thought about Evan over the years.

Plus all the interviewees she didn't hire . . . all the Sundays she missed church . . . and splurges she'd indulged in with money that should've been saved.

Didn't she just pat herself on the back this morning for having good credit and padded finances? Ah, the world can be so cruel.

Brenna paused her packing and changed from her hands-and-knees-on-floor position to a butt-on-heels slump. *For all the money I have in the bank, will it cover my life for six months?*

Experts recommended a half-year's stash in case of emergency. But she knew that even without daily espressos and monthly shoe binges, her account wouldn't cover her mortgage alone for more than three months—let alone everything else she needed to live.

How do you file for unemployment? she wondered, picturing long lines of ousted workers awaiting checks doled out from expressionless tellers behind dingy Plexiglas windows. She shuddered at the humiliation of becoming one of Michigan's jobless mass.

"I can't believe they blindsided me like this," she hissed. You can't undertake these types of company-wide actions without somebody knowing. Brenna knew from experience. Human Resources always got a heads-up. So did Internet Technology Services.

Evan?

Had he been clued in to today's events this morning—or even last week? Perhaps that's why he was job-hunting. And maybe ice-skating was a ruse to avoid talking about something that might later feel like salt in her wounds. The way it did now. After all, he never did tell her his so-called news.

He had to know.

Brenna pushed up from the floor and scurried to her computer. She'd activated her screen saver before leaving for lunch, the way she always did. But when she opened her laptop, there was no neon-lit school of fish swimming across her screen. Instead there was an empty network log-on box holding court on a gray screen. She quickly keyed in her user name and password.

A simple line screamed at her: ACCESS DENIED.

How could you let them do this? How could you not warn me?

No wonder he was being so nice. Evan obviously felt guilty about his role in her termination.

That she'd never noticed a mean streak or vengeful tendencies didn't matter because he typically veiled his kindness in nonchalance that made her regard his compliments, chivalry, and refusal to eat "dutch" as little more than protocol for a well-raised man. And today he dared to look in her eyes as if the gesture was just for her.

Certainly nothing more than sorry-for-you sympathy, she huffed. Squatting near her half-empty box, Brenna began filling it with desk knickknacks—Bible verse calendar, sorority trinkets, employee awards (that she was tempted to toss in the wastebasket)—and tried to wish her keys back from Evan's hands.

"Wait till he gets back here," she hissed, sliding a lid onto the final box of her workaday world.

"Brenna, you okay in there?" the voice of the office fashionista crackled through the closed door. She knocked before calling out again, this time in a coarse whisper, "What's going on? We know you've got the scoop."

Her coworker's irony stung; the cocky assumption that Brenna was in the position *opposite* where she now sat stole her breath. Retreating inward, she reached for her mental cache of Sayings for Every Occasion and scrounged up a reply.

"Staff will be notified shortly of everything's that's taking place today." Brenna sighed heavily and pursed her lips. "Please give me a few more minutes, if you don't mind, and I'll be out. Thanks!"

She sighed again and thought of Evan. *Evan will be back soon. Then I'll be out of here for good.*

She stopped her mind's racing rant.

As hurt as you are, don't you want to say good-bye? she admitted. *Don't you want to say you'll miss them, wish everyone well, remind them to scratch your name off the pot-luck dessert list for tomorrow because you won't be bringing your famous peach cobbler after all?*

The door opened. Evan entered. Water droplets twinkled in the top of his hair and along the collar of his coat.

"It's started snowing?" she asked, standing up for a closer look.

"You didn't know? The news says we're supposed to get a couple of inches this afternoon," he answered with a shudder that sprinkled her packed items with shattered droplets.

"Since my schedule didn't include moving boxes through the elements earlier today, what did I care about more of Michigan's usual?"

"I parked right out front." Evan ignored her somber tone. "How about I grab one of those carts from the back to load all this at once?"

How dare he play the levelheaded helpmate? His calmness inflamed her irritation.

"Sure, Evan—create an even bigger show." She rolled her eyes and turned her head to look out the window. "Let's turn Brenna into the spectacle of the day."

"What's up with you? I'm just trying to make this as quick and easy as possible."

"Just do it, please. I'm tired." Her eyes welled again as Evan turned from the office with a huff and a head shake. "Leave the door open. My thirty minutes are up. Let's get out of here."

She listened as the hum of chatty coworkers in the cube across the aisle quieted. They listened. She waited.

The information piranhas would appear any moment now. They'd watch her struggle in the deep water, then swim in for the ambush: asking her a million questions, seeming sympathetic, offering hugs.

Suddenly, sneaking out and sending a farewell e-mail from home (the way some departed employees did) felt more cowardly than necessary.

"Why am I sitting here like I've done something wrong? Why shouldn't I go out with my head held high?" Brenna hoisted her chin just a bit and hoped the bleariness had dried from her eyes. In the style of the human resources director she'd been to her coworkers, she decided to go first; providing enough information to shush speculation, withholding enough detail to protect her privacy, and leaving the vicinity before the shock set in on them. "Sorry, but there'll be no employee question-and-answer session today," she'd say.

She stepped toward the door, and held her toes at the threshold between familiar and unknown. Evan returned with the cart and caught her eyes for the third time that day. He'd make a great executive in time. It takes a certain moxie to look a colleague square in the face and express such empathy while your head and heart are already on to the next order of business. Brenna couldn't resist the inner smile that crossed her lips at the idea of Evan suited up in a corner office.

Like hers.

Undoing her expression, she furrowed her brow and pointed—nicely—to her meager takeaway for three years of work. She allowed her gaze a quick pan of the place she no longer belonged. "Mind taking them down for me?" she asked. "I'm going to say my good-byes. Meet you in a few minutes."

Chapter Four

"You going to be all right?" Evan asked after lowering the last box on the floor of her home.

Should I curse him out now for not telling me I was walking into my own funeral, or should I be the bigger woman and drop the issue?

"You're good, Evan Shephard." She rolled her eyes and pursed her lips in disgust.

"At being nice?" His eyes narrowed. "Thought you knew that already," he teased.

Any other day Brenna would give a quip back. But this man, her former coworker, was now the senior staff member at Sandstone Personnel's Michigan office. He was smart, too, wanting to part on good terms with the employee everyone used to admire.

"I always—well, used to—tell people that challenge builds character." Brenna folded her arms beneath her breasts, leaned back on one hip, and began tapping the opposite foot. "It also brings clarity—because now I see how you really are, Evan."

"What? Okay, hold up." Evan raised both hands, palms forward in mock surrender. He dipped his head and backed toward the front door. "I really didn't want to drop you off, dump your stuff, and drive off with you acting half crazy. But I think that's what you want." He muttered, turning around to walk away. "I try to do right . . ."

"*After* the fact, maybe." Brenna marched after him and jabbed him in the shoulder with a forefinger. "If you were *so* concerned, you could have at least told me they were laying off people today."

He stopped and, for a moment, the house fell perfectly silent. He rotated his body, slowly, deliberately, to face Brenna. His heavy coat and her low ceilings joined forces with a smug sneer to inflate Evan to larger-than-life proportions. Her accusation hung in the foot of space between them, keeping them miles apart.

"So, the HR person—Sandstone's own classified information officer—thinks that the company told the computer-tech something you didn't even know?"

"You're the one who locks people out of the system when they're fired."

"Brenna, we haven't fired anybody from that office since I've been there." He frowned and tossed up his hands. "When people *quit*, I work with national to transfer access to their files. What are you thinking?"

Brenna's head exploded. "That you would be the logical employee—"

"To do something like that to you?" He turned back toward the door with shoulders thrust backward and footsteps hard enough to shake the floor statues he passed. "Guess that clarity you were talking about works both ways, 'cause I sure don't know you now."

"Nobody warned you about me being let go?" Brenna asked with surprise.

"You should have warned me you have a tendency to be paranoid," he teased again.

Really, I don't. She thought the words that wouldn't leave her lips. "None of this makes sense, Evan," she said, her anger abating.

"Neither have you. All day." Evan's tone softened, but

he continued facing the door. "Is it something besides your job?"

Yes. I'm afraid of losing you, too, she admitted only to herself. *Ever since you stopped into my office this morning I've thought you were leaving the company, abandoning me.*

"They cut me off," Brenna said instead. "They cut me off from my career, my income, my colleagues . . . my friends . . ."

Now he swiveled to face her. "Might not be the best time to remind you, but aren't you the one who was looking to break out in a couple of years and do your own thing anyway?"

"Launching a business takes proper planning," she retorted. "There's research I haven't conducted yet, start-up capital I don't have, expertise I haven't refined."

"I'm not trying to be insensitive, Brenna, but now you do have time to make all that happen." Evan eyed her with a mix of sympathy and reprimand.

Brenna interpreted his look to mean "Haven't you figured that out?" and instinctively declined the idea. "I'm not ready."

"So the Divine Order explanation you apply to other people's situations doesn't apply to yours?"

"No." She wished she could shake the smug look off his face. "In the 'All Things Are Meant to Be' school of thought, I could live with being laid off to find a better job, go back to school, or maybe get more involved in the community."

"Do you really think the Fates are pushing me to morph into an entrepreneur now, with Detroit at the bottom of the country's economic heap?"

"Brenna Campbell is no ordinary office worker. I think those 'Fates' see something you won't."

"Don't try to run my spiel on me." Brenna laughed.

Funny that Evan had been listening to her HR rants over the years about insecure employees or nonvisionary companies. "I'm the Queen of Skills Assessment. I know what I've got and where it fits. 'Founder' belongs off in tomorrow, not today."

"Wow, Brenna." Evan's eyes widened. "This afternoon I pegged you as nervous. But after all this rhetoric and denial, I see I sized you up wrong. You're flat-out scared, aren't you?"

Had she been writing off Evan's insight as male arrogance all this time? He did have a way of spinning a situation positive. While she wasn't ready to accept her unsketched future, he saw realization of potential she hadn't even acknowledged yet. Still, . . .

"Just let it go, Evan."

Instead, he pressed his point. "Okay, they say it's optimum to have a bunch of money stashed away—enough to live on for six months, enough to run your business for a year—but you'd also have to deal with the constraints of a rigid nine-to-five, two weeks' vacation time, and trying not to juggle your side objectives with your boss's expectations. This way you can spend all day researching, networking, making appointments, finding cash resources, without anybody watching over your shoulder. Right?"

"Yes, but . . . I *don't want* to start a new venture at this point in my life."

"Sure about that?" He winked. "What's it take to change a chicken's mind?"

Not certain he was still talking about work, Brenna fielded the question as if he was. "It's not that simple, Evan. I have this list—"

"Oh, but of course you do." He folded his arms. Then smirked.

"Stop thinking you know me." She fumbled for an explanation she felt she shouldn't have to offer. "Let's call it a road map—"

"That takes you where?"

"Professional, financial, and personal security."

"Job, money—should've known you'd plot your love life, too." He shook his head and raised her defenses. "So as of today, your map's off course with two areas anyway. Third one on track?"

"N-no." In barely a whisper, Brenna stammered her confession. He'd worn her down, sucked the secrets out of her inner confidential files. She'd worked so hard at being together, not just pretending she had it going on. And, dang it, Evan, of all people, knew the truth.

"Just reroute, Brenna."

The walls seemed to draw nearer, pulling him closer. Which of them was walking she couldn't tell.

"Creating a new map can't be that hard, can it?" Except that the mere idea of starting over did seem that difficult on the heels of a very bad day and too much talk about its consequences with a man who held no stake in her life. "What do you care?"

"You might not know it, Brenna, but you've been a lot of help to me these past three years. You deserve better than what you got today." A finger's length away, he seemed to tease.

"Then this could be the perfect time to step out into the universe and claim what I want." *Like one little hug.* She craved a single meaningful moment to shake loose the day's grief. "Will you hold me?"

Evan enfolded her in the repeat warmth of his earlier office hug. "Ten minutes ago, you thought I was playing games with your universe."

"All this stuff you're telling me now isn't what you wanted me to know at lunchtime, is it?" Okay, so he'd brought her comfort, yes. Convinced her, not yet. "If you didn't know about the layoffs, then what was your news?"

She felt him tense within the circle of her arms.

"I signed up for ballroom hustle classes. Wanted to know if you'd ever heard of Mr. Smooth."

"You? Gliding across the floor? Spinning some poor woman dizzy?" She laughed even though she could picture him perfectly in a fairy-tale scene surrounded by strangers looking on as he danced with a woman in white.

Without a word, he bent her backward in a sensual dip that left her light-headed and tingly. "I'll teach you to doubt me," he teased.

Her heart raced. Her body pulsed. Evan was much too close. "Let me up."

"Not till you take that stuff you said back." He swung her slowly back and forth.

Brenna struggled to pull herself up, pressing harder against his body and sparking a new round of inexplicable pulsing and tingling. Her attempt to rise was quashed by Evan's stronghold.

"Okay, I'm sorry. I had a rough day." She began to squirm, playful yet serious.

"Apology accepted." He leaned over Brenna, lifting her slightly, into the cloud of his cologne. "Come on."

He lifted, she slipped, and seconds later, Evan lay atop Brenna on the soft white carpet, his coat tented above their bodies.

Maybe if his arms hadn't cushioned their tumble, she'd feel really clumsy right now. And if he wasn't cradling her in his warmth, she'd feel much more awkward. Instead, he lay atop her gently, reminding Brenna just how long it had been since she'd put herself—literally—in this position . . . and just how good it felt. She looked up into Evan's eyes.

Um.

From "just a hug" to "just this once" in the space of a smile, Brenna accepted the "please" in his gaze and closed her eyes.

He kissed her.

Um.

She melted, warm and sugary like Christmas's home-made peach cobbler dessert. Sensations she'd forgotten how to harness spilled from her lips in an "ooooo."

Memories of her last lovemaking session nearly a year ago tried to cool her desire. Brenna remembered how trying to shape that man into The One didn't work, but he hardly compared to *Evan.*

Evan's lips disappeared. She opened her eyes and watched him search her face.

"You okay?" he asked. Not smiling, but obviously hopeful, he continued holding her much too close to elicit anything but agreement.

"I'm fine," she answered. "As long as you don't let me think."

Shy, but unashamed, Brenna reclaimed her kiss, opening his mouth with her tongue and sliding it slowly between his lips. He shut his eyes first. She followed suit, relaxing into the force of his tongue tangoing with hers and the sense that maybe he was overdue for a little affection, too.

She rocked him onto his side, rolling with him as she shimmied loose from his embrace and began removing his coat. Brenna shuddered—less from the removal of the coat than the feel of his mouth as he nuzzled her ear and nibbled her neck. Every touch was like liquid heat thawing the iced-over desires she'd long since stored away.

When his lips reached the V of her suit jacket, his hands took over, undoing the snap that concealed her cleavage, the buttons along her belly, and the front hook of her bra. He shoved aside the fabric and pushed himself back onto his heels.

Her nipples tensed in the cold. Her stomach tightened as he lifted. Her brain interjected.

"What's wrong?" she asked, feeling so selfconscious all of a sudden.

"How'd *this* happen?" he asked, shaking his head.

A man with a conscience? In the middle of The Deed? Brenna stifled a groan and struggled from beneath him to sit upright. Even with her plush carpet, the floor was still hard. But so was he.

"Maybe we've been wanting *this* all along," she offered, pulling her jacket across her exposed breasts.

His eyes followed her motion, then returned to her face. "Never crossed my mind, Brenna. I swear."

"Mine either." She smiled. "Does it matter?"

"I have a lot of respect for you and—"

"So you'll think less of me now?"

"No. But differently, yes."

"I'm a big girl, Evan. I'll still think you're a good guy when you walk out the door." She stood and reached for his hands.

"You say that now," he laughed, rising to one knee, then the other, finally shadowing her once more.

"What's that you IT guys do—test systems?" She kicked off her heels and tugged him toward the couch. "Test me and we'll see how it works."

Brenna played coy, but her heart was pounding so fiercely she knew he had to hear it. A concoction of desire, personal emptiness, and professional inadequacy squelched her better judgment. In an hour he'd be gone and after this they'd probably never speak again. But right now she needed him.

With shaky fingers, she began unfastening Evan's shirt. Her jacket fell open. He cupped her breasts in his hands. Her breathing quickened. She slid the shirt from his shoulders and tugged at the undershirt beneath. He released her to raise his arms so she could undress him, then returned the favor by pushing her jacket and bra to the floor.

He pulled her against his body and kissed her forehead.

So nice.

Brenna unzipped her skirt, stepping out of it and her stockings, and sitting on the couch. She listened as he undid his slacks, heard the snap of underwear elastic against his skin. Her breath caught in her throat. He sat beside her and took off his socks.

"Only for you," he teased, tossing them to the floor. He ran his fingers through her hair, looking at her so intently she wanted to believe that their feelings were real.

Seconds later, she'd laid herself beneath him once more—this time, unhindered by clothing, unconcerned about the cold. Her hands ran the length of Evan's taut body. His muscles clenched beneath her fingertips as his own hands coursed over her skin. The fire in his touch seared her inch by inch until she begged him to enter.

"Now," she gasped.

"You're sure?" he asked, breathing heavily, but hesitating still.

Brenna groaned in response.

Evan reached between their bodies, rubbed his hand between her legs, and pushed himself inside.

He lifted her hips, sending her deeper into that place where you lose yourself and the world turns to stars. Brenna threw her arms around his neck and screamed into his skin as he brought pleasure to her body. He pulsed, she writhed, and finally they gave in as the heavens exploded around them.

Ready to run, Evan lay atop Brenna without daring to make another sound. Until an hour ago, she'd been his last female "friend," the only confidante of the opposite sex he hadn't slept with. And, thus, the only unrelated female he trusted to have his best unbiased interest at heart.

Screwed that up, didn't you?

He cursed his testosterone, her perfume, and the act of fate that shoved them together.

"Well, *that* wasn't supposed to happen." Kay strolled to the edge of the station she shared with Jay and tipped an ear toward the scene below. "At least not yet."

"Why'd I listen to you?" Jay fumed. "*Merging assets, one incredible deal.* Looks like two big ole disasters if you ask me."

Kay gasped as she monitored her masterpiece and found her charges out of control. Driven by instinct, Brenna and Evan sealed a deal without a contract.

Unwilling to watch the catastrophe unfold, Kay wished for magic she didn't possess. While she could arrange possibilities, she couldn't predict actions. How would she know Brenna and Evan would jump to the end before they had a solid beginning?

"Okay, let's say at the meeting they jumped ahead to agenda item number twelve," suggested Jay. "What do we do? Send 'em back to cover one through eleven?"

"Neither one will understand the reason," said Kay. "They're both smart enough to recognize a great opportunity and they pounced."

"Literally," snickered Jay. "But without the paper they've got no real deal and neither do we."

"I'll fix this and you're going to help," huffed Kay. "First, we're going to assist them in restructuring so they have a stronger foundation for launching this initiative. And then *you* are going to introduce a third party to get our partners back on task."

Chapter Five

This was not the Christmas Eve Brenna envisioned one year ago; attempting to suppress regret with a steady stream of Christmas songs and busy work. Beneath the hustle and bliss, Brenna tried to pretend she stopped counting the number of days she hadn't heard from Evan. Three, if she included today.

What a lie.

The only thing she'd admit to doing differently was that she stopped imagining a workday with Evan. No longer would she think that at 9:00 a.m. he'd be leaned against her doorway, offering coffee, brightening her day. Noon would find him bugging her to pack up and leave for lunch. No matter how swamped with work they were, he always found time to eat. And the end of each day brought the unacknowledged promise that they'd see each other tomorrow.

It took three days, six hours, and a handful of minutes to realize just how many fantasies she'd jammed into their one-day stand: images of phone calls, text messages, visits, another round in the sheets, constant company to take the edge off her aloneness.

In reality, their only bond was a former shared workplace and accidental sex that both ended Tuesday, Wednesday, and Thursday, ago. Today—Friday—left her wondering what he was doing and why he hadn't called.

So she spent her Christmas Eve belatedly honoring her

holiday ritual—despite the change in her finances. After a day of lot hopping, she'd finally found the perfect blue Spruce to fill the den corner ordinarily occupied by a columnar floor lamp.

Light fixture temporarily relocated to a corner housing CD racks, she settled the tree into a red metal stand filled with water. She strung a new set of miniature lights and thoughtfully hung a collection of ornaments that ranged from new sale merchandise to childhood favorites she'd repossessed from her mother.

After the tree was dressed and lit, Brenna littered her fireplace mantle with cinnamon scented candles, wrapped her stairway banister with pine garland, clamped a wreath to her front door, and placed a small-scale nativity scene in the center of her coffee table. Lastly, she poised a handmade satin angel atop her tree.

"Now what?" she asked the glowing cherub.

The dimming light of the darkening evening suggested that she would have fared better calling a girlfriend to use the coming hours spending money she no longer had; not retreating to the couch and her pajamas as acknowledgment that she'd given up on *his* company.

"But why not?" she asked herself. There were worse fates than watching *It's a Wonderful Life* or *Meet Me in St. Louis*. Again.

So she did surrender to her PJs—the pink floral flannel ones reserved for extra crampy periods that showed up on cold winter nights. Thick scrunchy white socks with a tiny hole in each big toe accessorized the look she completed with a top-of-head ponytail and a freshly-scrubbed face that shined just so.

In six hours, midnight would deliver Christmas, just another day she'd make it through without a job or a man or enough motivation to address either issue. But, right now, her primary concern was pizza heaped with all the wrong toppings. She called to place an order, then phoned her mother.

"Hey, Ma, how's Jamaica?" *and the new man*, she wanted to add.

"Better than Michigan, I'll bet—except for missing you." Her mother paused. "Sure you'll be okay without my cooking?"

Ma's dinner served as the ultimate salve for Brenna's frequent boyfriend-less occasions. Except this Christmas the new addition to her divorced mom's life chose to whisk her away from the stress of the city and the annual ritual she shared with her daughter.

For a second, Brenna wondered how Evan would spend his holiday. His family was as scattered as hers and the restructuring at Sandstone would probably keep him tied to Detroit for weeks.

"Beverly invited all us solo sorority sisters to her house tomorrow." Brenna reassured her mother—who really didn't sound *that* worried.

"What are you wearing?"

"Those wide-legged black pants and that red velvet tunic I bought last year. The one with the peasant sleeves."

"Show your shape, honey. Maybe you'll meet somebody while you're there."

"No prospects in this crowd, I promise. But—"

"I just wish you weren't alone."

"I'll have plenty of people to 'eat, drink, and be merry' with." Brenna finished her statement with a sigh. "I don't expect daddy to fly in from Houston and babysit me while I wait for Santa to leave a guy in my stocking. I'm grown up now just like you and him."

"So you say. But no husband and now no job . . . I worry."

"Don't, Ma. You taught me well. We Campbells are survivors, remember?"

"True. Still I can't wait till these tough times are behind. Or at least you don't have to face them by yourself."

Brenna feigned a laugh. Her mother wasn't helping her already pensive mood. "Isn't that why I have you? You know, that *family* thing?"

"Not the same, sweetheart."

The doorbell rang at its thirty-minute delivery deadline, cueing Brenna to say good-bye to her mother and collect her food.

She rose like an automaton to answer. Habit required a cursory glance through the peephole, which revealed a pimply-faced delivery boy who brought the pizza she wanted and not the Prince Charming she wished for.

"Veggie Supreme, two-liter diet cola, bread sticks, and dipping sauce," he said as he handed over her bounty.

Brenna in turn placed each item on the floor inside the door and withdrew a crumpled twenty-dollar bill from her pocket. She thought of him being out in the frigid temps, and being greeted by stingy, non-tipping recipients. Maybe she could appease her guardian angel by being different. "Keep the change."

"Wow, thanks!" He reached into his jacket pocket and withdrew a fortune cookie. "This is left over from my other delivery job. Thought I'd give it to you. Have a great night!"

"You, too." She shut the door and picked up her food, careful not to crush the future-telling cookie in her hand, and spread her buffet on the coffee table—without disturbing the Nativity Scene in the center. Before turning up the volume to listen to Judy Garland sing "Have Yourself a Merry Little Christmas," she anxiously unraveled her fortune.

The life you desire awaits your permission to begin.

* * *

The engine in Evan's two-seater Lexus coupe purred beneath his roaring thoughts. Parked across the street from Brenna's house, he hoped the car's bright pearl exterior camouflaged it among the knee-high snowdrifts created by a long winter and busy plows. He sat staring at her wreath-clad door, the view intermittently disrupted by the swish of his wipers washing away wave after wave of an encroaching snow-rain mix—"snain" to Michiganders, a hindrance to his surveillance.

Finally, movement.

Within the pause of one thirty-second swipe, he caught sight of a pizza delivery car pulling into Brenna's driveway with what must be her Christmas Eve dinner.

To think I could have saved her from this. Evan regretted his decision to spend so much time contemplating his next move. He may be too late to court a woman he should have called three days ago.

The door opened and she appeared—half shadowed by porch light—but he could still see her smile. And a ponytail, a little more ragged than the one she had worn to work last Monday. And a mismatched jogging ensemble that said no way she had company.

He'd dressed the part of a suitor, deciding after a day of contemplation to "drop by" her place with her favorite Chinese takeout instead of watching basketball with his single, aimless frat brothers while the married ones were off having a real holiday. Theirs was not the company he sought. Tonight was for saying sorry.

Brenna paid the delivery boy. He turned from her porch. She turned off the light. Evan watched his chance at redemption disappear. He slumped into the blanketlike folds of his leather seat as his resolve melted away.

Whether the car was overly warm from his nerves or

the heater, he couldn't tell. But he turned the temperature down to seventy degrees to help clear his mind and cool the memories of how much he had enjoyed their impromptu lovemaking days before.

"Okay, man. Be honest," He said to himself. "That's what's really going on here. I enjoyed it. Her."

That's why he hadn't called.

That's why he couldn't step out of the car.

That's why he couldn't apologize to a woman he had to admit was now more than a colleague.

"I can't say sorry for something I'm not sorry about." A tinge of guilt for giving in to her emotion and his libido lay at the base of his dilemma.

Sure, he'd loved and left many a woman in his time; not returning calls, forwarding calls to voice mail, ignoring e-mails and text messages, driving around entire city blocks or declining nights out at his favorite clubs all to avoid the aftermath of his disinterest. But Brenna was different.

They had no foundation. There was no reason for what they did. No easy banter to fall back on. No relationship to cradle the one instance they fell into. He wasn't even sure she *wanted* to hear from him. She was professional, independent, certainly sure of her sexual needs.

He lifted his head from the cushioned neck rest to find the delivery boy standing at his driver's-side window with an ear-to-ear smile. Creeped out, but cool, Evan rolled down the window.

"Hey, you lost?" he asked.

"No, but you seem to be," the young man replied. "I'm passing these out this evening with my deliveries. Maybe it can help you find your way." He thrust a crinkly-sounding object toward Evan.

"Yeah, sure. Appreciate it." Evan didn't want to touch whatever this fella was sharing and tried to hurry him off.

The delivery boy smiled and walked away.

The guy didn't look like a drug dealer or porn trafficker. He'd definitely be out of place here. This looked like one of those neighborhoods where original owners still resided in the first homes they'd ever bought, raised their children here, and now welcomed their grandchildren on Sundays. It was hardly a hotbed of illicit activity. Curiosity prodded Evan to peek.

The gift was a fortune cookie. Evan didn't partake in their trite prophecies, though he did believe in wisdom that came from mentors and role models, experience and lessons learned. But here he sat outside the home of a woman who had his insides in knots, looking like a stalker.

He laughed at himself, threw his head back, and watched the wipers clear a path from his eyes to the moon. Light swathed the cookie in his hand.

Evan tore the wrapper, cracked the treat, and read, *You are the answer to a riddle.*

What he was looking for was a solution to his own problem. If the fortune couldn't do that, it didn't deserve to be kept. He scoffed, pitching the cookie and its plastic onto the seat beside him. "I don't have time for this."

Armed with only his lame excuse of "I didn't know what to say" at this unusual hour—post-dinner, pre–booty call—and bringing food she didn't need, Evan knew ringing Brenna's doorbell was pointless.

Grumbling, he grabbed the car's gearshift and jerked himself upright. He pulled the sports car onto the quiet street and left Brenna with no explanation.

Chapter Six

Sorority sisters made great surrogate families—until they all want to play the mother. Holidays especially seemed to inspire gushing bouts of maternal instinct among Brenna's peers and most of it revolved around her "Quest for a Man."

Did it matter that she'd maintained her weight, gotten promoted at work, or had money in the bank (unlike the shop-happy contingent)? Not much.

"A little more meat on your bones and maybe you could get somebody's attention."

"Come out of that office once in a while and you could get somebody's attention."

"Hit a couple of these sales with us and you could find clothes that look like you want to get somebody's attention."

The well-meaning critiques sounded so similar that the women's voices blended to a monotone inside Brenna's skull. Right now, they hit her head and her heart in time to a driving beat thudding from Beverly's living room stereo. They were all seated in the kitchen, gathered around the table finishing up Christmas dinner preparations.

In the absence of male affection, sister love was cool. It kept craziness at bay that would surely develop after too much tell-all reality TV. It prevented occasions for gathering from becoming I'm-all-alone-eating-ice-cream pity-fests. And for Christmas Day, its collective spirit distracted Brenna from tallying all the more moments she hadn't heard from Evan.

The room fell quiet as a slow song entered the musical mix. The women sprinkled cinnamon, buttered rolls, passed out plates in silence broken only by occasional humming or the clattering of forks.

"Don't you all get dry on me," Beverly admonished her guests.

"Where's that wine?" the stuffing-spooner asked. "Bet Brenna needs a glass."

"Just one," she replied, knowing a single round would calm her nerves, but two would put her to sleep.

"Who is it this time?" The sister stirring gravy asked what they all assumed.

"Nobody." Brenna hoped her answer would catch them off guard and convince them to leave her alone.

"Quit lying."

Brenna huffed and spilled the truth. "I lost my job Tuesday."

Beverly abandoned the ham she was carving and scurried to Brenna's side. "Girl, how come you didn't tell anybody?"

"Shocked. Embarrassed. Pissed the heck off." Brenna laughed. "What am I going to do without a job to wake up for?"

One by one, the other sorority sisters came to comfort Brenna, surrounding her in a circle of sympathy and hugs, offering ideas—serious and not—for ways to spend her time.

"Sleep in."

"Shop."

"Try relaxing for a change."

"What's that?" Brenna pretended to tremble uncontrollably. "Must have work."

"Get a life Brenna." Beverly laughed.

I used to say that to Evan all the time. Wonder if I offended him, too.

Not wanting to be caught brooding, she quipped with a smile, "You're right. I can do much better than hanging out with the likes of you all."

Laughter exploded throughout the spacious kitchen, bouncing from face to face, ricocheting off the copper pots and pans strung from a ceiling rack, until the joy settled around Brenna's spirit with soft giggles and shaking heads. It elicited her gratitude for good friends and lured Beverly's husband out of his upstairs confinement.

"Oh, goodness!" He rolled his eyes and circled the table with his eyes. "You all are drinking before dinner? We're never gonna eat, are we? I might as well go get a burger before I starve."

Joining in the fading laughter with a gentle snicker of his own, he stretched his neck around the tabletops and counters, examining the imminent feast. "You all did good! Let me get a little piece of that ham."

He followed his wife to the kitchen's center island. Beverly carved him a thin slice, stood on her tiptoes, and placed the ham on his tongue as if it were a gourmet delicacy.

"Um," he murmured, licking his lips and winking an eye.

Brenna remembered having the same reaction to Evan when he kissed her. Um. She fanned a hand in front of her face as if waving away the heat. "Hey, you two. Put your fast behinds on pause for another four or five hours. We don't want to see all that."

"Hater," he teased, patting his wife on the bottom and backing out of the kitchen.

"Ten minutes," she told him. "Tell your boy, too. I know he's coming."

She turned her head from her husband to Brenna. "Got you a little company."

The doorbell rang as if it were cued. To Brenna's shock, dismay, and hidden relief, Evan stepped through the back door wowing the women with his charm and cologne.

She felt both perturbed and possessive, wishing she could punish him with silence for ignoring her all week, yet wanting to claim him as her own to keep her single sorority sisters off him. He slipped off his leather jacket and handed it to "his boy," revealing a pair of relaxed fit designer jeans—loose in the thigh, tighter in the butt— a dark plaid button-front shirt open at the neck, and those doggone Timberland boots, this pair in black.

Bet he tastes better than the food, thought Brenna, biting back a grin.

"You look familiar. Do I know you?"

Brenna shook her head. "I have one of those faces," she teased.

"My mistake." Evan stared into her eyes, speaking words no one in the room could hear but her.

Beverly eyed them suspiciously. "What's going on here? Did you all go to prom together? Date in college? Or did you meet in a bar and have a one-night stand? It's something like that, isn't it?" she joked. "Well, it's time to wipe the slate clean and get to the table before the food gets cold. Let's eat. You can pretend you don't know each other later."

They continued the charade through the entire meal. Seated next to each other, they made sure to bump elbows when passing dishes from one side of the table to the other and their feet rested beside each other's beneath the table, barely touching.

The proximity kept Brenna preoccupied with erotic thoughts of Evan all evening. She couldn't brush his hand without wishing it was holding her. If it wasn't for the fact that he'd disappeared on her for three days, she'd invite him back to her house for an encore. No, tonight she'd use her head.

Dinner and dessert finished, the group moved from the dining table to the lower-level recreation area. Laughter and loud conversation flowed with the drinks. New guests, unknown to Brenna, began to arrive. Some making the stop their second or third holiday visit, others coming just for the good times they knew were waiting. Brenna was glad for the growing crowd; it helped shield her and Evan from her many "mothers" in the room. She smiled at their protectiveness.

"I'm surprised you're talking to me at all." Evan leaned and whispered in her ear.

"Surprise is the key. If I knew you'd be here, I probably wouldn't have come."

"If I'd known we were going to wind up having sex the other day, I wouldn't have taken you home."

Sex? That's all? No wonder he hasn't called since. "Well, I know not to let you in my house anymore, don't I?"

"Not if you can't control yourself." He laughed.

Brenna searched for her most controlled tone. "I thought you could handle me waiving my ninety-day rule." She shook her head. "You weren't ready, though."

"Please, girl." He furrowed his brow and studied her face. "What do you mean I wasn't ready?"

"All I'm saying is that I'm still Brenna. Treat me the way you have for the past three years."

"Really?" He raised his eyebrows. "Hmm. Okay. If you say so." Evan looked totally perplexed. "Most girls want more after you sleep with them—not the same—"

"Well, you *can* call—"

"Hey, no problem." Evan shrugged. "If you're saying we're still cool, same as before, that's all right with me."

What did she just give him permission to do? Had she managed to chase off the polite, thoughtful Evan who always listened to her work rants, took her to lunch, and escorted her home on the worst day of her professional life?

One thing felt certain: she'd probably ensured that she wouldn't be getting that "sorry I didn't call" apology she wanted so badly. That would mean he cared, and she just convinced him he didn't need to.

She checked her watch. "Wow, it's almost eleven."

"You ready to go?"

Her hopes brightened. Maybe she hadn't totally botched a start with Evan. "Yeah. I've been here all day."

Evan walked to the bar and set his glass down. "I'm going to hang out for a while longer, but go ahead and grab your coat. I'll walk you to your car."

"Oh, sure. Thanks," Brenna said, feeling incredibly silly. She began weaving through the crowd toward the stairs, her sedan, and the safety of misunderstanding. After all, nothing had changed and that was cool, right?

She gathered her winter wear from the hall closet and wished her hostess and sorority sisters merry Christmas while Evan went outside to start her car. Brenna stood in the doorway peering through the steamed glass of the storm door, watching Evan clear a dusting of snow from her windshield and headlights. What should she do?

He ran up the walk. She stepped outside as he shook flakes from his coat and stomped his feet. "All set."

"Thanks, Evan."

They stood staring at each other like awkward teenagers. Falling snow swirled in the glow of the porch lights. Their shine gave Evan a godlike quality against the royal-blue night. Her insides twisted and tingled. She shifted from one foot to the other.

"The car should be warm by now." He hesitated. "Drive safe."

"I will. You, too." She turned toward her car, then looked back at Evan. "Call me?"

He took too long to answer. "Based on what we said and everything, I just don't think it's a good idea."

"Well, you take care, then, Evan Shephard," she snapped, stepping into the car and slamming the door. "I don't know what got into me anyway, making love to you, waiting for you to call, letting my mind wander to 'us.'" She chided herself. "What in the world got into me?"

Chapter Seven

"Good morning. My name is Brenna Campbell and I'd like to speak with someone about what opportunities are available through your Small Business Incubator program."

"Certainly. My name is Karlethia Young and I'll be glad to help you."

Brenna appreciated the cheery voice on the other end of the phone. The speaker's warm, familiar tone reminded her of hot chocolate on a cold day.

"Can you tell me a little more about what you want to accomplish?" Karlethia continued. "Do you have an existing company you'd like to strengthen or do you want to launch a new business?"

"I'm exploring the possibilities of starting my own venture," Brenna thought aloud. "Perhaps HR consulting or outplacement services. Even relocating displaced workers from one state to another and what that might involve in terms of matching training and skills with employment opportunities that are available in other parts of the country."

"Well, that sounds relevant," said Karlethia. "And if you set yourself up right, you ought to get plenty of business helping people get to where the jobs are."

"I just have no idea about the licensing, what certifications might be required, taxes, accounting, all that. Would you be able to help me?"

"Well, if you could at least sketch out some of your thoughts in terms of who your target market might be, what capital you have access to—those kinds of basics—that'll help us get our conversation in perspective and we should be able to move through our discussion a little more effectively."

"Absolutely." Brenna responded quickly.

"What's your availability to get together for about an hour today?" Karlethia asked. The women arranged to meet that afternoon.

"Thanks. I'll see you, then, at two o'clock." Brenna hung up with her mind swirling. "Goodness! That call was so much simpler than talking to *MARVIN*."

Rolling her eyes in exasperation, Brenna recalled her morning escapade with Michigan's automated unemployment system. Tapping in her Social Security number and all the other identifiers they asked for in order to validate, claim and eventually cut the check she'd earned.

She'd heard on the news last month that MARVIN was a month behind. Good thing she had some savings; not half a year, but enough to get her to spring. She hoped.

But at least she'd invested her energy in moving her life forward today. If the fortune cookie was right, and the universe was waiting for her go-ahead to bring on the blessings, she'd now given the order.

And until this moment, she'd managed not to let Mr. Evan Shephard interfere in her planning. One day, she'd give him his due in a book or an interview for jump-starting her courage. But today, she thought it best to keep him out of her mental mix.

Brenna swiveled in her office chair toward a set of oak barrister's bookshelves, lifting the protective glass that covered a set of books on business and personnel management. She traced the titles with her forefinger and stopped on a volume called *Building Your Business Brand*, tipped it backward, and let it fall into her opposite palm.

"I'm sure there's a business plan in here," she murmured, flipping through the pages until she found the information in chapter three. She spun back toward her laptop and opened a new file in her project management software. "Four hours is plenty of time to get BC Enterprises ready for Karlethia Young."

She jotted her thoughts on a tablet atop her desk as she turned back and forth from computer screen to book page, typing action steps and target dates into the project file. Brenna liked the feeling of being productive again.

Under different circumstances, a week away from the grind of Sandstone Personnel would have left her rejuvenated. The sudden separation instead left her purposeless and insecure. But the old Brenna had suddenly showed up, working without stopping, through the battling background sounds of R & B on her radio and judges on TV.

She emerged from her work on the other side of noon, pleased with herself and the business she proposed.

"Evan Shephard, please." The unfamiliar voice, youthful and radio-like, prompted Evan to sit upright in his chair.

He instinctively pulled up the black DOS screen administrators used to tap into troubled network computers, thinking he was being called in rescue action of some sort. "This is Evan. How can I help you?"

"My name is Jebran Adams and I was referred to you by a former colleague in response to my search for a senior network engineer," he said. "We are quite impressed by your credentials and wonder if you would be interested in exploring new employment opportunities."

Wow rushed through Evan's brain, but he managed to

speak with calm. "May I ask what company you represent?"

"I am recruiting on behalf of a West Coast film production company looking to establish a satellite office here," Jebran answered.

"The governor's goal of luring Hollywood to Michigan seems to be getting people's attention," Evan noted aloud. "What would the position entail?"

He'd seen news of "cattle calls" for set extras, coverage of star visits for movies in production, industry spin-offs settling in locally to provide accounting, production, and talent services to incoming filmmakers. Yet even in this age of digital enhancement, working in the entertainment field held no appeal—until the industry sought him out. They made plans for an extensive meeting.

"I'll see you then," said Evan. Confidence soaring, he hung up the phone and tipped himself back in his chair.

Brenna would be proud of him today; not just his navy and gray sweater and slacks outfit, but the fact that he was giving time to a venture outside his typical job parameters of small company, good benefits, nothing flashy, decent pay. He seemed to be attracting positive energy—at least on the professional front. He hoped she was, too.

Evan opened his e-mail and composed a brief note to an IT colleague at another company and asked if he was familiar with Vidayo Productions or knew anyone who worked there. He sent the message and clicked his Internet browser to search for the company's site.

He arrived at a page under construction that told site surfers information would be available soon about their Midwest satellite office to be located just outside Detroit, Michigan, in summer 2010. Disappointed that the site wasn't developed yet, Evan also appreciated the fact that corporate executives would allow the new IT person to determine the look and feel, content, vendors, and time-line for launch, as opposed to coming in behind someone else's work.

Evan hoped he'd be the one chosen to lead the team. His thoughts floated a month into the future by which time—if all worked out—he would have given notice and settled into his new job. His thoughts went back to Brenna.

"I hate your missing out on my news," he whispered aloud, wondering whether she was job-hunting, had considered his suggestion to launch her own company, or—heaven forbid—wallowing in her circumstances and taking no action at all.

"I'm not ready to be here in Heaven," Kay said.

It's true what they said, there are no tears in heaven, so she could not cry to express her frustration at being called away before completing her life's list of to-dos: Traveling, writing a book, fostering a child, running a company were a few of her unfulfilled earthly passions.

"Sure, it's a surprise, but how can you not like relaxing all day, floating to any spot in the world, reuniting with everyone you lost over the years?" Jay asked over her thoughts.

Kay ignored the question and continued to flounder in her own pitiful tactics. "I was always a know-how indi-vidual and now all they want me to do is keep watch over someone else. What about the afterlife *I* wanted?"

"But isn't this fulfillment of your talent and more?" Jay tried a new approach. "Brenna's still down there living and struggling—in need of the wisdom you can share with her. Are you telling me that's still not enough?"

"I just needed a little more time . . ." Kay whispered,

hoping something could transform her white robes and halo to blue jeans and boots, and set her back on Ashcroft Street for another day or two.

"Funny you feel disappointed. I gotta admit that I've been waiting on you all this time and you still don't act like I exist."

Stunned by Jay's statement, Kay rose from her pool of self-pity and looked at her fiancé. Without voice or comment for the first time she could remember, she stared at Jay, her dutiful hero, unfailing friend, now perfect angel. She'd taken their heavenly reunion for granted.

Before they'd had children, before they could put down roots, before they said their vows, illness brought Jay here where he'd waited as faithfully as she had on earth. While he had the joy of eternity, she lived embroiled in her bitterness.

"I'm sorry I died so early in our lives together." Jay paused, stepped forward, and clasped her hands. "I can't tell you how often I came to your bedside and whispered into your dreams that I would always love you, just like I promised."

"I did hear you!" she gasped. "Only I thought my loneliness was driving me crazy. There was no way it could be real."

"It was. And so is this." Jay opened his arms as if embracing the wonder around them. "Now there's no need to miss the days we didn't get to share, Kay. The things you wanted, the goals you hoped to accomplish, the existence you always wanted can be ours."

She hugged him tightly. Even in their angel forms of nebula and mist, she felt him strong beside her. The distance of their separation condensed to nonexistent, Kay stood youthful beside him the way she looked the day he died.

"Did you know how much I love you?" she asked.

"I suspected it," Jay laughed.

They gazed on the pair, separated by the death of hope the way Kay and Jay had been parted by tragedy.

En route to separate lives, Kay suddenly realized her heavenly assignment was more than a babysitting job.

"Let's show them the way to love."

Chapter Eight

"I need a major change." Brenna sat in the salon chair draped in a cloth leopard-print cape pondering what new direction she wanted to take. She'd picked out black slacks and a matching tunic that would look great for her meeting and the date that followed. Now she wanted a look to match. "Cut it all off."

Brenna and her stylist looked in the mirror at each other's reflections.

"Define cut," the stylist said flatly.

"I'm talking Jamie Lee Curtis and Tinkerbell or Toni Braxton and Halle Berry back in the day."

"Are you serious?" The stylist caressed the ends of Brenna's hair, finger-combing the strands and arranging the bouncy curls around her shoulders.

"Yep." Brenna nodded for emphasis. "Plus color."

The stylist raised her eyebrows and chuckled. "Since we're feeling dramatic, what do we want? Blond?"

Brenna studied her coffee-brown hair. "Almost. I'm thinking from this to copper with a few sunny highlights. Can you touch up my eyebrows, too? I've got a big day." She closed her eyes and envisioned her new look.

The stylist set to work and two hours later, the mirror reflected just the face Brenna imagined. What didn't show was a new layer of confidence she was about to audition on her HeavenSent.com match—Mr. Decent AKARon.

I sure hope he's worth this trouble. Not that she would

transform herself for the perfect man she had yet to meet. The makeover was for herself. This way, when she came across photos of herself with her new style, she'd remember that this look belonged to all the right things that were happening in her life.

Next stop: Karlethia Young.

Brenna left the salon and hurried to extract her car from the space she squeezed into at the curb. Her impromptu glam session left little extra time until her meeting. She inserted herself into the stop-and-go neighborhood traffic.

As she drove in time to the syndicated radio's afternoon banter, Brenna thought about Evan. She replayed the words she shared with him about not being ready—not even wanting to be an entrepreneur. The old notions chipped away at her optimism, eroding it to uncertainty with each city block she passed. Soon she was toying with the idea of not attending the appointment, not stepping out on faith, taking no action at all.

Brenna only continued because she'd already come this far. No sense wasting a good business plan that Karlethia could certainly help strengthen. If she didn't use it now, it would be ready later when she had a better idea of what she wanted to do. She approached the downtown center with her uncertainty becoming foreboding.

Two exit ramps later, she pulled onto Woodward Avenue and began searching storefronts for the address Karlethia had given her. Passing it once, she circled around a block of medical office towers and university administration buildings, jumped back into the midday traffic, and found the trendy soul food restaurant she was supposed to meet Ron at in an hour and the small business incubator offices housed atop the eatery.

"A little too convenient," she muttered, silencing her car beside a curbside meter two blocks away.

Sliding her preliminary business plan into her tote, she gathered her financial grids hoping Karlethia planned to offer more than referrals to pamphlets, Web sites, or some 1-800 number to get her started.

The quick jaunt wasn't a bad walk, even on a brisk December day in Detroit. Real air was refreshing after a morning spent inhaling hair chemicals, dyes, and sprays. Gusty winds lifted her spirits along with tree branches and streetlights around her. The breeze ruffled the short layers of her new hairdo.

Yesterday she would have worried about arriving for her afternoon appointments appearing tousled or unkempt. Today she relaxed, knowing everything—hair, business chat, and blind date—would fall into place as they were meant to.

"Apparently, I needed an outside perspective," she said to herself. Change would leave her different, but not undone.

She scanned the list of occupants shown on a tabloid-sized sheet inside a flat glass frame beside the door. Nothing said small business incubator or Karlethia Young, so Brenna pressed the doorbell labeled START-UPS INC., NEW VENTURE ADVISERS and waited.

Within seconds, the buzzer sounded, the lock magically unlatched, and Brenna climbed the stairs to the second-floor suite. Delight followed surprise as Karlethia's door opened to reveal a space that mimicked Brenna's own home décor.

A whitewashed wooden armoire opened to reveal rows to white binders, paper trays, even ink pens. A matching laptop displayed the image of a snowcapped mountain range on its screen. They walked across white industrial carpet to a sturdy circular conference table, white of course, with matching upholstered chairs.

"We have similar tastes," remarked Brenna, sliding into a seat and placing her tote on the floor at her feet. "But I couldn't resist a little color for accent—artwork, figurines, candles, and lamps. This is quite striking."

"I find it helps relax clients and keep our conversations focused," explained Karlethia. "So, tell me, what makes you want to start a business in this crazy economic climate?"

Evan, thought Brenna. *No way I'd strike out right now without prodding. He makes it seem so logical, but what makes him an entrepreneurial expert?*

"You don't think it's a good idea right now?" Brenna asked, jumping into her manager mind-set.

When she worked for other people, she had always prided herself on a proactive outlook that emphasized planning and preparation. That meant pursuing valid strategies and avoiding actions that might result in negative consequences. She expected the same thinking if she worked for herself. Her internal high-risk meter was wagging wildly right now.

"Do I detect second thoughts?" Karlethia asked, homing in on Brenna's inner turmoil.

Brenna shook her head, amused with her own confusion. "I came fully equipped with *my* written plan—as you asked—but someone *else's* motivation for moving it forward."

"May I see what you've put together?"

Dutifully removing the folder from her tote, Brenna handed one set of papers to Karlethia and began reviewing her copy of the documents aloud. "I've outlined goals, objectives, marketing tactics, and a proposed budget for our discussion," she said.

"I'm sure you covered every aspect in its entirety," said Karlethia, "except one."

Brenna halted her presentation, annoyed at the oversight Karlethia had already uncovered.

"You've missed the most obvious and vital component," Karlethia continued. "*You.* Where's Brenna Campbell among the facts and figures, paperwork and jargon?"

"Right here." Brenna flipped to the organizational chart on page two. "President and chief executive officer."

"In that post, I give you one year. But if you could run any enterprise you wanted, regardless of your career path to date, what would that be?"

Brenna paused, leaned back, and thought of her biggest little-girl dream. "A comprehensive hope network for special-needs kids. I'd find a way to connect children suffering from chronic or incurable diseases with each other for support and to provide their parents with resources for insurance, research, caregiving—everything."

"So that's the 'you' that's missing from the hard work you brought to show off." Karlethia spoke slowly, leaning back in her chair.

Brenna smiled sadly. "I lost a good friend last year to a disease that plagued her since she was a child. She passed a few months after her fiancé, who died of the same illness. Not that I claim the expertise for that type of undertaking, but if I could do *anything*, why not something for someone like Kay?"

"Well, that's why you went searching for me, isn't it?" Karlethia reminded her. "So let's create a plan to help fulfill your heart's desire."

* * *

"Mr. Shephard, you are one heck of a find." Evan pretended to be the recruiter he'd interview with in less than half an hour. "It's an honor to welcome you aboard."

With one final approving glance, Evan smoothed the lapels of his indigo interview suit—which also served as his board meeting, first date, and Easter suit. He loved the way he looked in expensive clothing, but with few opportunities to dress up, preferred to invest his wardrobe allowance in his one-day-I'll-need-a-house account instead.

He strode through the apartment grabbing items from each room on his way to the door; wallet from his dresser, portfolio from the breakfast bar, shoes from the hall closet, keys from the hook by the back door. He punched in the code on the alarm keypad and opened and closed the door around him as he moved through in one quick motion.

Jebran Adam's office was only three blocks from Evan's apartment, but he chose not to walk in the winter muck. The half-melted snow and ice would wreak havoc on shoes he hated to wear in wet weather. And it would be just his luck to get pelted by a drive-by splash in his cashmere overcoat.

Nope. He started up the Lexus and prepared to valet park to save himself any potential annoyance. Except that when he arrived, Jebran's office was one block over from the place he thought it was. There was no valet parking. And the spot he left his car in was farther than walking would have been.

Evan took the inconvenience as an omen, but rang the buzzer beside START-UPS INC., NEW VENTURE ADVISERS with confidence anyway. He distracted himself by taking in the mixture of home-cooked smells from the soul food restaurant below the offices as he waited. A little peach cobbler and ice cream following the interview would be the perfect way to relax.

The door buzzed and unlatched. Evan entered and followed the signs to Jebran's suite, adjacent to a similarly titled office with a different name on its door. He wondered if Karlethia Young was a partner, division director, or coincidental suite mate. Shifting focus to his own mission at hand, Evan turned the knob on the neighboring door, straightened his shoulders, and walked inside.

A minimal lobby furnished with a tiny unstaffed receptionist desk, phone, two armchairs, and a stack of news magazines greeted him. Before he could process what the minimalist surroundings said about the search firm, Jebran appeared, hand outstretched in greeting. "Mr. Shephard, right?"

Evan responded with a "Yes" and a nod, returning the handshake and easing a bit at the sight of Jebran's gray and navy suit. The ensemble style was a men's magazine-perfect complement to Evan's own attire. *Great minds think alike*, he thought.

"Obviously you received my memo on attire for the day." Jebran laughed and motioned Evan forward. "My temporary quarters are right through here."

"You're not based locally?" Evan asked. He pulled a simple wooden chair from behind its matching square table, the surface just big enough for the two men to lean forward on their elbows and not bump heads.

"No. I stay on the road these days, traveling wherever the company needs me to facilitate a connection. Today, Detroit is the spot and you are our link." Jebran opened a folder containing Evan's résumé and a handwritten list of bulleted items. "So tell me, Mr. Shephard. What does your life look like five years from now?"

If Evan wasn't suited up, sitting across from a career headhunter in a makeshift two-dollar office, he'd swear he was online, under fire at HeavenSent.com. The question bore that same ambiguous tone that made you wonder what specific part of "life" it referenced—personal or professional.

Here, of course, Jebran must mean work. But the future Evan envisioned for himself included a whole new personal life replete with a good woman and cute kids. New responsibilities would, in turn, demand different priorities. Maybe even a complete change in career.

The interviewer raised his eyebrows.

I'm taking too long to answer, Evan realized. "Five years from now, I will have expanded my security credentials through on-the-job experience and additional certification. With those qualifications, I can see myself in an executive position with even regional oversight or providing consulting services at that type of level."

"Are you targeting any particular industry?"

"Up to this point, I've worked primarily in human resource operations. But I am not opposed to a change in venue. That's why your opportunity intrigues me."

"Just what we hoped to hear," Jebran continued, detailing a laundry list of day-to-day duties the position involved.

The job would definitely keep him challenged, requiring the network support Jebran shared in his initial phone call, along with network expansion and upgrades, process development and staff management—for the Detroit, Chicago, and St. Louis satellite locations. He'd spend one to two days per week on the road most weeks out of the year.

While that information soured him somewhat on the position's fit with his long-term goals, the salary weasled the prospect to the forefront of his short-term needs. Making a hundred and fifty thousand a year would give him plenty of time to save and secure the house and family. If Jebran offered the job, he was taking it.

"How does all this sound to you, Mr. Shephard?"

"Excellent. Really. The position is right in line with where I'd like to grow professionally and it offers the chance to travel the country and take on a supervisory role critical to the company's success. Job relevance is very important to me."

"Smart outlook. In this market, everyone should aim to become indispensable," Jebran said. "If you're interested, I'd like to set up a phone conference with you and a few folks from Vidayo's senior team. I believe you're just what we've been looking for."

Brenna hurried from Karlethia's office suite feeling reinvigorated. Hopeful. She stopped off in the hallway ladies' lounge to fluff her hair and refresh her lipstick before meeting Mr. Decent in the restaurant downstairs.

She left the office suite, returning to street level through the same door she'd been buzzed through an hour before. Directly to her right, a steady stream of late afternoon snackers, coffee drinkers, and wireless patrons entered Shileen's Soul Food. She followed, tentatively searching rows of vinyl-clad booths for a face like the photograph Ron displayed in his online profile.

No matches. Brenna checked her watch. The time was 2:01. Was he the punctual or tardy sort? Or one of those who would arrive early, check *her* out, and escape through the men's room if he didn't like who showed up? Was he spying her now, trying to decide whether to keep the date?

The idea unnerved her from a self-protection point-of-view and disheartened her from the dating perspective.

She chose a four-person seating area along the wall midway through the eatery and started waiting.

"When was your last date?" Brenna asked her reflection in the napkin holder, smoothing red lipstick into the matching liner outlining her lips. Her mind wandered back to the afternoon with Evan. "No. That was nookie, not a night out. It doesn't count."

The last time anyone—except Evan—took her out to eat would have been last Fourth of July, when she attended the Greek fraternity/sorority picnic with that Kappa guy who simply wanted to show her off to his frat brothers. Not a good time.

All her dates had been like that since she broke up with Roland. That had been well over a year ago—and they only dated three months.

It's been forever, so behave yourself.

Brenna watched guests enter and leave the restaurant. Others who'd entered before her were now receiving drinks and appetizers. Annoyance overruled the urge to be patient. She checked her watch again: 2:15.

Come on, Mr. Decent. It's time to see if the nickname holds true.

A smiling waitress in a black outfit much like Brenna's approached the table. "Are you ready to order, ma'am?"

"I'm waiting for someone. But . . ." Brenna debated holding out for her date's arrival. "Can I get some hot tea and a fruit plate, please?"

"I'll be right back with that." The waitress walked off, probably not shaken by the fact that Brenna looked as if she worked here, too.

Since she'd skipped lunch in lieu of her hair appointment, Brenna felt famished. And, because Mr. Decent didn't show up on time, she felt entitled to a snack while she waited. But she wished for a laptop and smaller booth to avoid looking so obviously alone.

Is that Evan?

Yes. Standing at the front of the restaurant, flirting with the hostess, listening as she was telling him he was free to seat himself anywhere, he had the nerve to laugh loudly—freely—as if he was in a really good mood.

Brenna groaned and tried to sink into her seat.

He unbuttoned the dress coat she'd only seen at Sandstone Personnel board meetings, revealing a suit she'd seen him in at those functions as well. He looked good enough to eat; tastier than those ribs on the menu, better for her than the fruit plate en route, warmer than this empty seat she now sat in. Alone.

Is Evan by himself?

Brenna fished her PDA out of her purse and opened its Web browser. She opened the HeavenSent.com site and logged in to her account. Mr. Decent was no longer among her Favorites. She searched the profiles she'd Nodded at and found his account no longer existed.

"Anything else?" Brenna's server twin placed a small pot of hot water, a teacup, and a tiny bowl of strawberries, grapes, and cantaloupe on the paper place mat.

"Thanks," Brenna murmured, paying little attention to the food or her stifled appetite.

Instead, her eyes followed Evan as he made his way through the waning crowd to a table directly across from hers on the other side of the restaurant. He seemed to notice and turned to her with an expression she didn't know how to read. No longer giddy, but not angry. Neither sad, nor sorry.

Brenna sat paralyzed between being stood up by Mr. Decent and ignored by Evan Shephard. A wave of "miss you" melancholy brushed over. Part of her knew she had no right to demand anything from Evan. A whole different side of her wondered why she'd never considered getting what she needed from *him*?

He gave her half a smile.

She returned her gaze to the empty seat across the table. Reaching into her wallet for a ten-dollar bill to leave on the table, Brenna gathered her purse, coat, and pride, and left.

Chapter Nine

"She did it again," Kay exclaimed. "Even *we* can't seem to get them together."

"What would you have done in her position?" asked Jay.

"Same thing, I suppose." Kay sighed. "Did I tell you what she said about her true career passion?" Kay changed the subject. "She wants to help me, and the other kids like we were—sick, sad, and feeling all by themselves."

"Who knew she was paying such close attention to us at work all that time?" said Jay.

"She is . . . was . . . good at her job, understanding what was going on with our health, getting our claims processed, giving us time off," Kay reminded him.

"Still, we thought we were just tasks on her list of things to do," Jay countered.

"So let's not let Evan feel that way," Kay suggested.

"He's going to get this new job—"

"And they could use each other's help." Kay poked a finger into Brenna's world while Jay did the same with Evan's.

Brenna refused to let Mr. Decent dampen her outlook. Karlethia had provided her with a wonderful outline for creating a nonprofit organization, a very different tool than the resources she was working with to launch herself as a human resources consultant.

She now had a whole new set of personal convictions to examine, funding sources to explore, and professionals to connect with. Sorting the hows and whys of her Cherub Coalition occupied her mind throughout the never-ending hours of Tuesday evening, right up until the edge of night.

That's when she realized she'd run out of romance options. Nothing in her e-mail, on the Internet, or among HeavenSent.com's promises held any appeal following her afternoon exploits with Mr. Decent and Even Shephard. Once again she'd shower, sleep, and awake alone. What she needed was a Karlethia for her love life.

In bed by eleven o'clock, she awoke around nine. Her thoughts resumed last night's failed relationship analysis and instead of diving into her nonprofit business plan, she decided to log in to her HeavenSent.com account one last time. She opened her in-box to delete the chat messages from Mr. Decent and found a new Nod from someone who called himself The Unexpected.

"Yeah, right," she scoffed. "I, StillWatersRunDeep, am above all surprises these days. Enough is enough."

A mailbox filled with lies was worse than any unanswered Nod. Clicking on The Unexpected's profile revealed no photos, but plenty of telling details. He worked in the entertainment industry and registered on the site to find a wife who was well read, trying to make a difference in the world, and loved to dance.

In exchange, he offered to share his love of the arts, life in the entertainment industry, and home computer know-how. This man, The Unexpected, also claimed to be of above average height, an exercise buff, and better in person than he was on-screen.

"How do I know that if you won't show yourself?" she asked.

He sounded charming, but so did Mr. Decent. And though The Unexpected's Nod was flattering, she'd lost faith in men and HeavenSent.com—at least for today.

She stared at the icon on her screen symbolizing his Nod: a simple colorless face that bounced forward and back every time she moved her computer mouse over its surface.

"Oh, stop it already," Brenna snapped. She clicked on the Settings link and checked the box beside *Delete My Account*, then paused to set her fingers on the keyboard to compose a quick, polite reply.

Thanks for the attention, but I'm leaving HeavenSent. Perhaps you'll find another woman to your liking. SEND.

There.

The properly mannered good girl in her felt better about giving notice than walking away to leave him wondering the way she'd done so many times. She inched her mouse toward the link that would delete her account once more.

A pop-up box ambushed the center of her screen. *You have one new message.*

"You're kidding me," she muttered in disbelief and clicked the *open* tab, curious to see whose timing beat her typing.

Did I sound that bad? The Unexpected wrote. *Sorry if I scared you away.*

Brenna laughed and wrote back, *No, it's not you. I'm just tired of the games here.*

Atypical, yes. A jokester, no. If I wanted to play, I'd be on the basketball court.

If you're so great, then why are you here? she snipped, hitting SEND.

Maybe I'm waiting for you.

* * *

"Good save!" Kay rubbed her hand across Jay's back.

"Your girl won't make it easy." He cupped Kay's chin in his palm and stared into her eyes.

"Well, how did you get him to do that?" Kay asked, genuinely intrigued by her charge's determination to dodge affection and Evan's skill at blocking her escape.

Jay zoomed his vision onto Evan's faraway computer screen, double-checking spelling, sensitivity, and the timing of his next move. "More like practiced persuasion. It's not that I know *him* so well—he's not as shy as me. But girlfriend? I just know she's going to rewrite every good scenario you try to cast her in."

"You paid more attention to me than I thought."

"Studied every move you made." Jay tapped Kay on the nose with his forefinger. "I hoped one day paying attention would pay off for me."

"Are we giving them our happily ever after?"

"They think and act a lot like we do," Jay agreed, "but once our work is done, they get to weave their own story."

"Until then we . . . nudge." Kay understood, remembering that so much of love was nuance.

"Exactly. And only when necessary." Jay wagged a finger at Kay as if reminding her to exercise restraint.

"So how much rerouting did he need to visit the Web site?" she asked.

"Not much. He was headed to the vending machine for some midmorning cola."

"Which reminded him of how she used to chew him out about his nutritional choices—"

"And *gently* forced him to confront why he didn't want to think about her."

Amazed at how the pieces came together, Kay put her hand over her mouth to smother a squeal of excitement. "So he tried to find someone else to think about instead?"

"Exactly. He decided to pursue the one woman who matched his new criteria on HeavenSent-dot-com."

Kay never thought she'd admire Jay more than she did on earth. This moment proved her wrong. "Sure I'll be as good as you one day?"

"Absolutely. I'll have you winning hearts before you can flap your wings three times."

"I have to earn those, too, don't I?"

Favorite singer? typed Brenna.

Prince, came the reply.

Seriously? You seem like the Brian McKnight and Jon Legend type.

There you go boxing me in again, wrote The Unexpected. *I like those guys, but I respect Prince's versatility in front of the mic and behind a control board.*

Is that your way of forewarning me that you're overcompensating for some critical shortcoming—like honesty, fidelity, gainful employment? Brenna phrased the question as a joke to disguise her seriousness.

Why bother lying to someone I don't know? Why commit to a woman if you want someone else? And why hasn't that man called and offered me the position I interviewed for?

Maybe the guy just thinks like me: somebody who's obviously so perfect doesn't need their job. Or this woman.

The hour of anonymous banter had been loads of fun. Playing online footsies refreshed her faith in her own appeal and let her know that somewhere out there a guy was waiting to discover Brenna Campbell, Miss StillWater-RunsDeep. But she'd had enough of The Unexpected's charade, his perfect answer to every question.

He was full of crap and she had a nonprofit to start.

Gotta go. She sent the message quickly.

Chat later?

Don't think so, but thanks, Brenna wrote. Then added, *Take care!* to ease the blow of her sudden departure.

The Unexpected sent back, *Good luck with your search!*

Brenna hesitated to allow her second thoughts a say before returning to the Web page she'd started at earlier. She placed a new check mark in the *Delete My Account* box and clicked SUBMIT.

Are you sure? The page asked.

She clicked YES and stood, unable to watch her carefully crafted profile and pages of criteria fold on themselves and melt into cyberspace. The notion that she'd deleted The Unexpected, too, and moved him to the Recycle Bin seemed cruel and creepy.

But she'd logged on to opt out of the imaginary friend realm and let go of the idea of finding a man by New Year's Day. With her life list rearranged by the layoff and business venture, staying single and self-centered seemed the better choice for her new direction.

Love could wait a little longer.

Chapter Ten

"I quit," muttered Evan. "From great connection to closed account just like that?"

Either she held standards he couldn't meet or she was afraid to commit. Whatever her so-called reason, he appreciated being dumped before she dragged him in too deep. Until she threw out that line about him being perfect, he was definitely game for a face-to-face round of conversation. So who played with whom?

"Never again." This was the last time HeavenSent.com got to disappoint Evan Shephard. He decided Miss Still-WatersRunDeep had the right idea about cutting losses, found his profile Settings page, and deleted his account as well. "Hmmph."

"The server's not going down, is it, Evan?" A passing coworker retraced her steps to peek into his cubicle.

"Nope." He almost forgot he was on the job. "Minor aggravation. Nothing that'll affect you."

"Shucks. I just knew I was about to have an hour to run out and wrap up my shopping because the computers went down." She walked off laughing at her joke.

"Sorry to disappoint you." He tossed the comment at his colleague but meant it for the woman who'd wasted a good part of his morning as well. Evan logged off Heaven-Sent.com admittedly wounded that his decision to Nod at such a great match resulted in a huge letdown.

If everything happened for a reason, he chose to believe that the female drought in his life left room for the new job opportunity.

Evan had a network server to back up and an end-of-year technology audit to complete, but instead he chose to e-mail Jebran Adams about the status of Vidayo's search for an IT compliance officer. Being at work was always tough the days before New Year's Eve; this year focusing was even harder—without Brenna.

He should've called after they made love last Tuesday.

He should've dropped off her Christmas gift Saturday.

He should've walked over to her table and said "hi" yesterday.

Three chances. Three strikes. No way she wanted to hear from him now.

The phone rang. Not Brenna, as his mind dared think for half a second, Evan recognized the number as New Venture Advisers'. *Come on. Tell me what I want to hear.*

"Good morning, Evan Shephard here."

"Good morning, indeed, Evan. This is Jebran Adams calling to invite you down to our offices for a follow-up interview."

"Absolutely. When would you like to meet?"

"Well, I just realized how close we are to the holiday and we really wanted to wrap this process by year's end if at all possible," Jebran explained. "How soon can your schedule accommodate a one-hour meeting?"

Resisting the urge to shout "Now!" Evan paused to pretend he was scrutinizing his calendar. "I can rearrange a couple of in-house meetings and free myself up late this afternoon if that's not too soon for you."

"Let's shoot for three thirty," Jebran said. "Most of your time will be spent on a conference call with Vidayo's chief operating officer, who's at a conference in Miami this week, and our human resources manager, who's based in the New York corporate office. I'm also trying to confirm one of our field consultants for the meeting. They're all looking forward to speaking with you."

"Likewise. I'll see you at your office this afternoon."

Being senior manager on staff since Brenna's departure, he had no problem giving himself the afternoon off. He'd leave work at one o'clock to go home and get ready.

"So what happens if I get the gig?" he asked himself.

He debated with himself. With the reinvention of Michigan's economy, chances were good he'd have to shift his career path sooner than later anyway. Some part deep inside him wasn't sure the moviemaking business was the journey he wanted to start.

He searched his memory for something Brenna would say right now. She always had the right words for difficult on-the-job situations.

In fact, when everything fell into place with Vidayo, he'd call Brenna—finally—and let her know he appreciated her prodding him to reach further than he might have, keeping his confidence afloat through the day-to-day boredom that came with being underutilized, and letting him know about additional certifications that would someday—now—work in his favor.

"Work and women." Evan laughed at himself. "I'll eventually get one of them right."

The afternoon jitters caught Brenna by surprise. Her nerves kept her running back and forth to the bathroom mirror, powdering her nose and fluffing her hair, to the laptop to tweak her nonprofit proposal, and to her PDA to re-re-reconfirm her afternoon appointment with Karlethia.

Her business adviser had called this morning—just

after her online debacle—with exciting news that she'd uncovered several sources of funding, support that could be quite useful for Brenna's planning and implementation phases during the New Year.

But Karlethia also mentioned that one of the opportunities involved an application that needed to be submitted before Friday, the end of the year. Despite the short notice, Brenna agreed to pursue the grant—with Karlethia's help—and now gathered her items for that three o'clock meeting.

Only one week after losing her job, the professional life check marks displaced by her job loss could reclaim their spots today. Instead, Brenna decided to let go of The List—permit herself a "Leave Due to Personal Circumstances"—and allow her career to take this uncharted upswing.

Still, the planner in her wondered what other impromptu items lurked on her upcoming agenda: a worse economy? lack of supporters? Evan Shephard? Would he appear out of nowhere again today?

If so, don't run away this time. You at least owe him a thank-you for turning you toward the direction you're about to pursue, an incredibly worthwhile cause that's going to make a difference in the lives of kids and communities.

The awkwardness of their one-afternoon stand and subsequent Christmas confusion aside, he deserved the credit for opening her eyes to this possibility. Hoping for a run-in redo with Evan might be pushing fate too far, but why not?

Chapter Eleven

"Have we Brenna-proofed today's plan?" Jay raised an eyebrow at Kay, implying he had doubts.

"I've got her figured out now," Kay said, crossing her arms across her chest and huffing with self-assurance. "She can duck and dodge, bob and weave all day if she wants. But Brenna Campbell will not escape true love this time."

"Then, too, he's finally ready," said Jay.

"I see it," said Kay, "And it's breathtaking. Their life roads have converged at one simple question—can I take the next step?"

"It's time," whispered Jay.

Chapter Twelve

The speed of the interview amazed Evan. If his watch didn't say otherwise, he'd swear he'd flashed from arrival to wrap-up in the space of a handshake.

"I did manage to locate that field consultant I told you I was trying to reach. She'll be in shortly. Let me give you a little background," said Jebran, not seeming to notice Evan's bewilderment. "Vidayo is committed to establishing a legacy in each community in which it opens a satellite office. Typically that requires varying types of support so each project is managed differently. We have identified the local project with which we'd like to be affiliated. This nonprofit is in need of infrastructure support, so you'll be handling the effort."

Evan raised his head to the sound of a gentle, but familiar knock.

"Come in, please." Jebran stood and motioned for Evan to do the same. "I'd like to introduce you to my partner Karlethia Young."

Evan nodded and shook the woman's hand, keeping his eyes on the opening door.

"And this," said Karlethia, "is my client, Miss Brenna Campbell, soon-to-be proprietor of the Cherub Coalition. Seems she had this notion of what kind of venture she wanted to pursue, but just needed to convince herself it was okay to proceed."

"I can not believe this," Brenna murmured to herself

but only Evan needed to understand. "Evan actually answered this riddle of where I should point my life."

"I'd say the same for you, Brenna." Evan tried not to sound as shellshocked as he felt, staring only into Brenna's eyes. "Really, it's an honor to be a part of such an important initiative, Jebran. I can't wait to hear more about it."

"Based on what you've each shared about your goals and aspirations, we think you two partners have just been waiting to connect," said Karlethia.

Brenna and Evan couldn't stop smiling at each other.

Chapter Thirteen

"So what do we do now that they're together?" Kay asked.

"We'll probably get new assignments," Jay guessed.

"You mean someone else gets to help them bloom and grow now that we've done the hard part?" Kay pouted and slumped. "It doesn't seem fair—having to let go now."

"That's all that was required, Kay, to unite Brenna with Evan and let love take it's course. You've played your role. I played mine."

"Well, if I can say so, I think I had the harder part, being a newcomer and all."

"You think guiding Brenna was more difficult than orienting you?"

Kay stopped to weigh the implication of Jay's question. "Yes, because if that's what you were doing, you failed. I have no idea what you're talking about. What orientation?"

"Technically it's Lay Your Burdens Down 101. Freeing you from those last bits of anger and fear you brought with you," said Jay. "We all go through the phase—with help. Otherwise, you can't get your wings."

"Stop it!" Kay giggled. "I'm fine with the gown. I thought halos and wings were storybook fantasies."

"They're real, but earned. And they come with a gift."

Kay squealed. "Where is it?"

Jay pointed at Kay's chest. "There. Your heart's desire. Just ask."

She stood silently, overwhelmed by the thought of receiving the only thing she remembered wanting. Kay closed her eyes and bowed her head.

"When you died, my whole world ended. All I could do was think of the wedding we never had."

Blue sky parted behind Kay, revealing a faraway sunrise of peach, amber, and rose. Mountains rose from the horizon, oceans cushioned the earth below.

"Our mothers, friends, coworkers—they all thought I was crazy to still be talking about our wedding even after I'd gotten sick again."

She recounted the memory as the clouds surrounding them thinned to rows of spiral fluff, swirling at their feet and above their heads. Snowflakes, like millions of pale rose petals, began to fall, capping the mountains and rippling the waters.

"I kept imagining our New Year's wedding. It made me happy then." Kay's mouth formed half a smile, wistful and wanting. "None of that should matter now, I suppose. We're together now."

Jay stepped forward and took her hands in his. "Here's your heart's desire, Kay."

"What?" Kay opened her eyes. If heaven permitted tears, she would have cried with joy.

To her delight, throngs of smiling faces encircled the couple. Long-gone relatives hovered near. She recognized public figures she considered heroes and family friends and neighbors she'd forgotten.

Bebop rhythms rose in the background, played by a white-suited troupe of jazz musicians; just the songs they'd planned to hear when she stood before Jay at their wedding.

The simple gown she'd worn since her arrival had been transformed as she reminisced into a sheath of satin and pearls accented by her bare feet and brand-new wings.

And her Jay, radiant and handsome in a white jacket and slacks, bared his feet and wings as well.

"Dearly Beloved," began the minister who'd wed her parents and baptized her as a baby. "What God has brought together, let no man put asunder."

"Look, Evan, the sun's coming out after all." Brenna grabbed his hand for balance and half skated, half stumbled to the edge of the outdoor ice rink. Above the high-rise buildings of Detroit's sleeping downtown, heaven seemed to be waking up.

He skated up close, hugging her from behind to rest his chin atop her knit beret. They stood watching the clouds part and rays pour down. Brenna couldn't remember seeing a sunrise so breathtaking.

"Thank you," Evan whispered. He turned her slowly around to face him and cupped her chilled cheeks in his thick wool gloves. "Dragging me out here at the crack of dawn was a wonderful surprise."

"I owe you," she said, reflecting on the lunch she'd botched just weeks before. "I'm just glad *you* didn't say no."

"Promise me you'll return the favor this time next year and say 'I do.'"

JANA DeLEON

"DeLeon is excellent at weaving comedy, suspense and spicy romance into one compelling story." —*RT Book Reviews*

Everyone in Mudbug, Louisiana, knows that when Helena Henry shows up, no good will come of it. Especially now that Helena is dead. And more meddlesome than ever.

Sabine LeVeche needs to locate a blood relative fast—her life depends on it. Her only ally is the smart-mouthed ghost of Helena Henry. Until Beau Villeneuve agrees to take the case. The super-sexy PI is a master at finding missing persons— and all the spots that make Sabine weak in the knees. But as they start to uncover the truth about the past, it becomes clear that someone out there wants to bury Sabine along with all her parents' secrets. And she realizes what they say is true: family really can be the death of you.

Mischief in Mudbug

A Ghost-in-Law Mystery Romance

ISBN 13: 978-0-505-52785-1

✂ ☐ **YES!**

Sign me up for the Love Spell Book Club and send my FREE BOOKS! If I choose to stay in the club, I will pay only $8.50* each month, a savings of $6.48!

NAME: _____

ADDRESS: _____

TELEPHONE: _____

EMAIL: _____

☐ I want to pay by credit card.

☐ **VISA**   ☐ **MasterCard**   ☐ **DISCOVER**

ACCOUNT #: _____

EXPIRATION DATE: _____

SIGNATURE: _____

Mail this page along with $2.00 shipping and handling to:
**Love Spell Book Club
PO Box 6640
Wayne, PA 19087**
Or fax (must include credit card information) to:
610-995-9274
You can also sign up online at **www.dorchesterpub.com**.

*Plus $2.00 for shipping. Offer open to residents of the U.S. and Canada only.
Canadian residents please call 1-800-481-9191 for pricing information.
If under 18, a parent or guardian must sign. Terms, prices and conditions subject to change. Subscription subject to acceptance. Dorchester Publishing reserves the right to reject any order or cancel any subscription.